PERHAPS LOVE

SALLY PRITCHARD

For Adeline and David

Chapter One

1985

Marcus Johnson looked around the classroom, he had just taken the afternoon registration. The upper sixth had completed their A-level exams over a week ago and had left school. His class, the Lower Sixth, had finished their mock exams. This had been his first teaching post since leaving University and he was surprised he was given the responsibility for the Lower Sixth tutor group. All in all it had been a good year. Mr Johnson stood up.

"For those of you who have worked hard, I'll see you here in September, for the rest of you I'll see you stacking shelves in Gateway!"

It had the reaction he'd hoped for, a lot of laughter with some of the boys telling each other, that would be them.

"Right you can all go home now, have a good summer break."

Some of the pupils broke into song 'schools out for summer'. Samantha Thompson looked at her friend Megan, she grinned and rolled her eyes, Megan responded with a laugh. There was a great deal of excitement in the air. The class, rather than leave, were homing in on Martin Parker who had suddenly become the most popular boy in the school. His parents were hosting a barbecue at their farm that evening, and Martin with help from his friend Richard, had organised a disco. Mr Johnson looked up and smiled, most of the girls were in small groups planning their wardrobes and lifts for the evening.

"Sir," called a voice from behind him.

He turned, Oh no he thought, it was Savannah Marshall, a well endowed girl who had crept up on him thrusting her double D's.

"Are you going to come to the party?"

"No Savannah, I'll be busy marking homework."

"Oh sir," she said disappointingly "I'd look after you."

Over my dead body he thought.

"That's very kind Savannah, but I'm afraid the answer is still no."

"Spoil sport!"

Savannah pouted then wandered back to her friends. Mr Johnson started to clear his desk and looked up in time to catch Samantha's eye, she smiled at him, he gave a small nod and bent his head again. Now, if she was to ask him, he thought. She was stunning, tall, naturally beautiful, and had a figure to die for. Deep breath Marcus she's Jailbait!

The level of noise in the classroom was increasing, Mr Johnson raised his voice.

"I know you're all excited about tonight and the summer holidays, but I'm sure you've got homes to go to. Remember the rest of the school hasn't broken up yet, so go quietly!"

He closed his case moved across the classroom and stood near the door. The students started to file out, 'Bye sir', 'Have a good summer sir', 'See you next year sir'. He could see Savannah loitering at the back of the group, hell he didn't want to be left alone with her, she would flirt outrageously at every opportunity. He took advantage of a gap that appeared in the line of pupils exiting the room. He made his way out down the stairs to the café area which only the six form used, thankfully there was still a couple of catering staff clearing up after lunch and Mrs Henderson, head of History. Safety in numbers thought Mr Johnson.

"Mrs Henderson, we don't usually see you over here."

"No, I have a free period and I thought that the sixth form block would make a nice change. I didn't know your students would still be here, I thought they'd be flying out the gates."

At that point Megan and Samantha walked passed.

"Bye, Mr Johnson, oh hello Mrs Henderson," said Samantha.

"Hello my dear how are you?"

"Fine thank you, have a good summer."

"And you." Looking at Mr Johnson,"What lovely girls, both so polite."

"Shall I get you a coffee?" he replied.

"That Samantha really is quite attractive I could imagine she'd be quite a distraction in class."

Luckily Mr Johnson had turned away from Mrs Henderson so she didn't see him blush. It probably was a good thing he didn't actually have to teach her. Mrs Henderson continued.

"I had so hoped she would choose History, she has real flair, but alas she's determined to do Science."

Mr Johnson carried the coffee's to the table. Savannah suddenly appeared at his side.

"Oh Mr Johnson have you bought me a coffee?"

"No Savannah this is for Mrs Henderson."

He hoped that would put her off, but Savannah wasn't going to be intimidated. Mrs Henderson was already sitting, he gave her the coffee and sat himself.

"Miss, tell Mr Johnson he needs to come to the sixth form party."

"I'm sure Mr Johnson can make up his own mind without me."

"Oh miss," Savannah continued her whining, "it's a tradition, the form teacher goes."

Mrs Henderson raised an eyebrow.

"Young lady, I've taught in the school for over 30 years. This is the first sixth form party I'm aware of and it's only happening due to the generosity of Mr and Mrs Parker."

Savannah didn't scare easily.

"Well tradition has to start somewhere!"

Mr Johnson looked at her.

"Savannah, as I said earlier, it's very kind of you to invite me, but the answer is no, I think it's time you went home."

Savannah realising he wasn't going to budge, sulked out of the building. Mr Johnson relaxed.

"It must be very difficult for you Marcus, a young good-looking man, I expect many of the girls have a crush on you."

Marcus Johnson blushed, had she just called him good-looking? He looked at her for the first time, did he see a twinkle in her eye?

"They're not too bad Mrs Henderson but Savannah is in a league of her own. She creeps up on me almost shoving her breasts into my face!"

Shit, he thought, he hadn't meant to say that out loud, but to his surprise Mrs Henderson threw back her head and laughed.

"Oh Marcus, you must be terrified."

"You're right."

"I thought you coped very well," she patted his hand, "and you must call me Mavis."

She must've caught the look of panic on his face and laughed again. Marcus smiled at her.

"Would you be able to teach me how you do that with your eyebrow?"

She gave him the sternest look.

"If I did that, I'd have to kill you. Thank you for the coffee but I must get on now."

"Thank you for your company,.......Mavis."

Smiling to himself he thought how on earth could have been scared of her? She was delightful.

Sam and Megan wandered out of the school together as they had been best friends since meeting in the first year. Megan was a petite strawberry blonde, which was incredible as her mother was a voluptuous glamorous dark haired Italian. Megan had three older brothers who looked like their mother, she took after her blonde father. The family owned a vineyard in Italy and ran a successful wine business which meant Megan spent most of her summer holidays in Tuscany.

Sam on the other hand was an only child. She looked like her mother, who was a local artist and sculptor. Sam had turned down the offer of staying with Megan in Italy as she had just passed her driving test and desperately wanted to get her own car. She had planned to work as much as possible during the summer holidays and she also knew Megan's boyfriend Tim was going out to stay with her. Sam definitely didn't want to play gooseberry.

"Can you believe this is the last time we'll ever wear a school uniform."

"Well unless one of us becomes a stripagram!"

Megan laughed at Sam's quick response.

"That will be you, you'd probably earn more than working in Mills the chemist."

Sam grinned.

"Maybe not a bad idea Megs, anyway what are you going to wear tonight?"

"Don't know, I'd planned to wear a skirt but the forecast isn't so good, so probably jeans how about you?"

"Definitely jeans, it is a farm after all. Mum is happy to take us and pick us up."

"A lift there will be good but I'll be leaving about 10 as we have an early flight tomorrow."

"Megs you're so lucky, off to Italy, all that sunshine and Mediterranean food!"

"Sam I've asked you to come."

"Yes, but you know I can't."

"Tim is not going to be there the whole time, you can still join us."

"I'm not even sure I've got a passport."

The girls had reached the main road known as 'Old Way'. It was a busy road, but as it was the middle of the afternoon Mrs Jones the lollipop lady wasn't there. They managed to cross and walked down a steep footpath to the river, over the bridge where Megan went left and Sam went right to their respective homes.

"See you about 6.30," Sam called back.

"Okay, I'll be ready."

At the school gates a determined Savannah waited for the unsuspecting Mr Johnson.

Chapter Two

It was 5.15, Samantha's mother called up the stairs.

"Sam do you want anything to eat love?"

"Mum I'm going to a barbecue they'll be food there!"

"Yes, but not proper food!"

Samantha had had a leisurely bath and washed her hair. She was going through her wardrobe, jeans were fine but which top should she wear?

"Mum have you washed my white blouse?"

Her mother appeared at her bedroom door.

"Do you mean this one?"

She held up Samantha's favourite blouse.

"Thanks Mum you're a star. I won't put it on until the last minute."

"Food?"

"Actually go on then I'll have a sandwich please."

She followed her mum downstairs.

"I'm going to phone Meg."

"Sam you'll be seeing her in an hour!"

"I know I won't be long I just need to check which shoes she's wearing."

Sam was at the bottom of the stairs and picked up the phone situated on the small table and started to dial. Her mother turned to her.

"Something flat would be sensible, it could be uneven underfoot being a farm, you wouldn't want to get stuck especially if you've had a few drinks."

"Drinks! Oh hells bells Mum, I'm supposed to take some drink!"

The phone connected.

"Oh hello Mrs Robbins, it's Samantha here, I wonder if I could speak to Megan please?"

Sam's mother walked back into the hallway with two bottles, one of cola and one of lemonade, she waved them in front of Sam who acknowledged her with a thumbs up.

"Megs Hi, which shoes are you going to wear, heels, flats, boots ?..Okay,... are you, okay, see you soon."

Sam walked into the kitchen. Her mother presented her with a plate.

"There you go, cheese and pickle."

"Thanks mum, Megs is taking wine for Mr and Mrs Parker why didn't I think of something?"

Sam's mother Laughed.

"Love, they own a vineyard, a bottle of wine from them actually doesn't mean much, your mum on the other hand thinks of everything, a box of chocolates!"

She produced a box of Milk Tray and placed it on the table. Sam smiled at her mother, sat down and proceeded to eat her sandwich.

"Do you think I should take some alcohol?"

"You don't drink, stop talking and eat up."

"I know, but I think everyone else will take some."

"I'll see what I've got."

Her mother disappeared into the dining room, where the drinks cabinet was kept. She called out.

"I've got wine, no, not a good idea, Whisky?"

"No!" Sam answered.

"Brandy?"

"Mum is there any lager or anything?"

"Cider?"

"Yes perfect, thanks Mum"

Her mother returned to the kitchen.

"You better get ready, make sure you brush your teeth, you've got a bit of something... there! You may get lucky tonight!"

"Mum, behave! All the boys in my class are gross, now if Mr Johnson was going I wouldn't say no!"

"Samantha Thompson, that poor man. I bet half the girls have a crush on him, he is rather good-looking."

"You should see Savannah Marshall today, she almost pushed her boobs into his face!"

"If I remember rightly she is a rather well endowed young lady."

"Thats putting it mildly! She must have asked him to come to the barbecue at least 10 times today but he told her no!"At 6.45 they picked up Megan and drove to Binden farm. There were lots of cars parked in the farmyard. Fairy lights were strung up from the house to one of the barns. A voice boomed out.

"Testing, testing, can you hear me Martin?...Okay."

The barbecue was already lit, Martin's father and older brother were in charge. Sam and Megan presented their gifts to Martin's mother who thanked them as she engaged in conversation with Sam's mum.

"You're very welcome to stay Adeline"

"That's very kind, but I must go, I'll be back about 11 to pick Sam up, see you later."

The girls went into the barn, more fairy lights were intertwined through the beams. It had been completely cleared out of animals and farm machinery. It smelt clean and fresh, bales of straw lined the walls, a few of their friends were sitting on them. Megan and Sam walked across to their friend Rosie, who was accompanied by a younger girl.

"Hi Rosie, this is great, who is this?"

Rosie look gloomy.

"Hi Sam, this is Lilly, my little sister. Mum said I could only come if I brought Lilly so she could have some peace."

"Never mind we'll make sure you have some fun!"

Sam looked at Lilly and wished she had a little sister.

"Do you know what to do with the drinks?" Sam asked holding up a carrier bag.

"I'll show you. Come on let's get some food"

They followed Rosie and Lilly to the end of the barn where they found a table covered with paper plates, cups and plastic cutlery. Guests had started filling the table with their 'bring a bottles', along side a glass bowl of Mr Parker's home made fruit punch. The girls got themselves a drink and made their way to the barbecue.

By 7.30 the barn was full of hungry people eating their sausages and burgers. Richard and Martin announced the disco would start.
The first song had to be Alice Coopers 'Schools out' which was greeted with a cheer encouraging everyone to get up dance and singalong. The evening was a great success. Mr Parker had kept the fruit punch topped up, at one point it was suspected someone had added gin, as nearly everyone was more than merry. At 10 o'clock two of Megan's brothers came

to pick her up. They stayed for a dance, much to the delight of most of the girls who were attracted by the Anglo Italians.

Sam was sorry to see Megan leave ,she gave her a hug.

"See you soon, have a fab holiday."

Rosie's mum turned up soon after and Sam found herself sitting alone in the corner of the barn.

Dean Williams, the captain of the school rugby team, very good-looking but also very cocky, possibly to compensate for his shorter than average stature swaggered over to her.

"Hi Sam do you wanna dance?"

"Hi Dean, no thanks just having a bit of a cool down."

"Do you wanna drink?"

"Oh go on then."

Dean felt encouraged by her response as on previous occasions when he'd asked her out she had always declined.

He returned with two cups of punch and sat down next to Sam. This was his chance.

Chapter Three

Samantha woke the next day, the sun was streaming through the gap in her curtains. Her mouth felt disgusting and she had a splitting headache. She looked at the bedside clock 9.30! She never slept on like this before. She staggered to the bathroom to have a pee and a wash then lay back on the bed. A few minutes later there was a tap on her door, her mother walked in with a cup of tea.

"Morning sleeping beauty how do you feel?"

"Headache!"

"Shall I open the curtains?"

"Oh no!"

Her mother sat on the bed.

"Well you were certainly having a good time when I picked you up. Good job Dad stayed outside talking to Mr Parker he would've had a stroke if he'd seen you."

Oh shit, she thought, it all came back to her, Dean coming over with a drink, she couldn't remember why or when they started snogging but that's what they were doing when her mother arrived.

"Oh God, sorry Mum."

Her mother smiled.

"Don't worry love, we've all been there!"

"What with Dean Williams!"

"Ha ha, you can't be feeling too bad, now plenty fluids and if you can stomach it, a bit of toast."

Dean Williams, what had she been thinking? He was the best looking lad at school, but boy didn't he know it. Hopefully he'd been too drunk to remember.

Samantha had a very quiet day, thank goodness she decided to take the Saturday off work. She was now on holiday, but would work the following Wednesday through to Saturday. That evening she settled down to watched TV with her mum and dad. After a good nights sleep she felt fully recovered.

Sam's mum had never been very conventional. Sunday roast was not on the menu, it was replaced with lasagna and garlic bread.

Samantha helped clear up and she was just wondering what to do for the afternoon when the front door bell rang. Anyone who knew the Thompsons knew to use the side door. Her father answered it as Samantha and her mum were clearing up in the kitchen. He walked back in.

"There's young man to see you Sam."

"Who is it?"

"Some short arse, he said his name was Dean."

"David!" Exclaimed Adeline

Samantha looked aghast.

"What does he want?" she whispered

Her dad shrugged.

"I'm guessing you."

Sam's mother interjected.

"Don't keep him waiting love."

"Mum you're not helping."

Her mother was grinning, Samantha threw down the tea towel she'd been using and walked into hall.

"Hi Dean."

"Hi gorgeous, I thought we could go down to the park."

Samantha was about to say no then realised she had nothing else to do.

"Oh okay I'll just get my shoes."

She went back into the kitchen, passing her dad.

"Don't wear heels" he mumbled.

"I'm going for a walk down to the park."

"Have fun!" her mother said grinning.

Samantha glared at her and poked her tongue out.

They had walked side-by-side in silence, Samantha decided to break it.

"Good party Friday night."

"Yeah."

"I had quite a headache on Saturday did you?"

"No, I can take my drink."

Maybe I should've stayed at home and read a book thought Sam.

They arrived at the park where they met a couple of Deans rugby pals. One of them looked Sam up and down and nudged Dean.

"Looks like you've won the jackpot Dean mate."

Sam rolled her eyes, tosspots the lot of them, she thought.

"I can't help it if girls fancy me."

His friends moved on.

"Jackpot!" protested Sam.

"It's just banter darling."

They continued to walk down to the pavilion.

"Shall we sit here?" asked Sam.

"It's a bit exposed."

"Exposed?"

Dean grinned.

"Yeah we want somewhere more secluded."

Sam sat down.

"Here's fine."

They sat in silence, again Sam gave in.

"Any ideas what you're going to do when you finish school?"

"My problem is I've got too many options," replied Dean.

"Okay like what?"

"Well for a start you must've seen me playing rugby, I could actually play for England, probably Captain. Mr Rawlings reckons I'm the best player he's ever seen," he continued, "you know my dad works at the hospital in the surgical department with Mr Jefferson, Dad says, with my grades I could get into medicine. Although, the best job I reckon is teaching."

Sam looked puzzled.

"Teaching?"

"Yeah absolute doddle. Teachers get it so easy. They've got all the answers, right, it's the kids who do the work, then all that holiday, bloody easy!"

Sam looked at him, he couldn't really be that thick could he.

"You know they have to plan their lessons and research their subjects."

Dean snorted.

"Bollocks!"

"I may go into medicine," said Sam.

12

"Yeah? My dad says it's no place for a woman, to hormonal. Anyway enough chat."

With that he turned to her, pulling her into him he started to kiss her. She went along with it for a while, thinking it was to be expected. Her lips started to feel sore so she pulled away.

"I should probably be getting back," said Sam.

"Okay," he said reluctantly.

All the way home he kept his arm around her waist, it was really awkward to walk. He spent the whole journey telling her about a rugby game he recently played, how he was the best player and was able to run rings around the other team. By the time they reached her house she wanted to scream. She wasn't interested in rugby. They walked around to the side door.

"Thanks Dean, that was……. interesting."

Before she could say anything else he was snogging her again, and suddenly broke off.

"See you," he said.

He swaggered down the drive. Sam looked on in shock, all he did was talk about himself and snog and she was bloody sure he hadn't brushed his teeth. All of a sudden she remembered the garlic bread she'd had for lunch and grinned, her breath must've stunk.

Sam closed the door, she needed a distraction so decided to call Rosie to see if she fancied going into Bath in the morning.

"I'd love to," said Rosie "I may have to bring Lilly though."

Sam didn't mind at all so they arranged a time to meet.

Monday dawned bright and sunny. Sam got ready, she was calling into Rosies at 10.30 and they would then get the 11 o'clock bus into Bath. She decided to wear a dress as it was such a nice day. She was ready by 10 o'clock so made herself a cup of tea before walking over to Rosies. There was a knock at the backdoor. She opened it.

"Dean!"

"Hi darling, you're looking good enough to eat. Home alone?"

He barged past her. Sam was still standing by the door.

"Sorry Dean I'm literally going out."

"Where?"

"To Bath, with Rosie Fairacres."

"Ditch her, you're going out with me, I'll take you to Bath."

Samantha was gobsmacked.

"Dean I have arranged to meet Rosie in," she looked at her watch, "exactly 7 minutes!"

"Oh Sam! What am I going to do?" he whinged.

"I don't know Dean, but we had nothing planned, so if you will excuse me, I need to get going."

"That really messes up my day," he moaned.

"Dean I'm going to be late, please come out so I can lock up."

Dean shrugged and walked out the house.

"Okay, but you'll see me tomorrow? I'll be round at 10, we could go to the pictures."

"Okay," she sighed. "I'll see you then."

Samantha locked up the house and walked to Rosie's leaving Dean to stroll back home. The three girls caught the bus into Bath and on arrival at the bus station transferred to an open top tour of the city, much to Lilly's delight. The day finished with a cream tea at the famous Sally Lunns, home of the original Bath bun. They had enjoyed themselves so much, arrangements were made to meet up again the following week.

Tuesday morning and as promised, Dean turned up. Samantha lied and said her mother was at home working on some sketches, so it would be better if they went out. Dean was disappointed as he'd hoped to see Sam's bedroom. They decided to go to the cinema, the latest Bond movie, 'A view to a kill' was showing which Samantha was keen to see. Typically they sat in the back row. Samantha struggled to follow the film as she had to keep slapping Dean's hands as he got carried away in the dark.

As they walked back to Samantha's house Dean spent the time criticising the film and moaning it had been a waste of his time and money. Samantha couldn't believe he could possibly make a judgement on a film he'd barely watched.

"I'll come round again tomorrow morning. Do you reckon your mum will go to work, we could have some fun indoors," he said leering at her.

"Sadly Dean I'm working for the next four days,"

"What! We'll go down to pavilion when you finish work".

"No Dean, I get really tired being on my feet all day".

Dean wasn't going to give up.

"Right Sunday?"

"Can't do Sunday, I'm visiting my Gran.

His patience was wearing thin. He all but shouted.

"Monday, then."

"I'm meeting Rosie again I'm free next Tuesday".

"Fucking hell Sam that's no way to treat your boyfriend. Carry on like this and I may have to dump you!"

Samantha was stunned again as she watched him walk away, then felt cross with herself. She should've told him to take a hike. At least she didn't have to see him again for whole week. 'Hallelujah' she said to herself closing the door.

Chapter Four

It was Wednesday morning, Samantha walked down to the town centre with a spring in her step. She enjoyed working in Mills the chemist although had been a little disappointed to have been allocated the cosmetics counter under the watchful eye of Mrs Thomas. She had hoped to be working at the dispensing counter with Miss Green the pharmacist who terrified most of the staff. Sam thought she was brilliant, an older single lady in her mid fifties who had a degree and seem to know every condition she dispensed for. Mrs Thomas was a petite lady in her 40s, she liked everything to be neat and tidy. She had taken one look at Samantha and nabbed her as she felt correctly, Samantha's glossy hair and perfect skin would encourage customers to buy more skin and hair care products. Despite the impression she was expected to give, Samantha only ever needed to use soap and water with a cheap moisturiser.

Working at the shop over the next few days made time fly by, It was now Saturday. Dean Williams entered the chemist and swaggered up to Samantha who was in conversation with Mrs Thomas. Samantha's heart sank, she'd forgotten about him.

"Hello ladies."

"Can I help you? We will be closing shortly," replied Mrs Thomas.

"It's okay I'm not buying anything, just wanted to let Sam know I'll come over later and take her out."

Mrs Thomas tutted.

"Young man this is a shop not a dating agency."

Samantha cringed.

"Sorry Dean, I'm meeting up with some friends, we are going over to Bella's to watch the Live aid concert on her Dads big telly."

"Live aid? What a load of rubbish, my dad says that Bob Geldof has never done a proper days work in his life."

Mrs Thomas tutted again.

"I must ask you to leave young man."

He looked at Samantha .

"I'll give you one last chance on Monday"
He turned and stormed out of the shop.
"Well I never, who is he?"
"Dean Williams, sorry Mrs Thomas."
"Not Barry Williams's son?"
"I don't know."
"I think he looks a bit like Barry did when we were at school, a dreadful bully. Be warned young lady."

Samantha didn't know quite know what the warning was for, so she just nodded politely.

After work she rushed home, changed, then made her way to Bella Smith's house where a group of excited girls were watching television. It was a fantastic event, Samantha forgot all about Dean.

The following week had started with the postponement of Rosie and Samantha's outing to the Tuesday. Samantha had decided Monday would be make or break for Dean and herself, as their going out together was something she couldn't be bothered with.

It was 11 o'clock by the time Dean turned up. Samantha watched him arrive from the front bedroom window, he was dressed in jeans and a white T-shirt. She had to admit he was very good looking with his blond hair and piercing blue eyes, but oh boy did he know it. Samantha sighed, she didn't know how much longer she could put up with him. His main topic of conversation was himself, his popularity, his sportsmanship, and how he could pull any girl he chose.

The doorbell rang, As her parents were out, Samantha didn't want him coming into the house. She had decided to wear shorts and a T-shirt, at least he couldn't get his hand up her shorts! She opened the door.

"Hi darling, I've got a surprise for you," he said smiling.
"Oh!"
"Yeah, come on."

They walked down the drive, thank goodness he hadn't taken her hand this time, thought Sam.

"What do you think of my new Jeans? They cost a fortune but Mum says I'm worth it," said Dean.

"Very nice."

He wasn't listening to her, he'd already launched into a monologue about his shopping expedition and how he didn't have to get a summer job as his parents weren't expecting him to work. In contrast, Samantha thought about how much money she would need to earn before she could get herself a car. Dean was still talking, so she attempted to stop his flow.

"Have you taken your driving test yet?"

"Yeah twice, stupid testers failed me for pathetic reasons. Can you believe it, they were both women. Hopefully I'll get a man next time and he'll realise what a bloody good driver I am. Women shouldn't drive.

"What!" she exclaimed, "I've already passed my test, first time."

Dean looked at her.

"I bet you had a bloke."

"Yes it was a man."

"Well that proves my point that men are better examiners!" he laughed "I bet you wore a low top and flirted with him."

"No Dean I didn't, I just drove carefully."

They had walked the through the town centre and headed towards a fairly new housing estate.

"When are you getting a car? It will be good when you do, I'll need a lift to rugby," said Dean.

"I'm saving up. That's why I'm working so much at the shop."

Dean looked at Samantha and smirked.

"I'm going to get a sports car as soon as I pass my test."

"How are you be able to afford that?"

"Like I said my dad will buy me anything I want."

They stopped outside a semi detached house, number 11 was on the door.

"Come on then, I don't know how long we've got," Dean said anxiously.

They walked up the short drive and around the side of the house. Dean took a key from his pocket and unlocked the back door.

"How long for what?" asked Samantha .

The back door led into a small utility area with a washing machine, a sink and a large coat rack mounted on the wall.

Everywhere was tidy, very different from Samantha's own home. A door led into the kitchen, Samantha looked around. The units were white, with grey worktops, grey and white tiles, it was immaculate. There was actually nothing on the worktops, the stainless steel sink and draining boards were gleaming.

"Wow it's so tidy," said Samantha .

Dean looked back.

"It's a kitchen! Dad has very high standards."

"Your dad keeps it clean ?"

"No my mum of course!"

The kitchen door led into the hall, there were two doors leading off, one went into the dining room, again immaculate and the second into the living room.

"You'd better take your shoes off"

Samantha removed her shoes before walking onto the hallway carpet and placed them by the front door. Dean was at the foot of the stairs.

"Come on I want to show you my room."

Samantha decided to ignore him and walked into the front room. Bloody hell she thought did anyone actually live here? There was a floral three-piece suite, a large television one side of the fireplace and a stereo system on the other. In the centre of the room was a large empty coffee table, not a magazine in sight keeping the theme of tidiness. There was a shelf above the stereo, upon which there were a few books but mostly photographs of Dean.

"Thats me captaining the rugby team," said Dean now standing next to her, "that's me winning a trophy."

Oh here we go again thought Sam.

"Do you have any brothers or sisters?"

"Yes I've got two sisters."

"Oh, where are they?"

Dean ignored the question. There were a couple of family photos behind the ones of Dean. Sam looked at them, they appeared to be taken on holiday, it was obvious he was the golden child. Dean grabbed her hand and lead her upstairs to his bedroom. It was a bright room with posters on the walls of various sports stars. Sam had no idea who they were but was surprised how tidy Dean's room was, she'd always assumed boys rooms would be messy and smelly. He pulled her onto the bed and climbed on top.

"At last," said Dean " let's have some fun."

"How do you mean?"

"Come on Sam you know you've been wanting me for ages now is your chance."

He pulled off his T-shirt and unzipped his flies. This was the last straw thought Sam.

There was a sound of a car on the drive, Dean leapt off the bed and looked out of the window.

"Shit they're back, go into the bathroom."

Sam was only too happy to oblige. In his panic Dean struggled to get his T-shirt back on. He ran down the stairs as his father walked into the hall. Sam waited in the bathroom listening.

"That was quick," said Dean flustered.

"Your blasted mother forgot to bring the paperwork for the car! Mr Jones wasn't there, only his idiot of an assistant who refused to touch the car without the paperwork!" said his father.

Dean's mother rushed passed them, into the dining room and opened the bureau.

"Come on Evelyn we haven't got all day," barked his father, "Bloody women."

He looked down at Sam's shoes.

"Who's are those?"

In her self imposed hiding place Sam smiled to herself, she wouldn't have noticed any odd shoes in her house! Deans reply wasn't what she was expecting.

"Sam come down Dad wants to meet you."

Sam thought she'd pull the flush to pretend she used it but then decided against it. She felt self-conscious walking down the stairs in her bare feet and shorts. Dean's father didn't help, leering at her as she descended.

"Well well my lad, while the cats away the mice are certainly at play."

Dean grinned.

"This is Samantha."

"Samantha eh, are you at school with Dean?"

Before Sam could reply, Dean spoke.

"Yes, we're doing A-levels together".

At that point Evelyn came into the hall waving the missing letter.

"Here it is!"

"I'm speaking!" said Dean's father gesturing her to stop.

"Sorry dear."

Sam was astonished. Her father would never talk to her mother like that. Dean's father continued.

"What do your parents do Samantha?"

Again Dean answered.

"Her dad works in a bank and her mum is that arty woman you fancy, wears all those weird floaty things."

"Oh yes I know the one you mean."

Sam couldn't believe it, Dean was answering for her, she could feel her anger creeping up a notch at each response.

"What A-levels are you doing?"

At last, she thought, her chance to answer.

"Sciences, I'd like to be a doctor."

Mr. Williams roared with laughter.

"A doctor, let me tell you, I've come across quite a few female doctors no good at all, too emotional. Never get the work done, cry if corrected, no my dear, with your face and your figure you should get a job as a model or something," he thought for a second, " yet looks and figures fade, your best bagging a rich man while you're young and nubile."

Sam wondered how many years she'd have to serve for murder, he really was a most hideous creepy man.

Dean's father clapped his hand on his son's shoulder.

"Let the men be the workers and earners, that's the way of things, Dean is going to go far."

Sam decided that prison wouldn't suit her so she took a few deep breaths. She turned to Evelyn.

"What do you do Mrs Williams?

Dean's father answered for her.

"Her job is making sure the house runs smoothly. I have very important work, I don't expect any problems when I get home."

Sam looked at Evelyn to see how she'd reacted to him speaking for her. She just smiled and nodded. Bloody hell, thought Sam, it must be hereditary, the men speak for the women, what a weird family.

With that a teenage girl walked in.

"Mum, Dad how long are you going to be. I'm so bored waiting," whinged the newcomer.

"Susan, I said wait in the car we're just coming," replied her father.

"Well I'm bored so if you don't come now I'm staying here."

"Evelyn deal with her, she is developing a real attitude."

As he turned back to Sam, Susan stuck two fingers up behind her fathers back. Sam smiled and thought, good on you girl, at least you're is not going to be bullied and be walked over.

"We'll leave you two in peace, be good and if you can't be good be careful," said Mr.Williams laughing and winking at him "we don't want any little accidents ruining Deans future do we ? I know what you girls are like, I've seen too many teenage pregnancies. So the condoms are in the drawer by my bed."

Dean took a packet from his back pocket.

"Don't worry Dad, I'm all prepared."

Dean's dad laughed again as he ushered his wife and daughter out of the house.

"Well done lad."

Sam feeling embarrassed by Dean's father's attitude, spoke up.

"Actually I've got to leave now."

Dean looked at her aghast.

"Why?"

"Sorry, I told mum I'd meet up with her for lunch." Sam lied as she put on her shoes. "Do you want to walk me back to the High Street?"

Dean looked disappointed.

"What's the point?"

They were now standing outside the front door. Sam tried to change the mood.

"What does your dad do exactly?"

"He is private secretary to Mr Jefferson."

"Who is he?"

Dean was surprised by Sam's question.

"Who is he? He is the top surgeon at the RUH. You must of heard of him?"

"Why? I've never had an operation. In fact I don't know anyone who has so why would I know who he is?"

Dean kicked a couple of stones with his foot, his hands were in his pockets.

"Can't you come back in for a quickie, my dad said they'd be gone for at least a couple of hours, we won't be disturbed."

Sam couldn't imagine anything worse. The thought of his groping hands on her made her flesh crawl.

"Look Dean, I think this has made me realise it's not working. All you want me for is sex. That's not much of a relationship so I think we just call it quits."

There she said it.

"What, you ungrateful bitch, no one dumps me. I'm dumping you because you're so fucking frigid. I'll tell everyone at school, no one will ever wanna go out with you."

Sam looked at him. What an arrogant prick he was just like his father. She smiled, Mrs Thomas was right they were both bullies.

"Tell them what you like I'm really not bothered."

Dean stormed back into the house slamming the door. Thank goodness that was over thought Sam. However her euphoria was short lived, who was she kidding? Why was it she couldn't get a decent boyfriend? It was seemed so unfair. If Dean told them she was frigid, she'd have no chance. With a sigh Sam decided to go and see her mum.

Chapter Five

The summer rolled on, it was a particularly hot August. Sam spent her days off hanging out with her friends and visiting her grandparents. Life was looking up, her mother's artistic career had taken off with a successful art exhibition in London, her best friend Megan was returning from Italy, and she had got rid of that arrogant Dean.
Megan arrived home and made her way to see Sam.

"Megs you're back!" said Sam as they hugged each other.

"Obviously," laughed Megan.

"You know what I mean," Sam looked at her friend. "Megs you've been in Italy for almost a month, you're paler than me!"

"Sam you can't imagine how hot it is out there this time of year, all you want to do is stay indoors plus you know me I burn like mad. As for those bloody tourists!"

"But you've had a good time?"

"Yes my family are great fun, although I'm sure my cousins think I'm adopted."

"Megs have you thought about what you wear for school? I'm starting to wish we could carry on wearing our school uniform it would be much easier."

"When we got back to the UK, Mum and I stopped off in London for a couple of days, I'm sorted."

"I haven't got a clue, do you fancy a trip to Bath with me?"

"Yes providing we can have some English food, I've had enough pasta and pizza for a while."

"Cream tea?"

"Perfect.

Sam and Megan walked into the town centre and headed towards her mothers studio. Adeline was busy painting when they arrived.

"Hi mum, Megs and I are going to Bath to sort out my school wardrobe, I wondered whether I could have a bit of cash?"

"Hello Megan lovely to see you back, have you had a good time?" asked Adeline.

"Yes thanks Mrs Thompson but it's nice to be back home."

"Luckily for you I sold a sculpture this morning for cash!" Sam's mother handed over some folded notes.

"Gosh Mum, £50, I don't need that much,"

Adeline looked at her daughter.

"Sam you never ask for anything and you've worked so hard this holiday, spend it wisely, have some lunch out, and anything left over you can put towards your car."

"Thanks mum, you're amazing, I can't give you a hug, as you're covered in paint!"

Sam and Megan walked back along the High Street to catch the bus, it was a double-decker so they raced upstairs to get a good view of the journey. As the bus drove through the town they could see into the park.

"Sam, look! Is that Dean with Savannah? See, over there, by the pavilion."

Sam leaned across to get a better look.

"Yeah I think you're right. Oh my God Megs, I haven't told you about my little adventure with Dean after you and Rosie left the party."

On the journey to Bath Sam told Megan all about her disastrous time with Dean, finishing with a visit to his home and meeting his awful father.

"So he was planning to have sex with you!"

"Yeah. Oh Megs he was awful, he had no conversation or interest in anything I said. All he did was to talk about himself and want to snog and grope me. I swear he never brushed his teeth! Oh and you know he always brags how important his dad is, we all assumed he was a doctor and virtually ran the hospital single-handed, but no, he's only a bloody secretary, not that I've got anything against secretaries," Sam paused, "Sorry I went on Megs."

"It's okay I'm sorry I wasn't here for you. What did you do after you dumped him?"

"I walked down to see my mum and told her about it!"

"What! even the bit that he wanted sex?"

"Yes."

"Your mum is so cool, if I'd gone home and said that to my mum she would've gone ballistic probably got the mafia round."

Sam laughed.

"That's just what he needs. Shall we go tell her?"
Megan grinned.

"No, come on, what did your mum say?

"She was fab, she'd asked if I was still a virgin, which I am, and said the first time should be with someone I trusted and loved and I'd know when it was right."

"As I said, your mum is so cool. I can't imagine having that sort of conversation with mine."

"How did they cope with Tim then?

"Oh they think he's some sort of superhero he gets on so well with my family. He even learnt some Italian before he came out to stay for the summer!"

"You're so lucky, do you think he's the one?"

"Who knows we're both planning on Uni, so we have to see how it goes, but I hope it lasts."

The two girls arrived in Bath centre and spent a couple of hours in the shops trying on clothes and then stopping for lunch. The outing was a success, they returned home tired, and laden with Samantha's purchases.

Chapter Six

Sam's mock A-level results arrived the week before they returned to school. She opened them as she sat down to have breakfast with her parents. She was very disappointed as she hadn't done as well as she'd hoped.

"Oh Mum I only just scraped through my chemistry and physics."

"It doesn't matter love, you've done really well in your maths and biology."

Her father looked on.

"Perhaps you're taking on too much. Why not drop one of the sciences to take the pressure off," he said.

"Dad that's the sort of thing Mr Quilter would say, why do men think I can't manage? I need them both if I'm going to get to Manchester."

"Come on Sam, don't be dramatic, Dads just trying to help."

"Well it's not helping, I need to talk to Megs, I bet she'd understand, you're both too old to remember what it's like."

Sam's dad looked at his wife and tried not to smirk.

"Well this old man had better get to work before his body gives up! How about you Adeline? Are you still alright to walk to work or shall I get you a Zimmer frame!"

"Dad, you're not funny."

Her father got up and gave both the women in his life a kiss on the head.

"Chin up Sam, it really isn't the end of the world, speak to Mr Johnson, if needed we could get some extra tuition to help you."

"Thanks Dad."

Across town a boy called Robert Brown and his mother Mary were driving towards Oldway Secondary school. Robert had also received his mock results that morning and had achieved straight A's across the board. However, he was far from happy. They had moved to Keyford three days ago, leaving Derby in a hurry. He hadn't been able to speak to his friends and was told he wasn't allowed to contact them.

Life was hard he didn't want to spend his last year of school away from his friends, he just wanted to go home.

Katie, his sister, was with him but she would be okay as she was in her second year at Uni and would be away from all the upheaval. The house they moved to was a three bed semi on a quiet road. He had been able to bring a few personal possessions that were important to him, his guitar, stereo and his music collection.

He looked across at his mother. He'd never seen her like this before, constantly looking over her shoulder twitchy and nervous. It was if she'd never driven before, checking which gear she was in, getting confused with the position of the indicators and windscreen wipers, in reality it wasn't her usual car. He noticed how old she looked and had lost weight in the last week, she had dark shadows under her eyes from a lack of sleep. His smart bright mother now looked a wreck, it was so bloody unfair his life was shit. They drove through the school gates and turned into the parking area. Stopping the car Mary looked at him.

"Look, I know this is difficult and you don't want to be here, but," she hesitated, "we don't have any choice, with any luck the police can sort this out quickly and we can all get back to normal"

"Can we go back home then?" Rob asked.

Mary sighed.

"I don't want to be here any more than you do, I really don't know what will happen, but you've always been such a positive child, try and make the best of a bad situation hopefully it will be over soon."

"But I don't see why Dad......"

"William please don't be difficult, I really couldn't cope."

"Robert! Mum, don't forget, I'm now fucking Robert!

Normally his mother would've told him off for swearing, but she didn't have the energy, it made him feel worse he looked at his feet and mumbled.

"I'm sorry Mum"

She patted his hand.

"Come on love you can do this."

The school was a large modern building, Robert and Mary walked into the vestibule and were greeted by a smart man in his 40s. He walked towards them his hand outstretched and introduced himself as Mr Jarvis the headmaster. Standing next to him was a much younger good-looking man.

"Hello Mrs Brown, Robert, welcome to Oldway School. This is Mr Johnson who will be your form tutor for your time here Robert."

Mr Johnson shook their hands, he saw a tall lad with longish hair, a fringe that covered half his face, heavy glasses and wearing a brace. Poor bugger he thought he looks as if he's got the weight of the world on his shoulders and as for the mother, she was a nervous wreck.

Mr Jarvis led them to his office to go through paperwork, review Roberts results and plan his timetable. Mr Johnson joined them and was suitably impressed with his mock results.

"So Robert, now that's all sorted Mr Johnson will take you for a walk around the school. I believe Mr Quilter is in his office, he is the head of science, it would be good for you to meet him. School starts on Monday for all the six form, but you won't need to start until Wednesday as they spend the first couple of days sorting out results, options etc so no need for you to be here twiddling your thumbs. This year for the first time six formers won't be wearing uniform, but we do expect you to look reasonably tidy, no jeans"

Mr Jarvis looked disapprovingly at Robert dressed in his jeans and T-shirt and thought he may have to introduce a short hair policy. He shook hands with Robert and his mother.

"Mr Johnson will look after you, goodbye."

They followed Mr Johnson out of the office and started the tour.

"The school is in two parts, this building is the newer half and is known as the west building, the other side was the old grammar school and is as you might expect is the east building. I think all your lessons will be in the east building Robert, but I'll quickly show you around in case you need to come here"

The building was purpose-built with a long corridor, large bright classrooms leading off on the left, offices, cloakrooms, and a staircase on the right leading to a similar layout upstairs. Walking back outside a path lead to the east building, halfway between the two was a smaller newer building. Mr Johnson took them inside.

"This is the sixth form block," climbing the stairs in front of them they entered a large classroom, "this will be your form room, there are lockers along the wall for you to use, just choose an empty one when you arrive on Wednesday."

Robert looked out of the window onto a large playing field, he had to grudgingly admit the facilities were superior compared with his previous school. Back downstairs Mr Johnson showed Robert the cafeteria and study areas,

"I will show you around the east building and take you to meet Mr Quilter"

As they walked along the path Mr Johnson pointed out the gym and swimming pool.

"Sport isn't compulsory in the sixth form, but it is encouraged, if you have a sport we don't provide you can let us know, for example last year a group chose to go iceskating in Bristol, it was a great success"

The east building wasn't so well laid out as the west, Robert thought he'd probably get lost initially but despite being an older building the science labs looked well equipped and spacious. Turning down another corridor Mr Johnson knocked on a door. Robert and his mother were introduced to Mr Quilter head of science. He was suitably impressed with Roberts results and tried to engage him in conversation about his future plans. Robert felt exhausted there was so much to take in. Mr Quilter looked at him and saw an unhappy young man, why on earth would his mother make him move schools, he thought, especially in his final year and how he could possibly be accepted by other students, as well as obtain his full potential.

"Your results are outstanding Robert, said Mr Quilter, "I have a few students under my care whose results have been somewhat disappointing, I've decided to pair them up with more successful students such as yourself with the aim they can work together. Would you be interested in doing that?"

Robert appeared indifferent to the idea, he felt a discrete nudge from his mother.

"Yes sir, that would be fine," Robert replied.

"Good, good ,well I think I'll team you up with Sam Thompson," he stood and shook hands, " I look forward to seeing you next week. Mr Johnson show them out please"

The tour party left the building.

"Is there anywhere else you'd like to see Robert," said Mr Johnson, "or have you seen enough for today? I know it's a lot to take in."

"I would like to have another look at the six form block to familiarise myself where I need to go," answered Robert.

After a quick refresh, Robert and his mother said goodbye to Mr Johnson and made their way to the car

"Well done love, that's the first hurdle over," said his mother.

"Yeah not too bad without any students!" Robert replied sullenly

It was Monday morning. Sam had changed her clothes three times, she was wearing a light skirt and a blouse, tanned bare legs and sandals and was now panicking about pens and rulers. Her father walked into the kitchen and took one look at her.

"You going like that?" he said.

"What? Why?" said Sam agitated.

Her mother intervened.

"David don't wind her up, she is driving me mad already!"

"I'm Just saying, it's going to rain later."

Sam looked out the window dark clouds were now covering the sun, which had been out since first light.

"I don't believe it, I have to change", she shrieked as she ran back upstairs.

The phone rang.

"I bet it's Megan," said Adeline picking up the phone.

It was Megan, she wanted to know what was Sam wearing as the forecast says rain.

"Hold on Megan I'll give her a shout."

Sam reappeared in a short tartan skirt over thick tights she grabbed the phone. David looked at his wife.

"Can she wear something that short to school?" he asked.

"She's fine, stop worrying," assured Adeline.

Sam finished her call and ran upstairs. A few minutes later She returned.

"You've changed again!" David exclaimed.

"I felt a bit exposed in that skirt."

Her father gave her a kiss on her head.

"Much better topsy, do you want a lift?

"No thanks Dad I'm going to meet Megan, we'll walk together."

Sam and Megan walked to school picking up Rosie on the way. There was great excitement in the six form block as students greeted one another, catching up following the summer break, and the novelty of not having to wearing school uniform. Looking around it was obvious this policy was going to cause competition amongst some of the girls. Sam just wished she could have worn jeans.
The students settled into the form room where Mr Johnson welcomed them back and went through the anticipated timetables. A couple of students had decided to leave after getting their exam results, one of them was Savannah Marshall much to Mr Johnson's relief. The students would spend the next couple of days meeting their tutors, Sam was dreading seeing Mr Quilter.

"I bet he suggests I drop one if not both science subjects," said Sam.

"He might not Sam," said Megan trying to sound positive.

"Megs he is so old, and old men seem to think science is for men and girls should focus on home economics!"

"What time are you seeing him"

Sam looked at her watch.

"In about 10 minutes, wish me luck."

Sam made here way through the east building to Mr Quilter's office. She knocked on his door.

"Come in, oh hello Samantha , good holiday?"

"Yes thanks sir"

"Take a seat. Let's have a look at these results. I must say they are rather disappointing"

Here we go thought Sam, have you thought about cookery or needlework instead or maybe give up or taking up modelling, get a husband...

"So what do you think? Would that help?" asked Mr Quilter.

Bugger she's been so busy daydreaming she hadn't listen to a word he said.

"Sorry Sir could you repeat that?"

"I said I'd like to partner you up with another student, so you can work together. I know how important getting a good grade is to you and I wonder if this might help. We could review it in a couple of months and see if it works."

"You're not suggesting I give up science then?"

Sam couldn't believe it.

"Why would I do that? You are a hard-working student with a lot of potential, we can go over your papers and see where you need some help."

Sam looked at him suspiciously.

"The student you want me to team up with it's not Dean is it?" said Sam crossing her fingers in her lap.

Why do these girls get crushes on idiots like Dean thought Mr Quilter. He had hoped Samantha was better than that.

"No, Dean decided to drop science"

"Thank goodness, I don't think I could do it if you paired me with him."

Ah he thought, she was better than that after all.

Sam left Mr Quilter's office on cloud nine and vowed to work as hard as she could. What a blooming marvellous teacher he was.

Megan waited for Samantha to see how she'd got on, Samantha told her the good news. To celebrate Megan suggested they call into the little teashop on the High Street have a cream tea, on the way home.

The girls chatted away as they sat at their favourite table. The waitress came over.

"Savannah!" exclaimed Megan.

Megan looked at Samantha .

"Hi Savannah, we heard you weren't coming back how's things?"

"Couldn't face another year at school so I decided to quit and get a job."

"Good for you," said Samantha .

"I'm glad you came in Sam, I hope there's no hard feelings."

"Hard feelings? About what?"

"Well you and Dean. He told me about how upset you were when he dumped you."

Megan snorted and tried to turn it into a cough. Savannah didn't notice.

"He told me you were desperate and wouldn't take no for an answer," continued Savannah.

"Savannah! You haven't taken their order yet!" said a voice.

It was Mrs Trenwin who owned the teashop, Savannah rolled her eyes.

"Doing it now, what do you want?"

"Two cream teas please," answered Samantha .

Savannah strode off and gave the order to Mrs Trenwin then came straight back.

"So are you and Dean going out then?" Samantha asked. Savannah smiled.

"Oh my God he's gorgeous, we usually go to the park or his house. Did you go there? It's so nice, his dad is lovely too. Do you know he works at the hospital?"

"Savannah!" called Mrs Trenwin.

She had a tray ready with their order. Savannah went to the counter collected it and returned.

"No hard feelings, Savannah. I don't think Dean and I were suited," said Samantha taking the cream teas from the tray.

Savannah turned away, Megan was trying hard not to laugh.

"Don't you dare," glared Samantha , "bloody hell you wait, I might just punch him tomorrow!"

It was Wednesday morning and Robert was having an argument with his mother.

"I can walk mum."

"No I'm taking you"

"Bloody hell I'm not a baby you haven't taken me to school since I was eight!"

"I'm taking you, and that's final."

Robert stormed out of the kitchen slamming the door. He met his sister Katie on the stairs.

"What's all the shouting about?"

"Mum wants to drive me to school."

"Will, she's worried about you that's all."

"Why? Does she think I'm going to run away, or get mugged, or even raped!"

"Will, calm down, it's because she cares."

The fight had left him.

"You're supposed to call me Robert"

"I'll come with you and have a look at this crappy school if you want."

He gave her a hug.

"As Art would say 'like a Bridge over troubled water', thanks Sis."

Katie smiled at him.

"Go and say sorry to Mum."

Mary dropped him off a little way from the school, so he wouldn't feel too embarrassed. Robert got out of the car and followed the crowds of school children through the gates. Everyone was in uniform apart from him, he was sure the head that said the six formers didn't have to wear uniform. What if he'd got it wrong! He felt sick, he really didn't want to be there. He thought if he was back home he would've walked in with his mates, joking and messing around, he wondered what they thought about his sudden disappearance. Robert suddenly felt tears in his eyes, he couldn't let anyone see he was crying, thank goodness for his glasses. He looked up and found himself in front of the six form block. There were plenty of students milling around, no one was wearing uniform, thank goodness he thought.

"Robert!"

He turned, it was Mr Johnson.

"Follow me I'll take you to meet Martin, you're both taking the same subjects so I've asked him to look after you until you find your way around."

Robert followed Mr Johnson up the stairs to the form room. It was full of noise and bodies. Mr Johnson clapped his hands.

"Quiet!"

Amazingly silence fell over the room.

"This is Robert Brown who has moved to the area. He will be joining us for his final year. Please make him feel welcome. Martin Parker I'd like you to show him around as he is taking the same lessons as you."

Mr Johnson gestured at Martin to come forward and meet Robert.

"Show him to his locker where he can put his things. The rest of you take a seat while we have registration, then we're all going to the west building hall for assembly. You all know the drill, sixth formers sit at the front of the hall facing the room at the side of the stage. There will be a reporter and a photographer from The Keyford Gazette, so behave."

Martin showed Robert to his locker.

"What do we call you?" asked Martin,

Robert panicked for a moment.

"Rob, Bob, or Robert?"

"Oh, um, Rob, my mates call me Rob."

Panic over he thought.

Following registration they walked across to the hall and shuffled into place, Robert sat at the back and kept his head down. Mr Jarvis welcomed them all back to school, the teachers who were sitting on the stage introduced themselves for the benefit of the new first year pupils. Mr Jarvis made some announcements including the appointments of the school prefects for the coming year. As their names were called the pupils were asked to stand up. Robert had another brief moment of panic, then realised he obviously wouldn't be one. Finally the head boy and girl were to be announced.

"Dean Williams please come to the stage," said Mr Jarvis.

He seemed a popular choice, although watching him Robert noted he walked with a swagger.

"Sam Thompson you too, please come to the stage."

Robert's head shot up. Sam was a girl! He'd assumed Sam was a boy, she also was a very popular choice. Rob watched as she turned and walked in front of him, she was absolutely gorgeous. He muttered under his breath.

"As Cliff would say 'Goodbye Sam, hello Samantha'."

Martin sitting next to him chuckled.

"You're telling me, it's worth coming to school just to look at her. As far as I know she's going out with Dean, shame he's such a wanker."

The next half hour was spent with the photographer taking pictures of the first years, the sixth form, the prefects and the head boy and girl. Robert kept his head down allowing his fringe to hide his face. Walking back to the form room Robert turned to Martin.

"Apparently Mr Quilter has partnered me up with Sam for science."

"Really, you lucky, lucky, bastard!"

"Life of Brian?"

Martin smirked.

"Yeah, I'm a big fan"

"Me too!"

Maybe school wasn't going to be so bad after all.

Chapter Seven

School settled into a routine. Initially Mary insisted on dropping him off and picking him up. By the third week Rob had put his foot down, Mary relented but she said he must be home by 4 pm.

Katie Brown was packing for Uni and after a lot of arguing and phone calls, she was now going to Cardiff. Robert knew he would miss her terribly.

"It's the weekends Katie, you know Mum won't let me out of her sight , it'll be so boring."

"Stay cool little bro it isn't forever, this time next year you'll be at Uni, then freedom!"

"I know, but I've made a couple of friends, they've asked me over twice now and I've had to make excuses it's really awkward and I'd I'd like to go."

Katie didn't know what to say.

"Have you tried speaking to Mum?"

"Katie don't you think I've tried, what other 18-year-old has a 4 pm curfew?"

"Give her time, oh and don't forget you must call me Ruth."

Monday. Robert was looking forward to walking to school for the first time. His trek took him to the High Street, down the main road over the bridge and up Bath hill, along the Oldway and through a couple of footpath's to school. It had taken a lot longer than he had anticipated, maybe the car wasn't such a bad idea. At the end of the day he caught up with Martin and his friend Richard. Martin always cycled to school, but he walked with Richard for a short while.

"You're walking!" said Richard.

"Yeah although I was surprised how far it is.

"Which way did you go?" Martin asked.

Rob told them the route he took.

"Come with us, we'll show you a quicker way."

Rob followed them out of school, along the footpath to the Oldway. Instead of walking along they were ready to cross the road.

"Wait till Mrs Jones says we can go, she gets really pissy if you cross without her," said Richard.

Mrs Jones the lollipop lady walked into the road and stopped the traffic. They crossed then went down a steep footpath to the river.

"This is where we part company. I live just up here on the left," said Richard.

Martin mounted his bike.

"I now cycle a couple of miles out of town to the farm."

"Which way do I go?"

"Shit, I forgot you don't know, Sorry Rob.Turn right here, follow the river, that takes you to the park, basically you walk straight through and at the end turn right and you're home.

"Thanks mate, see you tomorrow"

It was a pleasant walk along the tow path, there were a few other school kids who slowly turned off at various points. Rob smiled to himself, his mum would have a fit if she could see him walking under the road bridge, just the sort of place to get mugged!

Walking home each evening with his friends however, briefly gave him a small sense of belonging and eased his isolation. He'd had to explain his parents had separated and his mum had had a nervous breakdown and that's why he wasn't able to leave her alone. He needn't have worried, Martin and Richard were very sympathetic.

Science with Samantha was a whole new problem. Mr Quilter, had as promised, paired them up. During the first lesson Martin had looked across at Robert and winked. She was breathtaking. Literally he could barely breathe, speech was impossible. When he tried he developed a stammer! Bloody marvellous Robert thought. Science was his thing, sadly he started dreading the classes. Samantha was pleasant and friendly, always keen, she often leaned into him to see how he worked something out. He didn't think she did it on purpose, but he could feel the heat from her body, it was like electricity running through him. He could smell her, it was intoxicating, twice he started to get an erection and had distract himself with images of Margret Thatcher to cool down.

Unknown to him Samantha was also dreading the science lessons. One Friday at lunch she had a good moan to Megan.

"It's bloody hopeless Meg, he's really intelligent, he works out the formula as soon as Mr Quilter puts them on the board, but he won't even look at me let alone speak to me. I have to lean across all the time to see what he's writing."

"Perhaps he does it on purpose Sam, to make you lean nearer him."

"I don't think so, he positively freezes when I get too close."

"Look at it from his point of view."

"Like how?"

"Well," Megan paused, " If I'd been paired with someone like Dean for instance, I would feel tongue-tied and awkward."

"Dean! Are you serious? He's a moron you're way better than that."

"What I'm saying Sam is you are pretty gorgeous, sadly he's really not got a lot going for him in looks or personality."

Samantha sighed.

"Et to brute."

Megan frowned.

"Why did you say that?"

"Why does everybody make assumptions because of the way I look? I know you'll think I'm mad but I wish I had acne."

Megan nearly choked on her sandwich.

"Plonker! What are you going to do? Do you think Mr Quilter could help you?

"I don't know, I'll give it another week, I've been trying to catch him alone, but he's always with Martin and Richard he even walks home with them. He doesn't seem shy or feel awkward with them.

The next week followed the same pattern. On Friday Samantha decided to walk through the park and visit her mum at her studio. The weather had turned a lot colder, Samantha was walking briskly to keep warm. To her surprise she spotted Robert walking ahead of her alone. This was her a chance to speak to him so she started to run.

"Rob, Rob hang on," called Samantha .

He turned to look at her. Oh shit what did she want he thought. She finally caught up and grabbed his arm while she caught her breath.

"Rob, we need to talk."

He raised his eyebrows.

"About what?"

Samantha looked around.

"Come on let's sit there."

She led him to a bench slightly off the main path, hidden by some Leylandii trees, she hadn't let go of his arm.

"It's a bit more sheltered here. Bloody hell it's cold. Rob I really do need to speak to you."

"About?"

"Why do you have such a problem with me?"

"Uh!"

"Exactly, as soon as I speak to you you become monosyllabic.I've seen you with Martin and Richard and you chat away. So what's your problem with me?"

Before he had a chance to speak she carried on.

"Megan says it's because of the way I look. Please tell me she's wrong."

"Well…"

He was cut short again.

"Because, you are super intelligent and hopefully don't judge a book by its cover. Science is really important to me, I want to go to Manchester, for that I need good grades. Mr Quilter obviously thought you and I could work together, which I'd really like. Could we please try and be friends?"

All through Samantha's outburst Robert had been looking at his feet.

"Here's an idea, if Meg is right..," Samantha paused and turned towards him, "look at me, really look, go on."

He looked up and took a deep breath. Where to start, he thought. Her hair was golden even on this dark dull afternoon, when she moved it was like a field of corn in a breeze. Her skin was like porcelain, absolutely perfect, not a blemish. Her eyes were the deepest blue, he stared into them and then her lips, full and sensuous, as he looked she parted them slightly to reveal her perfect white teeth. Oh to kiss those lips.

"See!" she interrupted his reverie, "hair, skin, nose two eyes and the mouth nothing special. Now it's my turn."

"What!" Robert exclaimed.

"Take off your glasses. "

He obliged.

"Let's start with your hair," she said touching it , " it's lovely and shiny , although I hate to have to say it I think it would look better if it was a little shorter."

Robert gulped, she still had her hand on his head. Did she honestly have no idea the effect she was having on him.

"For a boy you have really good skin, I work in the chemist on the High Street on a Saturday and the number of lads who come in with really bad acne, you're very lucky"

She then looked into his eyes continuing her analysis.

"Wow you've got gorgeous eyes, such a deep brown and your eye lashes, my goodness you need to get rid of those glasses, can you wear contact lenses? Your eyes are to die for. I wonder what colour eyes our kids would have?"

The last remark took Robert by surprise.

"What!"

Sam laughed.

"Sorry Rob I've been doing biology, we've been looking at genes, but I can't remember which eye colour is more dominant."

Robert grinned, he had never met anyone like her before.

"Do you ever stop talking?"

Samantha grinned back.

"Bloody hell Rob that's the most you said to me since you started at school!"

Robert went to put his glasses back on.

"Hang on, I haven't finished yet!"

He frowned.

"I haven't done your mouth, it's difficult because you've got a brace, but I'd say you've got a nice mouth and you'll have lovely straight teeth when your brace comes off."

"Have you finished?"

"Yep, what I'm trying to say is, we are no different really, so could you just think of me as one of your friends?"

Robert smiled.

"Sam I will do my best to help you achieve the grades you need . It's difficult to talk at school, especially with Dean watching me like a hawk."

"You're joking, he is a complete prat."

"According to Martin you two are an item."

"We were briefly at the beginning of the summer hols. It was a complete disaster, now he's seeing that gobby Savannah, I think he's met more than his match there!"

"Is she at school?"

"Of course I keep forgetting, no she left the lower sixth if you want to check her out she works in the little teashop on the High Street."

"Jealous?"

"Jealous! Relieved more like, I'm just pissy because he told her he dumped me as I was frigid and suicidal afterwards. She is welcome to him, I swear he never brushes his teeth."

He felt more comfortable looking at her now.

"Tell you what," she continued, "let's go there next week after school I want to go through the periodic table with you and you can help me remember it all, it's too blooming cold out here."

"Okay,Tuesday suit you? We'll have had double chemistry in the afternoon and if there is an issue we can talk it through. If there is ever anything you need to go over I always walk this way home."

He looked at his watch 16.15, his mum would be fretting.

"I better get on, see you Monday, bye Sam."

"Bye Rob and thanks, in anticipation."

Robert smiled.

"As Leonard would say 'I'm your man'."

Samantha frowned.

"Who is Leonard?"

Robert was already striding away. A smile spread across his face. He can now start to enjoy science again, thank you Mr Quilter he thought. It was 16.30 when he walked through the door. His mother was frantic.

"Where have you been, you're half an hour late? I was expecting the worst, I didn't know what to do," said Mary wringing her hands with worry.

He wanted to scream at her.

"I'm 18, its fucking 4.30, this is all Dads fault."

He knew it would only make things worse. He took a deep calming breath and put his hands on his mother's shoulders.

"I'm sorry mum, you know I've been helping a student with science I had to stay on at school today, forgot the time. I'll be helping Sam a lot leading up to the exams so I'll be late sometimes. I'll try and let you know the day before, but maybe expect me home at 4:30 from now on anyway."

Mary seemed to calm down.

"Sorry love, I'm just so scared that something will happen" He gave her a hug.

Chapter Eight

The weekend came and went, it was Monday again. Robert couldn't wait to see Samantha . They met in the form room.

"Hi Sam, good weekend?"

Samantha beamed at him.

"Hi Rob, yes thanks and you?"

"Not too bad, I'll see you in class."

He saw Martin staring at him his mouth open.

"What?" asked Robert

"What the fuck Rob, the hottest girl, probably on the planet, just...,you know?"

"Just what, she spoke to me"

"Yeah, how the fuck did that happen?"

Robert grinned.

"My natural good looks and charisma!"

Martin had a big smile on his face.

"Long may it last, because if looks could kill you'd be a dead man with the look Dean is giving you."

"Apparently he doesn't brush his teeth," replied Robert .

"You're a dark horse Robert Brown."

Robert was wishing the time away, he kept telling himself calling into the teashop with Samantha was no big deal. He knew he was kidding himself, he was sure she'd probably cancel. Double chemistry was hard work and Samantha felt like her head was spinning, but true to his word Robert explained his calculations which was a real help.

"Are you still free to have a cuppa later?" asked Samantha .

Robert shrugged, desperate not to appear too keen.

"Yeah if you're up for it."

"Okay meet me by the school gates, we can walk up together, as long as Martin and Richard don't mind."

Richard was just behind Robert , He poked his head around.

"Go for it man."

School had finished for the day Robert , Martin, and Richard walked towards the gates.

"Robert's got a date with Sam this evening," announced Richard.

"You're joking!" exclaimed Martin.

"It's not a date," protested Robert "we're just going to have a cuppa at some teashop to talk science, and I'm supposed to check out some girl called Sara or something"

"Oh God," said Martin "not Savannah Marshall?"

"Yeah, I think that's her name, apparently she's going out with Dean."

"No, you're joking. She's got the biggest pair of tits in the school."

Robert shrugged his shoulders and at that moment Samantha and Megan appeared.

"Hi guys," said Samantha .

Megan gave Samantha a hug.

"Have fun Sam," she whispered, "got to go, Tim's here."

Megan gave them a wave and got into a Mini.

"Who is he?" asked Richard.

"Meg's boyfriend, Tim," said Samantha looking at him, "Why, do you fancy her?"

"A bit," said Richard blushing.

"Oh Richard that's so sweet, do you want me to tell her?"

"How long has she been seeing Tim?"

"Oh I think it's over a year."

"Don't bother then."

"Do you mind if I walk down with you guys?"

"No not at all."

Although Samantha had been at school for six years with Martin and Richard she hadn't realised what nice lads they were. The four of them chatted as they walked down the hill to the river. Richard and Martin went their respective ways while Samantha and Robert walked up the hill to the High Street. A bitter wind was blowing and rain had threatened, the sky was getting darker by the minute. The teashop looked bright and cosy, they entered and looked for an empty table.

"I don't envy Martin having to cycle home," said Sam.

"Me neither."

"Oh hi Savannah how's life?" said Sam.

Savannah watched Samantha and Robert sit at a table. She came over, ignoring Robert and then launched into Samantha .

"Have you said anything to Dean?"

Samantha looked bewildered.

"About what?"

"He thinks we should split up because you're making such a fuss wanting to get back with him. You lied to me, you told me you were okay with him and me, why would you do that?"

"Savannah!" called a voice.

"I'm just taking the order Mrs Trenwin"

Savannah continued.

"How can you show your face here? Personally I'd throw you out, but it's not up to me."

"Savannah let me introduce you to Rob"

She seemed to register him for the first time.

"My boyfriend."

"Savannah!" Mrs Trenwin called again.

She walked off to the counter. Robert looked at Samantha .

"Your what?."

"Sorry Rob, it just came out."

"She hasn't taken our order."

Savannah was now serving an older couple. And enormous flash of lightning and clap of thunder made them jump as the heavens opened.

"Poor Martin, hope he got home okay," said Robert.

To their surprise Savannah reappeared with a tray laden with tea pots and cakes.

"So how long have you to been together?" Savannah enquired.

"We met in the holidays," Samantha took Robert's hand, "didn't we gorgeous."

"I would be careful," said Savannah looking at Robert, "I think it's probably on the rebound. Is Mr Johnson still your form tutor?"

Robert picked up the tea pot.

"Darling do you want me to be mother and poor tea?"

"Oh yes please, sorry Savannah in answer to your question, Mr Johnson is still looking after us."

"Can you tell him where I work, we nearly got together last year, but it was difficult what with him being a teacher."

"Savannah!," barked Mrs Trenwin.

"Bloody hell she's always on at me."

Savannah left them in peace.

"Did she really have a thing with Mr Johnson? I suppose it's possible, he's not much older than us."

"You must be joking whenever they were together he always looked terrified."

Samantha and Robert ate in silence for a while, the cakes were amazing, Robert hoped he had enough money on him. Samantha put her head in her hands.

"I can't believe I did that Rob, I really am so sorry but she was winding me up."

"As Carol would say 'You've got a friend'."

"Carol?"

"Carole King, you must of heard of her."

"Oh I get it, so on Friday you said Leonard something."

"Leonard Cohen."

Sam paused

"Mmm still No."

"Really? Do you like music?"

"Yes, love it."

"So who are you into?"

"You've put me on the spot, I can't think of anyone," Samantha stood up, "I've got to go to ladies excuse me."

Hope she isn't going to climb out the window thought Rob. As he turned to check the door he was faced with Savannah's chest he threw his head back quickly. Well he had been warned! Savannah presented him with the bill. He checked it and paid up.

"Quick," said Savannah, "while Sam is in the loo, are you two really going out?"

"Of course, why else would we be here together?"

"What's she like then? Dean says she was frigid that's why he dumped her."

"Frigid! You must be joking. I've never had such fantastic sex in my life!"

There was a loud cough, Samantha was standing behind Savannah.

Savannah picked up the tray and walked off.

"I can't believe you just said that!" said Sam.

"Don't blame me you're the one who started it. She asked if you were frigid, what else was I supposed to say!"

Sam stood there with her arms crossed.

"The rains stopped, it's time we left."

"She is watching us so you better smile a bit," said Rob.

"Come on," said Sam linking her arm through his, "shit we haven't paid!"

"I did it when you're in the loo."

"My treat next time then."

Robert inwardly rejoiced as they left the Tea shop.

"Forgiven me then?" Robert said sheepishly.

"Knowing Savannah we'll be the gossip of the school tomorrow."

"She's not there though."

"She has still got a lot of friends, not to mention Dean."

"Does that bother you Sam?"

"No, but I realised he's a bully like his father. So I hope he doesn't have a go at you. All the rugby he plays he's probably quite tough."

Robert thought about it.

"Don't worry I can look after myself."

They had made their to the chemist shop where Sam worked on Saturdays.

"Rob, I'm going to cut through here, thanks for the tea and the company. We didn't get much chemistry done, maybe next time."

"See you tomorrow... Oh and in answer to your question, definitely brown."

Samantha looks puzzled then realisation dawned and at that point she walked into the shop. Robert looked up at the sky more rain was on its way, he turned and made his way home.

Samantha made it home to an empty house having avoided the rain. After she made herself a drink she sat on her bed. She berated herself, what had possessed her to say that to Savannah? Then she laughed, well done to Rob for playing along.

He was actually a really nice guy, she realised she enjoyed chatting to him and he had even asked her questions about herself. She knew he was a grade A student but not once had he bragged about himself, unlike Dean. She ran downstairs and went through her parents records. Yes, Carole King's tapestry album, she set it up on the record player and listened to… You've got a friend.

By Friday the storms had passed and the sun had made an appearance. After school, Sam walked halfway home with Megan, then ran on towards to the park. As she hoped Robert was ahead of her.

"Rob, wait up", she called.

He turned and gave her a wave, she caught up with him puffing and panting.

"Blimey Sam, do you need to sit down?"

She nodded, as they walked across to 'their' bench. Samantha regained her breath.

"We left school at the same time how come you are so far ahead?"

"Two reasons, first I've got long legs and second I don't talk as much as you and Megan do!"

"Ha ha, funny boy."

Robert smiled.

"To what do I owe this pleasure?"

"Oh hark at you, you'll be quoting Shakespeare next."

"No I'm not into the Bard."

"I just wanted to say sorry about Tuesday, I hope no one has had a go at you, I feel really bad."

Robert didn't like to let her know his street cred had gone up big time, his friends Martin and Richard couldn't believe it.

"The weird thing is Sam, the more I try to play it down and say we're just friends the more they don't believe me!"

Samantha cuddled into him.

"Do you mind I'm cold. Hey, Perhaps we should have a big bust up in the teashop so Savannah can tell the gossip grapevine we've split up."

No, no, no, he thought.

"Yeah I suppose so, the trouble is we will still need to meet up to discuss school work, and it's going to be impossible to sit out here, much before the winter is over".

"You're right," said Samantha as she cuddled in even closer.

"Come here."

He put his arm around her.

"Any warmer?"

"A little, one thing I've noticed, you always smell nice what is it?"

" Aramis, my sister bought it for my birthday."

"Do you have any other siblings?"

"No just one sister, K...." he stopped himself and pretended to cough, "sorry her name is Ruth, she's at Uni."

"Lucky Ruth, although that will be us next year. What is she reading, as they say."

"Law."

There was a pause.

"You were right," said Sam suddenly, "definitely brown and my music choices are the Eurythmics, Duran Duran the Human league, Blondie, bored yet?

"No, you've not heard of my mate Leonard?"

Sam shook her head.

"What music did you think I was into?" he continued.

"I don't want to be someone who makes assumptions about people, because it pisses me off when they do it to me, but looking at you with your long hair, I'd have you down as a head banger.

"Go on then, elaborate."

"Um AC/DC!"

"Any others?"

"I don't know any others, Status quo?"

"I can see I'm going to have to educate your musical knowledge, hey you're shivering it's too cold out here."

"Mr Johnson said after Christmas we can start to do some of our free study periods at home. Will you be doing that? Because I was hoping we could go through some old papers together."

Robert looked uncomfortable.

"Can I trust you Sam?"

51

She sat up straight and looked him.

"Of course you can."

He removed his arm from her shoulder.

"It's, Mum. Since coming here, she's had some sort of breakdown. She gets anxious if I'm late home."

"Do you need to go now?"

"No, we've agreed a time, and Tuesday was okay because I told her on Monday I'd be late. I haven't been out over the weekend since we got here," he ran his hands through her hair, "so going to school is a sort of relief, I know that sounds terrible, but it's true. Please don't repeat this to anyone."

Samantha took both of his hands in hers.

"Robert Brown I promise this is between the two of us. We can study in the library at school."

"Thanks Sam."

"I know this is cheating but, as Carol would say 'You've got a friend'."

"Sam Thompson that is cheating, you need to work on some of your own song lyrics. Now it's time to go home, before you catch pneumonia."

Chapter Nine

Robert had been at school for over two months now and hadn't attended any PE lessons. It wasn't compulsory in the sixth form but it was encouraged.
It was early November, Martin approached him and asked whether he could swim.
 "Yes I'm not too bad, why?"
 "The school has a fun swim gala at the end of November and we need a team, they'll be me, Rich, John and hopefully you. Are you willing to give it a go?"
 "Yes, but I'm not sure I've got any trunks."
 "I'll see if we've got any spare between us that would fit you."
 "Are there any good swimmers that could beat us?"
 "Yeah, bloody Dean and his mates, they've won the past three years."
 "What, they're that good!"
 Richard had now joined them.
 "We may be in with a chance Martin, Matthew Perry left last year and he was their best swimmer. I don't know who they are replacing him with. Are you with us Rob?"

 The following Monday lunchtime the four of them were in the changing room dressed only in trunks. Martin looked at Robert .
 "Bloody hell Rob, no wonder you've pulled Sam Thompson you've got a bloody six pack!"
 Richard and John stared and cheered.
 "Come on hunk let's hope you can swim."
 Mr Winston the PE teacher was at the poolside, the four lads stood clutching their towels.
 "It's fucking freezing, where's the roof?" Robert said through chattering teeth.
 "Didn't we tell you it's an outdoor pool?"
 "Come on lads, we haven't got all day, stop behaving like a bunch of girls and get in the water," said Mr Winston.
 "There's only one way to do it," announced Robert dropping his towel and jumping in.

He was followed by his mates, shouting as they hit the water. After about 10 minutes of furious swimming they had warmed up and stopped to get their breath..

"Where did you learn to swim? Because you're bloody good," said Martin.

Robert smiled.

"I belonged to the local swimming club back home, I've swam for years, with the move here it was the last thing on my mind.

"With our new team member we might just win," said Richard confidently.

They swam for another 10 minutes and even Mr Winston who hadn't really been taking much notice started to time Robert's lengths. The lads climbed out of the pool Mr Winston approached Robert .

"That's the fastest lengths anyone's ever done. I coach the local swimming club, it would be really great if you could join us"

Robert's initial reaction was to say yes, swimming was such a distraction for him, he imagined training at the weekends, then realised he wasn't supposed to draw any attention to himself.

"Sorry sir, maybe next year I've got so much on with my A-levels"

"If you change your mind, let me know."

In the changing rooms Martin made an announcement to his 'team'.

"We keep Robs swimming skills a secret okay, don't say a word to anybody. We don't want Dean finding out he's got serious competition."

They all agreed.

Over the next couple of weeks the lads trained, Rob was able to give them some tips to improve their strokes and speed. He met Samantha a couple of times after school in the park, and told her about his role in the impending gala.

"How does it work? Does the whole school watch? There isn't much room around the poolside," asked Robert .

"They do it in year groups, although the lower and upper sixth all go together as there's not so many of us. How've you got on in the training?"

Robert trusted Sam, but he'd promised his mates he'd keep it a secret.

"I can't believe anyone can enjoy swimming in the pool it's so bloody cold!"

Samantha laughed.

"Normal pupils only swim in the summer not like you crazy buggers."

"It does nothing for my manhood!"

Samantha shrieked and slapped his arm.

"Rob behave!"

The day before the gala the weather was horrendous. There was great excitement in the staffroom as bets were being placed.

"Any tips then Roger?" Marcus Johnson asked.

"I am saying nothing," replied Mr Winston.

"Well Dean William's team has won for the last three years there is no reason it will be any different this year, they've got to be favourite. Roger?

"No comment!"

"You're bluffing!"

The school nurse Mrs Oswald caught Mr Jarvis's eye.

"I'm very concerned Headmaster, do you know what the forecast is tomorrow? I don't think it's appropriate for the children to be swimming if the weather deteriorates"

"Don't worry Mrs Oswald, I've checked and the weather is supposed to improve. Mr Winston has set up the covers for the spectators and staff."

More bets were being placed with Mr Fry the maths teacher.

"Dean Williams team is definitely the hot favourites."

The monsoon conditions of the previous day had eased to a light drizzle, Mr Winston was supervising in the boys changing rooms. The races started at 10 o'clock with the first year, and each year spent about 30 minutes in the pool, their respective year group cheering them on from under the canopy at the far end of the pool. The swimmers and judges sat at the opposite end under their own canopy.

Mr Jarvis was in charge of announcing each race and the swimmers names. Various teachers were checking, Mrs Oswald was anxiously making sure the swimmers didn't get too cold. There was a pile of extra towels to hand and jugs of sweet hot chocolate for the competitors once they had completed their events. There was a 10 minute interval between year groups arriving and going as there was only enough space for one year at a time to spectate.
It was 1 o'clock by the time the sixth form trooped in. The first couple of races left the field wide open all eight teams appeared to be evenly matched.

"The next race is the butterfly," announced the Headmaster. He listed all the boys that would be swimming. Samantha listened, shit, she thought this was Robert's first race, and butterfly? Why on earth had he agreed to do that? She felt cross with Martin, as team captain it was mean, especially as Dean was the only boy in the school who could swim that stroke properly.

The boys lined up, some were already in the water as they couldn't dive. Dean and Robert stood next to each other. Dean had swaggered out to the poolside, Robert had walked out wrapped in his towel. Bloody hell, thought Sam, he looked cold and nervous. Despite being taller than Dean, Robert looked small and vulnerable against Dean's confident posing.

Mr Winston drew the competitors attention.

"Ready, set go!"

The whistle blew, Robert executed a perfect dive. Samantha could barely watch, in amongst the splashing of all the other boys Robert gracefully swam the perfect stroke and won the race easily. The spectators went mad. Samantha grinned across at Robert. Who would've thought it, Dean didn't look very happy, which made Samantha even happier. Robert swam in the next three races, winning all of them easily. He had forgotten how much he enjoyed swimming, with each race he stood a little taller as his self confidence grew. Samantha watched in wonder, with his wet hair swept away from his face and with his swimming goggles removed she realised Robert was really good looking and what a body!

She chastised herself for being so interested as she always told people you shouldn't judge a book by its cover.

The final race was relay. It was agreed Robert would swim last.

"Ready, steady....."

They were off Martin started and made a good lead, then came Richard, not such a strong swimmer, Dean's team were now in close second. Next came John, but he swam against Dean, who now took the lead, and finally Robert, he wasn't allowed to dive in as he was going from the shallow end. He needed to swim hard to catch up Dean's teammate, but he managed and won the race. The spectators were shouting and cheering. Many of them glad someone had finally beaten Dean.

Mr Jarvis came on the tannoy.

"Well done all of you, now quickly shower and change, we need to get to the hall as the press will be here shortly, off you go."

Martin slapped Robert on the back.

"You were bloody amazing Rob, I wouldn't be surprised if you got top billing."

"What do you mean?

"Well someone gets awarded a special prize and the Gazette does a little piece on them. Dean is going to be so pissed off. He's won it for the last few years.

"Bloody excellent Rob!" said his teammate John.

Shit thought Robert , he so enjoyed himself he'd forgotten to keep a low profile. How was he going to get out of this!

Robert had just finished dressing when he received a shove in his back. He turned to see Dean standing there.

"You think you're so bloody clever don't you? First you steal my girl, then you try and show me up in the pool."

Robert was stressing about the press, he didn't need this.

"Dean, I'm not interested just back off."

"Fuck you!"

Dean pushed him again, harder this time. Martin had been watching.

"Dean, leave him alone, don't be such a bad loser."

This seemed to wind up Dean even more.

"Who you calling a fucking loser?"

He lashed out, and caught Robert in the face.

"Fucking hell!" Robert cried.

His lip had been between Dean's fist and his brace, now it was bleeding. All his pent-up anger with his parents, the move and his current situation came out as he punched Dean in the stomach. Dean responded by grabbing Robert's hair and punching him in the face. The situation was starting to get out of hand, some of the boys started to chant 'fight, fight!' The next moment the boys were pulled apart by a very angry Mr Winston.

"What in the hell is going on here?" he shouted.

He was greeted with silence.

"Everyone out, apart from you two."

The other swimmers picked up their bags and started to leave.

Martin hung back.

"Sir it wasn't...."

"Out Parker, Now!" Mr Winston barked. " You two pack your things away and follow me."

Mr Winston led the two boys to Mr Jarvis office.

"Wait here."

They stood in the corridor, Robert looking at his feet, how could he have been so stupid.

"I'm going to tell them you started it, I'm head boy so he'll believe me you're just a nobody," sneered Dean.

"I heard that Williams."

Dean swung round Mr Winston and Mr Jarvis were standing behind him. Dean glared at Robert who was still looking at his feet. Mr Jarvis opened his door.

"Go in."

He looked at both boys noticing Robert's split lip which was still bleeding and a large bruise developing on his cheek.

"Well, what have you got to say for yourselves? Brown? Robert looked up.

"Sorry sir, it got a bit boisterous."

"Williams what about you?"

"Rob was showing off after his win and was pushing and shoving so he started it. I just shoved him back and caught him."

"Robert, you and your team swam well today, but I will not tolerate this behaviour. I've a good mind to disqualify you."

Dean couldn't help but grin.

"Please Sir, disqualify me, but not the team, they worked so hard and they will be truly gutted."

Dean was feeling confident again, but not for long.

"Williams you may be head boy, but I will not tolerate liars and bullies."

Dean's mouth fell open.

"Three witnesses said you started the altercation, because in their words you were a bad loser."

"Three witnesses sir? Who was that? Martin, Richard and John?"

"Silent boy! I don't expect rudeness from you."

Dean was wishing he'd punched Robert harder.

"Robert, I was going to award you the top swimming prize, but in view of this incident I've decided against that. However I will allow the team to be given first place."

"Thank you sir," said Robert relieved.

"Now I don't want to hear of any more nonsense from you two. Robert I think Mrs Oswald had better have a look at your lip and you better keep your head down in the photos, we don't want to give the school a bad name!"

"No sir, thank you sir."

The boys left the office. Outside the door Dean sneered.

"No sir, thank you sir, at least I'll get the top swimmers prize which was rightly mine."

Dean swaggered off. Robert made his way to Mrs Oswald the school nurse, who cleaned up his lip as best she could and sent him back to the hall. He tried to keep his hair over his face as much as possible. All the swimmers were on the stage as Robert joined his team. They looked worried.

"What did he say?" John asked.

"It's okay we are still the winners."

"Phew, how's your face?" asked Martin.

Robert pushed his hair to one side.

"Shit! That looks terrible!"

"He told me to keep my hair over my face for the photos."

"Dean's been bragging he's getting the top swimmer award, that should've been you."

"Mr Jarvis said I wouldn't have it as a punishment for the altercation," said Robert emphasising quotation marks with his fingers.

"That's so unfair that would've been your minute of Fame instead of that bighead Dean."

Ironically, Robert sent a silent thanks to Dean, he'd been so happy swimming he'd forgotten he was supposed to remain inconspicuous . If it wasn't for Dean's jealousy it could've caused serious problems.

Mr Jarvis made a speech and thanked the swimmers for their courage for competing in the outdoor pool in November. Prizes were given to the winning teams, gold, silver and bronze coloured medals were presented . The local press took pictures of the teams amongst enthusiastic applause. Robert glanced across at Dean who was grinning like a Cheshire cat. Mr Jarvis then announced the prize for the top swimmers

"This year we are changing the format slightly. I'm going to split the honour between two swimmers."

Robert looked across at Dean again who looked a bit puzzled, then glared back at Robert .

"The awards this year go to Rosemary Bailey and Emma Thorne, both in the first year, the only girls to have taken part in the history of the November gala. Hopefully this will inspire others to follow their lead."

The two girls got up shyly to a rousing applause from the school. Robert grinned and joined in enthusiastically, John who was sitting next to him, laughed.

"Dean looks like he's swallowed a wasp, miserable bugger."

The pupils filed out of the hall and prepared to go home. Samantha waited for Robert to congratulate him. She was horrified when she saw him.

"Oh my God Rob! What's happened to your face?"

Robert smiled .

"An altercation."

"With what?"

"If you must know, Dean's fist."

"Rob! You're joking?"

"Actually no."

Sam looked horrified.

"You need to speak to Mr Jarvis. I can't believe he'd do that."

"Dean and I have already seen Mr Jarvis."

"What did he say?."

"It's all been sorted, so forget it."

Sam didn't know what to say, she felt like a goldfish opening and closing her mouth.

"Come on," said Robert,"let's walk home."

As expected his mum was horrified, when she saw him.

"Have you been in a fight? I'd better phone the school."

"No Mum, I was swimming in the gala today. Remember I said it's an outdoor pool, it was freezing I rushed to get back to the changing rooms and went flying."

"But your lip, it's cut!"

"It only hurts when I smile! It's because of my brace Mum, they made me go to the school nurse, she checked me over, I'm fine, honest Mum."

She looked at him with concern.

"I've never known you get into a fight."

Robert joked.

"You should've seen the other guy!"

She didn't laugh.

Chapter Ten

Christmas was only a couple of weeks away. Samantha did most of her Christmas shopping at work as the shop had a wide range of gifts which could be wrapped in store and she would benefit from staff discount. Christmas was never a problem, until now. She was in her bedroom with Megan discussing when to meet up over the holidays.

"Do you think it will ever snow over Christmas? When you watch the old films it always snows, and looks so lovely," said Megan.

Samantha didn't respond.

"Sam are you listening to me? You've been really distracted today. How's the Christmas shopping going anyway?"

Samantha sighed.

"Sorry Megs all done, bar one. The most difficult one."

She sighed again.

"Who is that then? You never normally have a problem, it's usually me who is worrying about everyone, I'm actually really organised this year. I was hoping we could go iceskating in Bristol. I've got a couple of free days over the holidays. You know what my family are like."

Samantha frowned.

"Bristol might not be a bad idea, we could have a look around the shops there."

"You still haven't told me who it's for!"

"Rob."

"Rob! I thought you said the gossip was a load of rubbish. Is there something going on there? I've barely spoken to him, he is so quiet, but he seems nice, bloody hell he looked really fit in his swimming trunks," she giggled.

Sam looked at her and laughed.

"Megs! As I keep saying we're just friends."

"Yeah right, I've seen the way he looks at you."

"Seriously we are just friends and that's what makes him so difficult to buy for."

"How about some baby oil to rub into his..."

"Megs! Behave!"

The girls shrieked with laughter.

"Megs, I need help here."

"Okay let's go to Bristol, operation Rob's Christmas pressie and iceskating."

The Christmas term ended with a concert. Despite being an excellent singer and guitarist, Robert decided to keep it to himself, after the swimming gala he didn't want to attract any more attention especially as none of the other six form lads were taking part.
The form room was buzzing with excitement as Mr Johnson finished the afternoon registration.

"This is your last registration," he said.

There was a loud cheer

"Now you've all got your revision timetables. Attending the revision classes is not compulsory, but you'd be silly to miss them, all of the revision can be done at home or here at school. I hope you all have a wonderful Christmas and I'll see some of you in my revision class, for the rest of you work hard and all the best for your exams."

The class broke into groups, there was laughter and hugs as friends swapped cards and gifts, most of the pupils had cards for Mr Johnson. Robert had cards for Martin, Richard and John. He also had a card and a gift for Samantha , but wasn't sure when to give it to her. Samantha broke away from her group.

"Rob," she gave him a hug, "Happy Christmas."

"Same to you Sam."

"I've got you a gift as a thank you in anticipation for all your help but I didn't bring it with me, I was hoping we could meet so I can give it to you when we're out of school."

"That may be difficult with, you know, my mum and everything."

"Oh, sorry I forgot, have you any Christmas shopping to do?"

Robert groaned.

"I haven't even started yet!"

"What! It's Christmas in five days, when do you usually do it?"

"Christmas Eve!"

"I finish work at lunchtime on Christmas Eve, meet me at the shop with a list and I'll help you if you like."

Robert tried to play it cool.

"If it's not too much trouble."

Robert decided to hang on to Samantha's card and gift until then, much better to wait until they were alone, rather than give it to her in front of her friends.

Samantha worked on the Saturday, it was extremely busy, she was exhausted and was glad she was having Monday off. She met up with Megan on the Sunday and they planned their trip to Bristol.

"Have you thought any more about a present for Rob?" Asked Megan.

"Not a bloody clue."

"If you're not going out, do you even need to get him anything?"

"I'm not going out with you, but I got you something."

"Ha ha very funny."

"The thing is I told him I had a Christmas gift for him on Friday."

"Why did you say that?"

"Because," she paused, "I felt sorry for him. Everyone else were exchanging gifts apart from Rob, and I want to give him something for all the help he's been giving me with my science revision. So here's the plan, I'll get here by 9 o'clock. We'll go straight to the ice rink, have an early lunch and then shop till we drop."

By 10 o'clock the following morning the girls were queueing outside the ice rink, they hired boots and soon were whizzing around the ice. Loud music played and they had great fun flirting with some local lads as they skated.

They left the rink, rosey cheeked and buzzing after their exertion they walked down to the Wimpy bar chatting away happily.

"Rather than shop in 'The Centre', why don't we go up to Clifton where there were lots of smaller independent shops?" suggested Megan.

"What if we don't find anything there?"

"I think it's worth the risk, and if all else fails we'll get him something from your work."

Samantha reluctantly agreed, although she didn't feel very optimistic. They walked up Park Street to Clifton a very exclusive part of Bristol. Megan was right, there were a lot of small interesting shops with unusual gifts in their windows. Samantha's spirits rose.

"This looks promising Megs."

They looked around a couple of gift shops, beautifully decorated with tinsel and fairy lights giving them a magical Christmas feel. However after perusing their wears Samantha's shoulders were starting to drop.

"There is nothing here and it's so expensive," whispered Samantha .

"Don't give up yet, come on."

Back outside, the next shop they came to was an art gallery.

"Oh my God, that's one of mum's paintings in the window!"
They both stopped and looked.

"She is really good Sam, the children in the snow, It's looks so real. Why don't you to get her to do a little sketch or something for you?"

"Bit bloody late now!" Samantha looked at her watch, "a couple more shops, then we better head back."

They visited two more shops neither had anything inspiring inside, they came out, Samantha was quite despondent.

"This is hopeless."

"Let's try this last one."

Megan dragged Samantha towards the shop doorway.

"It's an antique shop!" wailed Samantha .

"Let's at least look inside," said Megan hopefully.

Samantha looked in the shop window.

"It looks like I feel, bloody miserable. There is no Christmas decorations it looks really gloomy."

They went inside, a little bell tinkled as they opened the door. The shop was rammed with dark heavy furniture and on every surface there were clocks, china figurines, brass candlesticks and piles of books.

"It's like something out of a Dickens," Megan whispered.

Samantha agreed, she felt as if she'd stepped back in time.

"Can I help you young ladies?"

Samantha swung around expecting to see an old bespectacled man, but to her disappointment a rather ordinary looking man of perhaps 40 dressed in a smart shirt, bow tie and a waistcoat had appeared behind the small polished counter.

"I hope so, but I fear not.

"What are you looking for?" inquired the shopkeeper.

"Inspiration!"

"Ah, let's see if I can help you. Is it for yourself or a gift?"

"A gift," Samantha paused, "for a boy, not a boyfriend."

"But a friend who is a boy."

The shopkeeper looked at Megan.

"Me thinks the lady doth protest too much."

Megan acknowledged with a smile.

"Me thinks the same!"

Samantha Glared at them both.

"If you knew want me thinks….," She trailed off, "this isn't getting me anywhere!"

Samantha turned to leave.

"Hold on, how much do you want to spend?"

"Well between £2 and £4."

Megan raised an eyebrow.

"What does this young man like?" asked the shopkeeper.

Samantha looked around for help.

"Um, music!"

"Maybe HMV would suit you better. We have some musical instruments but they're all well over £5."

Samantha thought for a moment.

"He's really into science."

"I may have something suitable, wait there."

The man disappeared. Samantha looked at Megan.

"'The lady doth protest too much me thinks', he could at least get it right."

"Smart arse!"

The man returned with a large cardboard box.

"Let's have a look through this lot."

He started to take things out of the box, a globe, Sam grabbed it.

"Perfect!"

"A bugger to wrap," Megan quipped.

Samantha gently spun the globe as the shopkeeper continued taking unusual looking metal objects from the box. Samantha paused in her spinning, there was a large dent in the globe just over China.

"Oh!"

The man looked up.

"A meteorite I think," he said in a deadpan voice.

"Ha ha," replied Samantha .

Samantha looked at the collection of objects on the counter.

"What are these?"

"A couple of levels, a sextant a couple of apothecary weights, some glass test tubes, some glass petri dishes and," he opened a box, "an antique microscope."

Samantha gasped and picked up the microscope, she gently examined it. It was black and brass but filthy, yet she knew it could look amazing, all it needed was a good clean.

"This is it," she looked up, "how much is it?"

"I should tell you it doesn't work, the lens is cracked, you could get it replaced but it would cost a fair bit."

He hadn't answered her question.

"But how much?"

"How much have you got?"

Samantha got out of her purse and emptied the contents onto the counter. The man counted £3.74. He looked at Samantha's expectant face, he'd been hoping for nearer £20, but he sighed it was Christmas.

"How much do you need for your bus fare home"

"It's okay we got return tickets."

The shopkeeper gave her a grin and with that handed her back the 4p.

"There is your change Madam!"

"Really!"

Samantha's smile lit up the dingy shop.

"Yes, before I change my mind. Give it a good clean, get some Brasso on the brass bits."

"Brasso?"

He looked at sternly.

"You're going to bankrupt me, wait here."

He disappeared again and returned with a small blue and white striped tin with Brasso written in Red across the front.

"It's quite runny, poor a little onto a soft cloth. You'll have black streaks initially but just keep rubbing."

He put the microscope back in the box and placed into a bag along with the tin of Polish and handed it over to Samantha .

"Thank you so much, you've saved my life," said Samantha .

The shopkeeper looked at Megan.

"A boy who is a friend?"

Megan smiled.

The girls walked towards the door, Samantha turned back.

"Why haven't you got any Christmas decorations?"

"Bah humbug!" he replied winking.

Samantha gave him a beaming smile.

"God bless us, everyone!"

The shopkeeper roared with laughter and bowed to her.

Samantha and Megan left the shop.

"I think I'm in love, Megs"

"I knew it, all this crap about my friend who is a boy."

Samantha looked at her.

"Not Rob you plonker! With Mr shopkeeper!"

"He's old enough to be your dad!"

"But he was so funny. Shame we didn't get his name."

"Samantha I think the Christmas spirit it's gone to your head, anyway I'm sure he's gay!"

"No! You're just saying that to put me off. I'm just so glad I've got Rob's present sorted."

"When are you going to give it to him?"

"Tomorrow. I'm working in the morning, then he's going to meet me in the shop to buy his mum and sister Christmas pressies. So, I'll give it to him then."

The shopkeeper watched the two girls walk over the brow of the hill down to the bus station. He hummed white Christmas to himself, and couldn't wait to get home and tell his partner Lawrence about his unexpected role of fairy Godfather. He recalled how the girl was able to quote the last lines of a Christmas Carol, and with that he whispered Merry Christmas to himself.

They caught the bus home and looked forward to meeting again on Christmas Eve at Megan's house. Her mum always did a special meal for Samantha and her parents it had become a tradition for the past five years. Samantha couldn't wait to get home and start to clean up the microscope, she hoped Robert would like it.

Chapter Eleven

Christmas Eve, Samantha was up early ready for work. After spending a good hour cleaning and polishing the microscope, Samantha wrapped it in tissue paper and placed it in the box the shopkeeper had given her, then covered it in the Christmas paper she'd chosen especially for Rob. She agonised over how she should sign his card. Should it be with love, Love from, or simply from? Samantha finally decided on best wishes. Now, should she put a kiss or not? She always put kisses on friends cards, so why was this such a big deal? She signed it and put a kiss, quickly placing it in the envelope and sticking it down before she could change her mind.

Samantha loved Christmas at the shop. She had been allowed to help dress the window, to create a winter scene with the obligatory Christmas tree and fairy lights. The shop was busy with last-minute panic buyers, although it started to slow down by lunchtime, Samantha was glad as her feet were killing her. Robert walked in just after 12 o'clock looking rather sheepish, he was back to his hunched shoulders, and hair over his face look. He was loitering a couple of feet from the cosmetic counter, Samantha could see Mrs Thomas watching him ready to accost him as a potential shoplifter.

"Mrs Thomas that's my friend, he's here to buy some gifts, but he's a bit shy."

Mrs Thomas looked down her nose.

"He needs a haircut."

Samantha walked over to Robert .

"Hiya Rob"

Robert looked up with relief.

"Hi Sam, as you can probably tell I hate shopping."

Samantha took his arm.

"Come on, I'll show you what we've got, and you'll be pleased to hear, leaving your shopping this late most of it is now reduced!"

With Samantha's help Rob chose two gift packages of women's toiletries.

"Would you like me to wrap them?"

"Can you? That would be fantastic."

Robert was starting to relax a little and looked around the shop. Samantha looked lovely in her white coat wearing a little make up with the hair neatly plaited, she was the perfect advert for the cosmetic counter. Mrs Thomas was still watching them as Samantha wrapped his gifts, so mindful of manners he nodded and said.

"How do you do?"

This pleased Mrs Thomas no end, she smiled graciously at him.

"There, all done shall I put them in a bag for you?" Samantha asked.

"Yes please."

Robert paid for his purchases and thanked Samantha for her help.

"See it didn't take long," said Samantha smiling.

"Sam, what time do you finish? I wondered if you fancied a quick cuppa to say thank you?"

Samantha looked at her watch.

"About 10 minutes ago! I'd love a cuppa and maybe a sandwich?"

Robert waited while Samantha collected her belongings, reappearing in her coat and a bobble hat carrying a bag with Robert's gift. Despite being the middle of the day, the sky was black with heavy rain clouds, a chill wind blew. Samantha linked arms with Robert as they walked heads down towards the teashop.

The teashop windows glowed invitingly as they entered. Christmas music played, the whole place was adorned with fairy lights and baubles. There was steam on the windows, created by the occupants wet coats and umbrellas, the place was packed and noisy. Samantha and Robert looked around.

"I've never seen it so busy!"

A rather harassed Savannah greeted them.

"Wanna table?"

"If there is one."

Savannah noted Samantha's arm looped through Robert's.

"Hang on then."

Samantha was trying to think where else they could go but there wasn't anywhere apart from one of the local pubs.

Savannah reappeared.

"Okay you can squeeze into the corner there."

Samantha apologised to a very large lady, as they struggled passed to their table. They both shrugged out of their damp coats and hats and sat down.

"I don't know how Savannah is going to manage to take our order and serve us without doing serious damage to that woman with her chest!"

Samantha picked up the menu from the table.

"They've made a real effort, look."

There was a variety of Christmas themed sandwiches and cakes. They both chose a turkey and cranberry sandwich, a mince pie and of course, a cup of tea.

Savannah got as close as possible so Robert shouted their order to her. Thankfully the large lady had left before she had to bring them their food, although he was secretly looking forward to the entertainment. They chatted comfortably together.

"How are you spending your Christmas day?" Sam asked.

"My sister is back from Uni, so at least it'll be a bit more fun.
We'll probably play games watch telly you know, the usual stuff."

Although, he thought, it wouldn't be usual without his dad and at the new house which certainly didn't feel like home.

"How about you?"

"We will go to Meg's this evening for supper, then tomorrow we go to my Nanna in Gloucester. We always go there, she is such a great cook, if we stayed home with probably have beans on toast!"

"Do you usually celebrate New Year's Eve?"

"Yeah, I think my cousins are coming down for a few days they're twins Ali and Jill, I love it when we get together.
They're so lucky having each other, I've always wanted to have a sister, or brother at a push."

"I know I've got Ruth, but I've no cousins, both my parents were only children. I expect we'll stay up to see the new year in but no party"

Before she could stop herself Samantha blurted out.

"Come to mine and play a few games, Dad will probably let off a few fireworks at midnight and we could sing Auld lang syne."

"I'd love that but sadly I couldn't abandon Mum and Ruth."

"Rob, I'm sorry, I keep forgetting."

"It's fine."

He looked at his watch.

"I'm going to have to make a move soon."

He put his hand in his pocket and pulled out a small present and card.

"Um, this is for you, it's for your education!"

Samantha smiled.

"I've got something for you."

She brought out her carefully wrapped box and passed it across to him.

"Wow, I'm afraid yours is much smaller."

Samantha took Robert's parcel she laughed and gave it a little shake.

"Cassette?"

"How did you guess? I hope you like it, you probably won't have heard of most of the songs."

Samantha thanked him.

"Oh, I better warn you your gift is broken."

Rob looked confused.

"Broken?"

"Well, not exactly broken, but it doesn't work, you'll understand when you open it."

"Shall I open it now?"

"No, I think that's bad luck, isn't it? Keep it for Christmas morning."

She looked Robert in the eye and touched his arm. For a moment she felt like they were the only people in the café.

"Rob I hope you have a lovely day tomorrow and everything you wish for in the New Year."

Robert suddenly felt incredibly sad.

The moment was spoiled by Savannah appearing with their bill.

"We are closing soon. You two need to get a room!"

Robert realised he was holding Samantha's hand, how had that happened? He took a deep breath.

"Yeah, you too Sam."

He let go of her hand got out his wallet. Savannah was still hovering over them, he paid and they stood up together. Once outside the café the sky had got even darker. Robert looked up.

"I've never lived anywhere that rained so much, does it ever snow here at Christmas?"

"You sound like Megan. Sadly not often, we did have some a few years ago, Dad and I made an igloo you could get right inside, it was brill, but I don't think we'll have any luck this year."

They were standing outside the teashop door and had to shuffle to one side as more people exited after being evicted by Savannah. They both felt suddenly awkward, they started to speak at once then stopped.

"Got your parcels?" Samantha asked.

"Yeah, thanks again for your help and my broken present." Samantha smiled.

"It's not completely broken, it's just sort of, oh you'll see."

"Do you want me to walk you home?"

"No its only up the road."

"Well, have a good Christmas Sam."

Samantha stretched up to give him a kiss on the cheek just as he turned his head, her lips met his. It was as if the world had stopped, both paused their lips touching, then the door opened again as a couple of ladies emerged laden with shopping bags. Samantha and Robert stood staring at each other. Samantha realised she was breathing a little faster than usual.

"Could we try that again?"

Robert nodded.

Both of them had kissed other people before, but neither of them had ever felt such a connection. Robert gently bent his head and kissed Samantha, this was nothing like snogging Dean, this was so gentle but so passionate at the same time, she put her hand up to his face.The moment was broken by Savannah's voice.

"Oi! you two get away, You'll give the shop a bad name snogging on the pavement in broad daylight!"

They broke apart, feeling embarrassed, Samantha grabbed Robert's arm and dragged him further along the High Street. They both burst out laughing.

"Sam you trollop!"

She grinned.

"Speak for yourself. Where did you learn to kiss like that?"

"At my last school they gave lessons on the perfect kiss."

"Really?"

"No."

"Any chance we can meet up over the holidays?"

"Sadly no, I won't see you until we are back at school."

Samantha nodded reluctantly.

"Okay."

She wanted to ask if she could phone him, but didn't want to sound as desperate as she felt. Unbeknown to her Rob felt it even more. He would have no other distraction over the holiday and the memory of that kiss would have to keep him going. Large drops of rain began to fall, Robert took Samantha's and and kissed it.

"Have a lovely Christmas Sam and I'll see you next year."

She leaned up and kissed him on the lips.

"Just don't forget me please."

"No chance."

The rain was getting heavier.

"Go Sam, before you drown!"

She laughed.

"See you."

He watched her scurry away as the heavens opened. Robert lifted his face to the rain, let it rain he thought, He didn't care, she'd kissed him. Yes she'd definitely kissed him and then asked to kiss him again. He walked home in the pouring rain singing 'Oh the weather outside is frightful'.

Samantha on the other hand was deep in thought. Shit she'd kissed him, on the lips. The first had been by accident, they should've just laughed about it. She stopped walking. His lips felt so nice, she knew he'd felt the same, then she'd asked him to kiss her again, she blushed at the memory, oh God what would he think of her? He'd called her a trollop, she bloody hoped he was joking. She started walking again, bloody hell Sam, she thought, what were you thinking? She wouldn't see him again until after the Christmas holidays, was it going to be awkward, would he still help her revise? She'd ask Megan's advice, but no, forget that, she could imagine her saying, 'I knew it! Not just a friend, a boyfriend!!'

Megan was obviously more perceptive than she realised. She trudged on home confused with her feelings and wishing she could rewind the clock. Robert and her got on so well she hoped she hadn't spoiled it.

Christmas morning at Samantha's parents was a joyous affair, music played as they ate smoked salmon and scrambled egg for breakfast. Samantha and her parents exchanged presents, there was a lot of laughter, especially as her mum had decided to take up knitting and made them each a Christmas jumper. Samantha's was too big and her dad's was rather tight but they wore them with pride.

Her dad started to load the car up with presents for the grandparents.

"Hey Sam there's a small gift here for you, it feels like a cassette."

"Thanks a lot dad," said Samantha sarcastically.

"Why, what have I done?"

"Spoiled the surprise!"

"Well sorry, but it's fairly obvious love."

Samantha took it from him.

"Are you going to open it?"

Bugger, she thought, why did I put it under the tree? She'd meant to open it in her bedroom.

"You two ready?" called her mother,

"Nearly love, Sam's got another gift to open."

Reluctantly Samantha opened Robert's present.

"Surprise surprise it's a cassette!"

Adeline had walked in.

"Who is it from?" she asked.

"A boy at school."

"Anyone we've met?"

"What happened to that lad you went out with in the summer?"

Samantha rolled her eyes.

"Dad, he was a moron."

"So, if not him then who?"

Samantha gave a dramatic sigh.

"A friend, a boy but not a boyfriend, okay?"

Her parents looked at each other and grinned, before they could say anything Samantha continued.

"And don't you dare start quoting Shakespeare."

Her mum looked puzzled.

"Shakespeare! What's that got to do with anything?"

David was examining the cassette.

"He's written down all the artists and tracks, must've taken him ages.He's called it 'An education in music'."

"Who's on there?"

"Blimey, James Taylor!"

"Oh I love James Taylor he's got those most gorgeous eyes."

Samantha was embarrassed.

"Mum!"

"Leonard Cohen."

"Leonard Cohen! how old is this boy, unusual for someone your age to be into him, I'm surprised you like him Sam, he's quite an acquired taste."

"I've never heard of him."

"Oh you'll love this one Lyn, John Denver."

"Is it Annies song? That's one of my favourites, Sam."

Samantha had had enough.

"Actually it's my tape, so perhaps you'd like to hand it over so I can look for myself."

"Sorry love, tell you what let's play it in the car on the way over to Nan's."

They packed the last few things into the car and set off. Samantha handed the cassette over to her dad who he put it into the player. She looked at the carefully written list, Robert had worked hard making it, she was impressed, even if she hadn't heard of half the artists. The cassette started with a couple of Queen tracks which her parents sang along to, Samantha groaned and rolled her eyes. A few songs in, a lovely ballad started to play.

"I don't know this one, who is it Sam?"

Samantha drew her finger down the list of songs.

"Its by Bob Dylan 'Is your love in vain'."

"No way is that Bob Dylan!"

"Well that's what it says here and so is the next one."

There followed a couple of Elvis Costello songs which Samantha recognised.

"The next one is John Denver 'Perhaps love'," announced Samantha .

"Oh lovely I don't know the song but John Denver is one of my favourite artists, that voice."

"Mum!"

The song started, it was beautiful.

"I'm sorry love that's definitely not John Denver," said Adeline.

"Well that's what he's written here."

"His voice sounds exactly like the one on the Bob Dylan tracks, does your boyfriend sing?" added David.

"He's not my boyfriend!"

Adeline and David exchanged a look.

"Of course not love."

"Just give me my cassette and listen to your own music."

Chapter Twelve

Robert awoke, it was still dark, he looked at his watch, 7.15 Christmas morning. He stared into the darkness and thought back to a year ago, waking in his old room surrounded by the posters on his bedroom walls, he wondered if they were still there. He recalled hearing the murmur of his parents voices, already downstairs, then his dad knocking on the door with a mug of tea telling him it was pouring with rain and was he still game for an early Christmas morning cycle ride. Robert remembered jumping out of bed to put on his cycle gear and nearly tripping over his stocking which his parents had left there while he was asleep. The memories brought tears to his eyes.

They had cycled out to Breadsall Moor, the sky had cleared and a shaft of sunlight had shone down on them as they took in the view. Robert felt so alive and remembered smiling at his dad.

"Happy Christmas Son," said his father.

In that moment he'd felt a really strong connection with his dad.

Robert shut his eyes, he felt so homesick for his old life. God Dad where are you? he thought, how could you do this to us? He remembered his old friends, Simon, Jack and Joe and wondered if they knew what had happened, and if after all this time, had they even given Robert a thought. He continued to wallow in his self pity and as he turned on his side he dangled his arm over the edge of the bed inadvertently coming into contact with a hard object. It was Samantha's gift, the only bright light in his darkness. He caressed the box wondering whether she was awake, he wished he could see her, but knew his mum was completely paranoid about him being out of the house. He hoped the cassette was okay as he hadn't been able to bring many of his records with him, he'd had to improvise by playing and singing a lot of the tracks himself. On reflection he had recorded a lot of love songs. He hoped she wouldn't be offended, but it was her who had kissed him. He turned on his bedside lamp and started to unwrap Samantha's present.

It was probably something from the shop, he'd heard her telling Megan she'd always got her presents there because of the discount! He frowned, as he remembered she had said it was broken.

There was a knock on the door and Katie stuck her head around.

"Happy Christmas little brother, what's this?"

She picked up the stocking that had been at the foot of his bed. It was all too much he let out a sob. Katie jumped onto his bed and gave him a hug.

"It's okay Will."

"I just want Dad back at home with us, and that's not even my fucking name!"

They clung together and cried, Katie broke away.

"Come on, don't let Mum see us upset she'd never cope. Have you got any loo role here?"

"No, why?"

"I need to blow my nose and I thought boys always kept them by the bed."

"What! Bloody hell Katie you're gross."

Katie returned with some loo roll and her stocking. They both blew their noses and wiped their eyes.

"I assumed you did the stocking," asked Robert , "did you make one for yourself as well?"

"No, nothing to do with me, this was all mums work, shall we open them?"

"Let's make some tea and take it into Mum's room and open them with her."

"Good plan, off you go then, your idea, no sugar for me in case you forgotten."

"Cheeky bugger!"

He hopped out of bed and ran downstairs. Mary came out of her bedroom.

"Happy Christmas you noisy lot!"

"Back to bed mum."

Katie tried to steer her back through the bedroom door.

"I need to spend a penny, what's Will doing?"

"A pee, hand wash then bed."

Mary did as she was told. Robert returned with three mugs of tea and took them into his mum's room.

"Happy Christmas Mum."

He leaned across and gave her a kiss. Katie reappeared with three stockings.

"Will and I made one for you."

"Oh bless you."

Robert looked at his sister with new respect, Katie winked at him. They sat on the bed and opened the contents of their stockings. It was almost like old times apart from the obvious. Mary looked at her two children.

"I want to thank you, I know this has been really difficult, especially for you William. I know Dad would be so proud of you and how you have both coped, I've got a good feeling about the New Year, and William, sorry I've been so tense I will try to lighten up a bit more."

"Does that mean I can start going out now?"

Mary smiled at him.

"Not yet love."

Christmas day was pleasant, but very quiet. Mary had made a real effort with the dinner, turkey and all the trimmings. She raised a glass.

"To Dad wherever you are."

"To Dad," replied Katie and Robert .

They ate too much, played silly board games and then sat and watched television, so different from previous Christmas days.

That evening as Robert got into his bed and pulled the covers over himself, he found Samantha's present. He looked at her gift, he was reluctant to open it as the anticipation gave him a little thrill. The card was attached to the front, he opened it and traced his finger over her name and the accompanying kiss. He carefully unwrapped the parcel, inside was a plain box. So not toiletries he thought. Lifting the lid and layers of tissue paper, he pulled out the most beautiful brass antique microscope. Now he felt bad, all he'd had given her was a mix tape, this must have cost her a lot of money. He examined it carefully, he couldn't find anything wrong with it, yet she said it was broken.

It wasn't until the following day he discovered the lens was cracked, which came as a bit of a relief as he supposed it hadn't been so expensive after all.

As he hadn't told his mother or Katie about Samantha, he decided to keep the microscope in its box, along with her Christmas card hidden from them, thus avoiding any awkward questions.

Samantha and her family returned home a couple of days after Christmas, along with her two cousins Jill and Ali. That evening they decided to play truth or dare, a board game the cousins had been given for Christmas.

"Sam your turn truth or dare?" Jill announced.

"Truth!"

Jill picked up a card.

"Okay, what was your best kiss ever?"

"Oh God, really! Can't I change my mind?"

"No!" said Jill and Ali in unison.

"Best kiss, Christmas Eve."

"When?"

"Christmas Eve, six days ago."

"This Christmas?" asked Ali.

"Yeah."

"Wow, why was it so good?"

"Who was it with?" Ali interjected.

"Where did you kiss, was it at Meg's? Not one of her brothers? Oh my God they are so gorgeous."

"Hey I'm sure that's not on the card," protested Samantha.

"I don't care, we need to know," Jill demanded.

"Come on spill the beans," said Ali.

Bloody hell thought Samantha, she couldn't tell the truth, outside Mrs Trenwins teashop and accidentally at that.

"Alright, it wasn't at Meg's it was earlier in the afternoon. We finished school at lunchtime and a few of us went to a friends house, we stayed a couple of hours then I left as we are going to Meg's, he left at the same time. When we got into the hall we just happened to stand under some mistletoe. The first kiss…"

"First kiss!" exclaimed Ali, "how many times did you kiss?"

"As I was saying, it was quite a quick peck on the lips."

Her cousins were spellbound.

"And then?" Jill asked eagerly.

"Well, we kind of looked at each other, and then kissed again, it was amazing. Most boys I've kissed before just, I don't know, kind of attack your mouth with theirs, forcing their tongues down your throat"

"Gross," said Ali.

"Yeah I know what you mean," agreed Jill.

"Well this was so gentle, so perfect."

"Wow it sounds like true love Sam."

Samantha laughed.

"I don't think so, I haven't seen him since."

"Is he coming for New Year's Eve?"

"No, I did ask him but he is away visiting family. I won't see him until we're back at school."

"Is Meg and her family coming over for New Year's Eve?" asked Ali.

"What you mean is, are her brothers coming " Samantha teased, changing the subject.

"Now I bet they're good kisses."

Ali laughed.

"You've always fancied them."

Jill threw a pillow at her sister.

"You're jealous!"

The ensuing pillow fight knocked over the board game, thus ending the evenings fun.

Robert on the other hand found the days between Christmas and New Year dragging. When New Year's eve had finally arrived he and Katie spent the evening watching TV, drinking double diamond and some Carling Black label left over from Christmas.

Monday arrived, Robert returned to school. There weren't any set revision lessons, but it enabled him to escape the house, as he hadn't told his mum he could revise at home. If she knew he would have been expected stay in.

He was disappointed Samantha wasn't there, but assumed she would be the following day for their chemistry lesson. Robert was pleased to see his friend Martin.

"Hi Rob how come you've not stayed at home to study? If I'm not at school I'm expected to work on the farm, neither my dad or brother took A-levels so they don't see the point of them."

"What are you planning on doing? University, or getting a job?" Robert asked.

"I fancy going to Uni maybe study engineering, that way I'd have an escape route out of farming," he laughed, "what about you?"

"I'm hoping to take physics at Uni, don't know what I'll do after that."

They talked about Christmas and New Year, it seemed Martin's had been even quieter than Robert's. Work started early on the farm so there was no point staying up until midnight to celebrate.

The Following day Robert was in school early and went along to the science Labs to choose a seat at the rear second from last in the row, which he would keep for Samantha if she arrived. The students started to trickle into the room, Martin came over to Robert and slapped him on the shoulder.

"Thanks mate," sitting down in Samantha's place, "I hate sitting too near the front."

Before Robert could react Mr Quilter entered the classroom with a sheaf of papers under his arm.

"This morning I'd like you to perform an experiment as if you are sitting an exam. I'll hand the instructions out putting them upside down on your desks and when I say, you will turn them over and complete the experiment. You have everything necessary available, follow the sheet and record the data. You will have approximately 45 minutes then we'll discuss the results."

Suddenly the classroom door flew open, Samantha burst in.

"Sorry I'm late sir."

Mr Quilter turned towards her.

"You're lucky young lady as we haven't started. Take a seat, I'm not going to repeat myself."

Samantha looked round and caught Robert's eye and gave him a shy smile.

She had sat a couple of rows in front of him, all he could see was the the back of her head. The papers had been handed out followed by the signal for the test to begin. The class worked in silence until 15 minutes in there was a loud bang and a puff of smoke. The whole class gasped followed by some sniggering.

"Phillips! What are you playing at? Everybody stop!"

Mr Quilter hurried across to the embarrassed student. He then proceeded to chastise the pupil for not following instructions.

"Chemistry can be dangerous. As I said earlier follow the instructions to the letter!"

He emphasise this by banging his fist on the desk. The lesson continued, experiments were completed and followed by the discussion of the data collected. Apart from the minor explosion, it had gone well.

The students trooped out chatting to one another, Martin asking Robert about his results. Robert really wanted to talk to Samantha but he couldn't get away from Martin without appearing rude. They had reached the six form block, many of the students had drifted away with only a few staying on, luckily one of those was Samantha . Robert managed to break away from Martin.

"Hi Sam how was Christmas and New Year?"

"Oh, good thanks, yours?"

She seemed a bit awkward with him

"Okay."

He was starting to feel uncomfortable now.

"Look Rob, about Christmas Eve..."

Oh here we go he thought.

"What about it?"

"It's just, well, I think perhaps we should um…"

Before she had a chance to finish Mr Quilter interrupted.

"Samantha, Robert, good Christmas? Revision going well?"

Samantha swung round, ever polite.

"Yes thank you sir and yours?"

"Excellent thank you, I won't keep you I've got another lesson shortly."

Samantha turned back to Robert , but he'd gone.

"Martin, did you see Rob go?"

"Yes, he went out."

He pointed to the door, Samantha walked out and looked around, she could see Robert crossing the road outside the school gates. She hurried after him, why had she decided to wear heels she would never catch him. He looked like a man on a mission striding ahead. He crossed the Oldway and proceeded down the hill to the river. Samantha was hurrying as fast as she could but had to wait for a stream of cars to pass. Bloody typical she thought no lollipop lady today to stop the traffic! She continued to run down the hill calling after him. Robert stopped and looked back. He saw Samantha hurtling towards him, just pulling up in time to avoid a collision. She was bent double trying to get her breath back.

"Oh my God Rob I didn't think I'd catch you, why did you storm off like that?"

"Do you really need to ask me?"

He was thoroughly pissed off.

"Yes I do actually."

"Sam, you couldn't have made it any clearer, Christmas Eve was a mistake, so forget it."

"Wow are we having our first row?"

He glared at her.

"Okay not funny, but I didn't actually say that."

Robert sighed.

"Well that's how it sounded to me."

Samantha's breathing and heart rate we're getting back to normal, but her feet were killing her. She looked around, there was nowhere to talk privately, she took Robert's hand.

"Would you mind walking me home, as I can barely walk after running in these shoes."

They walked in silence, Samantha desperately trying to think of something to say to reduce the tension between them.

"Where were you going to go?" she asked.

"I don't know. I just wanted to get out once I thought you had given me my marching orders."

"Sorry, but I didn't actually say that."

"I know, sorry, oh it doesn't matter."

They walked up Queens Road and stopped in front of a large detached house that was hidden behind a hedge. There was a crazy paving drive, a large border filled with rose bushes and snowdrops covered the ground. They entered a side door, through a large utility space, into a bright kitchen. Samantha kicked off his shoes and gave a contented sigh.

"Oh my poor feet, that's why I was late, I realised I couldn't walk very fast but it was too late to double back and change them."

"Wow it's so lovely and warm in here."

"That'll be the Aga."

Robert looked around the kitchen it was large and cluttered, but felt very homely. Samantha filled the kettle and put it on the Stove.

"Mum always dreamed of having an Aga, but our kitchen was too small. This is nice, it reminds me a little of our house in Derby."

This was the first time Robert had talked about his old home, since the recent upheaval .Samantha spoke softly.

"What was it like?"

"Probably nothing like this structurally, but it felt like a proper home warm and welcoming."

"Here, sit down."

She pulled out a barstool as the kettle began to whistle.

"Tea?"

Robert nodded. Samantha made tea and sat opposite him at the breakfast bar.

"Rob, I do want talk about Christmas Eve and us, but please don't jump to any conclusions before I've had a chance to explain."

Robert looked worried.

"Okay."

"Good," she paused, "Rob I really like you a lot..."

"But?"

"There isn't a but, really it's, oh, I can't explain.."

Robert looked like he was about to stand up, she put her hand over his.

"Okay here goes. You know I saw Dean in the summer?"

He nodded.

"It was only for a few weeks, but it was an absolute bloody disaster, basically all he wanted to do was to get into my knickers."

Robert winced.

"Really?"

Samantha sighed.

"Really, it was bloody awful and that's been my experience with all the boys I've dated all they seem to want is sex."

He didn't know what to say, as he himself had fantasised about making love with her. She continued.

"You're different, you treat me like a friend, I never met a boy that I could talk to so easily. Next to Megan you've become my best friend and I don't want that to change."

Before he could say anything she carried on.

"Then you kissed me."

"Wait a minute I'm pretty sure you kissed me young lady and then you asked me to do it again!"

Samantha blushed.

"Are you sure about that?"

"Definitely, and now you're flirting with me."

Samantha smiled at him.

"Sorry."

"Don't apologise, I love it."

Samantha looked down at her mug and began to it twirl around.

"What I'm trying to say is…" she paused again, "I'm scared."

"Scared?"

"I don't want to lose you. The thing is, boys seem to think I've been having sex for ages, and when I don't want to go the whole way they think I'm frigid, I'm not, I'm just not ready yet. It needs to be with someone I love and trust, and, well…"

She sighed .

"I'm a virgin."

They sat in silence, Sam kept her head down she was too embarrassed to look at him. Robert was thinking frantically, what should he say, if he said the wrong thing there would be no chance of having a romantic relationship with her. The fact she was a virgin was actually a relief. How could he explain 18-year-old boys were testosterone fuelled machines. Samantha was still fiddling with her mug, she looked up.

"You're supposed to speak now, or have I completely frightened you off?"

He reached across and held her hand.

"Sam, you said our friendship was important, yes?"
She nodded.

"When I came here, I was so unhappy. I felt like I was being punished for a crime. Martin and Richard were friendly and made me feel a bit better but I really missed my old home and friends, then along came you. I felt so shy, here you were, are, the most beautiful girl in the school, probably the country and I could barely speak to you. You sat me down on our bench and made me realise how hard it was, people always making assumptions because of the way you look. I really like you Sam, it's not just because you're gorgeous but because you're funny and intelligent and you get my jokes, and even played along with the lyric game. Your friendship is important to me too, so I don't want to do anything that would scare you off, and you being a virgin is completely cool. When we kissed it just felt so right."

"Thank you Rob, so what do we do?"

He took a deep breath.

"What do you want to do?"

"Honestly?"

"Yep."

"I want to kiss you again."

"I think that might be okay."

He was trying not to grin.

Samantha stood up and walked around the breakfast bar. Sitting on the stool he was the perfect height for her. They kissed, at first very gently and then with more passion. Finally they broke apart, Samantha felt quite breathless, her heart was pounding, she felt such desire.
Robert held onto her hand.

"You okay?"

She nodded then pulled back looking into his eyes.

"I've never felt like this before, with anyone."

Robert grinned.

"Good!"

Samantha snuggled back into his arms, she could feel his heart beating fast, she knew he'd felt it too.

"If you like we can take things slowly and just see how things go," he held her perfect face in his hands, "If at any time you…" he thought for a moment.

"I don't know, want to...what I'm trying to say is I'll be guided by you, if we get a bit carried away and you get scared, just tell me. Is that OK?"

Samantha smiled.

"Rob, you're amazing."

They gazed at each other for a moment.

"Shit!" blurted Rob.

"What?"

"Samantha Thompson I want to thank you for my lovely Christmas present."

"Double shit. Thank you for mine, it must've taken you ages."

"I love the microscope it will always have pride of place on my desk. Have you listened to the tape?"

"Yes, although my mum wants to know who is singing half the tracks."

"Your mum? She's heard it?"

"Yes and my dad, we played it in the car on the way to my nans on Christmas day. So was it you?"

Robert covered his face with his hands.

"Yeah, this is so embarrassing."

"Rob is there anything you can't do?"

She ticked off her fingers.

"Maths, science, swimming, singing, oh and kissing!"

Robert laughed.

"I can't cook, or draw!"

"Talking of cooking, I'm starving. I'll see what there is in the fridge."

They shared Robert's packed lunch supplemented with some pork pies, cheese and some home-made apple pie. Samantha ran upstairs to get the tape and put it on in the kitchen.

"Do you have a favourite track on the cassette?"

"I like nearly all of them, but I think my favourite is 'Perhaps love'.

She started to sing along to the music.

"Sam you've really got a lovely voice."

Robert looked at his watch it was 14.30.

"I'll have to think about leaving soon, let's check on the timetables and make a plan to do some revision, would it be okay for me to come here sometimes?"

"Of course, we'll go to school for the set lessons and then back here for the rest."

Robert gave her a big hug, and they kissed.

"Sam, I've had a lovely day thank you."

"Me too, I don't want you to go."

"I'll see you at school tomorrow, don't be late, and wear some sensible shoes!"

Reluctantly he left.

"See you.

Chapter Thirteen

During the next couple of weeks they developed a routine, only attending school for the formal revision lesson, and spending more time at Samantha's house on their free days. They would study in the mornings, sitting together in the afternoons on the sofa talking and kissing.

Samantha had planned to sleepover at Megans one weekend, she hadn't seen much of her friend as they had revision classes on different days and Megan's parents had also organised some private tuition for her. Samantha was really looking forward to seeing her and had decided to tell her all about Robert .

Samantha worked as usual in the shop on the Saturday, then rushed home to shower and change before going to Megans with her overnight bag. When she arrived they gave each other a big hug but were unable to chat as Megan's family were around. Samantha realised something was bothering Megan, so as soon as it was socially acceptable, Samantha and Megan made their excuses and went to Megan's room.

They sat on her bed at which point Megan burst into tears.
"Megs what an earth is wrong?"
"It's Tim."
"Oh no, have you two split up?"
Megan shook her head.
"No. He's got a place at Cambridge."
"Bloody hell Megs, that's fantastic so what's the problem?"
"We both had offers from Cardiff and Exeter, now we'll never see each other, how will we keep our relationship going with him in Cambridge and me on the other side of the country. Do you think he's trying to break up with me?"

She started to cry again. Samantha put her arm around her friend.

"No way Megs, Tim is completely besotted with you. I bet he'd drop Cambridge like a brick if he realised how upset you are."

Megan dried her eyes.

"I know, I know, but I couldn't possibly ask him to give up such an opportunity."

They sat in silence for a while, and then Samantha sat up straight.

"Megs why don't you apply to Cambridge, you're guaranteed to get good A-levels, you did amazing in your mocks it's a no brainer!"

Megan smiled.

"Sam you're such an optimist. I'll never get into Cambridge, they like public school applicants. Tim is at King Edwards in Bath, we are at crappy Oldway."

"But it's worth a try!"

Megan thought about it.

"I suppose I've got nothing to lose I was hoping you'd go Cardiff or Exeter next year as well."

"There's no point Megs, with you at Cambridge!"

Megan laughed.

"Thanks Sam, you've cheered me up."

They spent some time discussing Universities, Samantha was starting to drift off to sleep when she remembered she hadn't told Megan about Robert , but then realised she wasn't ready to share her feelings about him yet.

Samantha looked forward to Mondays, the weekends felt so long she couldn't wait to see Robert . However this Monday there was a problem. Samantha woke up, it was very dark. She looked at the clock, 5.45 she groaned, why was she awake so early? She closed her eyes and smiled to herself, only three hours until she saw him. She sighed contentedly as she had had a lovely weekend, working as usual on Saturday, and then meeting Rosie, Megan, and a couple of other friends to celebrate Rosie's birthday. A pizza in Bath, one of Megan's brothers had been their chauffeur much to the girls delight and then it was back to Rosies to watch a video and a sleepover. She had slept most of Sunday, so maybe that was why was she wide awake so early. Samantha thought about Robert , they were having quite intimate cuddles now, on the sofa and true to his word Robert hadn't pressurised her at all in doing anything she wasn't happy with. She smiled, she had been very aware of his erection on a number of occasions even though he tried to hide it.

It was Valentine's Day on Friday and Samantha decided she would bring him upstairs to her bedroom, she wasn't sure she was ready to go all the way, but she trusted him enough now that they may be able to get naked and....her thoughts were interrupted by a crash.

She looked at the clock again, 6.05, she sat up and listened.

Aware of voices, she got out of bed put on her dressing gown and made her way onto the landing which was in darkness. A light was coming from her parents bedroom as the door was ajar. Samantha was surprised to see her mum up and dressed and having a whispered argument with her dad.

The Thompson's house has been built in the 1920s, her parents bedroom was at the front of the house it was large with a little dressing room accessed through two doors at right angles to each other. A large chest of drawers appeared to be wedged in the doorway of the dressing room.

"Morning," said Samantha .

Her mother swung round.

"Oh sorry love, did we wake you?"

"Not sure."

She looked around the room, the bed was covered in clothes.

"What are you doing?"

Her father's voice came from the dressing room.

"Trying to get this bloody thing through the door!"

"Why?"

"Why? Because Mr Williams is starting this morning, I told your father we should've cleared it yesterday, but no, it'll only take a short while to clear."

"Who is Mr Williams and what is he starting?"

"The ensuite."

Samantha climbed unto her parents bed.

"Why are you having an ensuite?"

"Your mother saw one in a magazine and now thinks we need one," protested her father.

"I still don't get it, the bathroom is only just outside your room!"

"This way we won't disturb you, if we want an early shower."

"In another seven months I won't be here!"

Samantha smiled, they only ever referred to each other as mother and father when they were stressed.

"Wouldn't it have been easier if you had taken the drawers out?"

She heard her father sigh.

"Push it back to me Adeline and we'll see if Miss smarty-pants is right."

Another half an hour saw them successfully negotiate the rest of furniture out of the room."

"How long will Mr Williams take?"

"It depends, 1 to 2 weeks."

"What! You know I like to study at home, It will be so noisy, I'll fail my exams over a bloody ensuite that you don't even need."

"Samantha don't be so dramatic! You'll just have to go to school, he may even finish this week."

Samantha went back to her room and got dressed, this had ruined her plans. After breakfast, she prepared for school and left the house muttering to herself, two bloody weeks!

Robert was turning into the drive as she came out, she quickly propelled him back onto the pavement.

"Everything okay?"

"No we've got bloody builders coming for the next two weeks."

"Oh."

"Yes, oh is exactly right!"

They walked down the road.

"I guess we'll just have to go into school."

Samantha was thinking, where could they go it was too cold and damp to be outside. They arrived at school, the six form block was deserted. Samantha and Robert entered the classroom and sat down ready to start their studies. It was the first time Robert had seen Samantha so grumpy.

"Sam it really isn't a problem, if it wasn't for you this is how I'd be spending my free study time."

Samantha suddenly brightened.

"How much money have you got?"

Robert checked his pockets and produced a handful of coins.

"Just shrapnel."

Samantha was rummaging in her bag.

"I've a couple of pound coins and some change. I have an idea. We'll get the bus into Bristol and, I don't know, what do you fancy, shops, the museums?"

Robert had mixed feelings, the thought of doing something like getting on a bus like a normal person would be fantastic, but what if his mother found out? Samantha looked at him expectantly.

"Well?"

Robert grinned.

"Why not. Let's go."

They stowed the contents of their bags into their lockers taking just the bare minimum and retraced their steps out of school down the hill, over the bridge, up the other side and along the High Street to the bus stop.

The day flew by, Robert really enjoyed his freedom. The museum was dry, warm and surprisingly interesting, they found a quiet corner to share his sandwiches. On the bus home, Robert held Samantha's hand.

"Thanks, it's been so good to do something normal. What shall we do for the rest of the week?"

Tuesday morning they both had a chemistry tutorial, then spent the afternoon walking around Bath. Wednesday and Thursday they were busy with school work. Friday morning, Samantha was loitering at the end of the road waiting for Robert . He arrived and gave Samantha a card and a box of milk tray.

"Hey happy Valentine's Day."

Samantha gave me a peck on the cheek.

"Happy Valentine's Day to you as well."

She handed him a card and a gift. They linked arms and started walking towards School.

"Do we have a plan for today?" asked Robert .

"Not really unless you fancy going back to Bristol or Bath."

Robert thought.

"I do have one idea, but you might not like it."

"Try me."

"I wondered if you'd like to visit my grandmother with me?"

"Okay, where does she live?"

"She is in a nursing home on the other side of Bristol, we would have to get a couple of buses if you fancy it, at least it'll be nice and warm."

Sam squeezed his hand.

"I'd like that."

They arrived at Hamilton Court nursing home just after 10 o'clock. It was a grand looking house surrounded by lovely gardens. They walked into the reception area, nobody took any notice of them, there was a visitors book on the table so Robert signed them in.

"Hopefully grandma is in the same room as before. I just need to warn you Sam, she gets very muddled and may not know who I am, she sometimes she calls people by the wrong name."

"Rob it's okay."

They walked along a picture laden corridor, an elderly man was in front of them walking with a Zimmer frame. Samantha couldn't help noticing there was an unpleasant smell. Room number seven was on the ground floor. Rob knocked gently and put his head around the door. He spotted his Grandmother sitting in a chair looking out into the garden. The contents of her handbag were scattered on the floor around her feet, she was singing to herself.

"Hi Nan."

Robert and Samantha walked into the room. His grandmother looked puzzled then smiled, she had a gentle voice.

"Oh are we going now? I haven't packed yet, I don't think Brian is ready, are you dear?"

Robert whispered to Samantha .

"Brian was my grandad."

He turned back to his grandmother.

"Don't worry Nan, I brought someone to meet you."

Samantha peered around Robert shoulder.

"Hello."

His grandmother smiled and clapped her hands

"Oh lovely."

Robert grabbed a couple of chairs and dragged them near her. Samantha knelt down and started picking up the items from the floor. Robert's grandmother watched her.

"Such a good girl, how long have you and William been married?"

Samantha blushed and started to stutter.

"William?"

"Don't worry, she's just rambling, best to smile and nod."

The old lady appeared to enjoy their company, even if she didn't seem to know what she was talking about. She asked Samantha to pass her a jewellery box that was sitting on top of the dressing table. She opened it and started to look through the contents muttering to herself, there were old earrings, bangles, beads, rings and at the bottom was a little box.

"Ah, there you are."

She lifted it out and passed it to Samantha .

"Open it, open it."

Samantha did it she was told, inside was a lovely silver locket.

"Oh it's beautiful!"

It was round with unusual engravings on the front and back.

"It's so delicate."

Robert's grandmother was nodding, pointing at the locket.

"Open it, open it."

Sam released the little clasp and the locket opened to show two little frames with portraits of a man and a woman.

"There!"

"Is this you."

Samantha showed the pictures to Robert's grandmother.

"Yes, yes."

Samantha looked at Robert .

"Is it?"

Robert looked at it.

"No idea, but I remember her always wearing it."

"It's yours now," said Nan.

"Oh no!"

Samantha hastily returned it to its box.

"Yes, it's for your daughter."
"Um, I don't have a daughter."
"Yes, yes, she must have it."

Samantha was feeling quite flustered and looked at Robert for help.

"Just say thank you, she'll forget all about it in a minute."

Samantha smiled at his grandmother.

"That's very kind, thank you."

This seemed to please the old lady. Samantha carefully collected the rest of the jewellery putting it back into the box, discreetly returning the locket at the same time.

By Friday the builders had finished, but Samantha's dad was home with a dreadful cold. She met Robert by the front gate.

"School I'm afraid, my dad is home."
"Not a problem, but we haven't planned anything."
"Let's go and see your Nan again I really liked her."
"Ok."

On arrival, once again Robert signed them in. They walked through to his grandmother's room, where they found her very agitated and had been tearing up tissues which were all over her lap and the floor. Robert spoke to her.

"Hi Nan, we're back to see you again."
"Where is he? Is he with you?"
"Who Nan?"

She became increasingly agitated as she tried to remember the name. Samantha didn't know what to do, she looked at Robert .

"Should we get a nurse?"

Robert shook his head.

"She's just very confused."

He took his grandmothers hand.

"Nan, it's me what's wrong?"
"He is missing, no one knows where he is!"
"Who Nan?"
"Andrew of course."

Samantha felt Robert stiffen beside her, she looked at him, he looked terrible.

"Rob, are you okay?"

She didn't dare ask who Andrew was as I seem to hit a raw nerve. Robert blinked and pulled himself together.

"He's okay Nan, he's safe and sound."

This seemed to calm the old lady. Samantha was desperately trying to think of something to say to break the tension between the two of them.

She knelt beside the grandmothers chair and quietly sang 'perhaps love'. It didn't take long before Nan relaxed and hummed along with her. At the end of the song Robert's grandmother clapped her hands and smiled, all anxiousness had disappeared. The same couldn't be said for Robert , he looked pale and tense. Samantha carried on chatting to Nan whilst collecting up the bits of tissue making it a bit of a game with her.

After staying for a while Robert announced they should leave. Samantha gave his grandmother a hug.

"We'll be back again soon."

They walked back to the bus station in silence. Samantha had never seen Robert so unhappy.

"Shall we get a cuppa before we get on the bus?
He shrugged his shoulders.

"Come on."

She dragged him into a little café and ordered two teas and a cake to share. They sat in the corner.

"Do you want to talk about it?."

Robert shook his head.

"Is there anything I can say to make it better?"

He sat back and looked at her.

"Sorry Sam, this is all a mistake, I can't have a normal relationship with anyone. My life is a mess."

"Rob, don't say that please."

He ran his hands through his hair.

"I can't explain, I can't expect you to put up with not being able to see each other at the weekend, having to pretend I'm at school so we can date. If my mum knew I was sitting here with you she'd go ballistic. It's all shit!"

"If it makes you feel any better my mum thinks I'm either at home or at school, I haven't told her about you, or that you come over."

Tears were stinging Samantha's eyes. Robert meant so much to her, the thought of not seeing him again was too painful. She rubbed her eyes.

"Robert Brown if you don't like me, or I've done something to upset you, then okay dump me, but," she mustn't cry she thought,
"If you like me as much as I like you, I don't mind the weekends I work on Saturdays I spend time with my friends on Sundays and watch 'Howard's way' with my mum."

"Not you as well, everyones watching it!"

"So you better not dump me."

It wasn't her best argument.

"Do you really mean that Sam?"

"As David would say 'I think I love you'."

The tension in Robert's shoulders dropped.

"Say that again."

Sam blushed.

"No, it was a one-time special."

"Samantha Thompson, if you don't tell me again, I'll dump you.

"That's blackmail, okay, but only because I don't want to be dumped. I think I love you."

"Sam, you only think?" He paused "you see I know I love you."

"So why are you thinking of dumping me?"

"I hate all this sneaking about, lying to my mum."

"Would she really get mad if you told her?"

"My home life is so complicated, sadly I can't explain it. My mum would love you, I'm sorry, I don't feel I'm being totally honest with you."

"Just know that I love you and I'm here for you if you want me. I don't want to make things harder for you, so I understand the situation isn't ideal, but we can carry on as we are, if that's what you want, and if anytime you're finding it difficult just let me know and we can talk about it."

"As Paul would say 'you're the best thing'."

"I didn't know you were into the Style council."

"How on earth did I meet someone like you?"

"Just lucky I guess."

"I don't know what I'd do without you."

They sat in comfortable silence, holding hands across the table.

"One day hopefully in the not too distant future Sam I can tell you about my family, you can meet them all and then we can date properly and.."

"Live happily ever after?"

"Yeah, something like that. Come on we don't want to miss that bus."

"Bless you."

Although the weekend dragged Sam's declaration of love kept Robert going, he couldn't wait to see her again. He was out of the house early on Monday and almost ran to Queens Road. He was surprised to see her mum's car in the drive. Samantha had told him, she would sometimes walk to the studio but he felt indecisive, what should he do? Taking a deep breath he walked up to the back door and rang the bell. It was answered by an attractive lady who obviously had a streaming cold.

"Hello?"

"Oh hi, I'm a friend of Sam's, I didn't know if she was going into school today?"

Adeline sneezed heavily.

"Bless you."

"Thank you, I'm afraid we are house of plague, Sam is still in bed, I don't think she should be at school until the end of the week, can I give her a message?"

Robert thought, tell her I love her and I miss her.

"Oh just tell her I hope she feels better soon."

"Okay."

Adeline shut the door. Damn she hadn't asked for his name, she'd have to describe him. Being an artist she was used to closely observing peoples faces, despite his heavy glasses he had very good bone structure, he would be interesting to paint.

Sam lay in bed, a box of tissues by her side, she felt grim her throat was so sore. Her mum appeared with hot honey and lemon.

"Thanks Mum."

"I've made us both one. You had a visitor, a boy from school, sorry I didn't ask his name."

She handed Samantha a piece of paper it was a rough sketch of Robert .

"Mum you're amazing how did you do that?,it looks just like him!"

Samantha put the sketch on her bedside table, she couldn't wait to show it to Robert.

Samantha spent the next few days wallowing in self pity and wishing the time away. By Thursday, she felt much better, the cold had left her with a croaky voice, but her head felt clear. She walked to school alone, Thursdays was one of the days when she and Rob had separate revision classes so she usually spent time with Megan and then would meet up with Robert when they had finished. He would usually meet her in the six form block about 2.30 and then walk into the park and sit on the bench or pop into the teashop.

Samantha looked at her watch, 2.30, no one had come. She looked out of the window, she could see Martin and Richard chatting to Rosie. Sam wandered out and joined them.

"Hiya Rosie, how's it going?"

"Sam, haven't seen you for awhile."

"No I've had a bloody head cold."

"You sound terrible."

"I feel much better."

"Hey you must've been snogging Rob," joked Martin.

"What! Why?"

"Because, he is off sick with a cold as well. Coincidence?"

They still hadn't told their school friends about their relationship. Samantha knew if she insisted Robert and her were just friends they would see through her. She rolled her eyes and tried to sound sarcastic.

"Oh no, we've been rumbled, we're obviously having a passionate love affair!"

Martin laughed.

"Probably in Robs dreams, he knows you're way out of his league."

Samantha wanted to protest but decided to keep it quiet as she walked part of the way home with them wishing away the time until Monday.

Samantha hadn't worked on the Saturday, her mother didn't think they'd appreciate a sales assistant who looked so pale and with a lovely red nose. The weekend again dragged for Samantha as Megan had also gone down with a cold and she wasn't even up to a long chat on the phone.

Monday at last Samantha looked so much better, she hoped Robert had also recovered. To her relief he turned up at the usual time. They hugged and compared sick notes over a cup of tea.

"We need a way of communicating to each other. I couldn't warn you last Monday and I was worried on Thursday when you didn't turn up at school."

"I know, I wasn't sure whether to knock on the door or not, but your mum is so nice, did she mind?

"Wait there, I've got something to show you."

Samantha ran upstairs and got the sketch from her bedside table.

"She forgot to ask your name," handing it to Robert , "so she drew you instead."

"Bloody hell Sam that's incredible."

"I know, she is so good. This is a bit cringy though, she'd like to paint you, apparently you have good bone structure."

Robert laughed.

"You're joking!"

"No, honestly."

"Shut up you'll make me blush."

"School breaks up on Wednesday for Easter do you have a telephone, I could just say it's about revision."

Robert hated lying to Samantha .

"Sorry no phone."

"Will we be able to meet up at all?"

Robert looked sad.

"Sorry Sam, I've tried to explain," he paused, "Mum is…"

"Rob please, it doesn't matter."

"Doesn't it?"

"Well yes obviously it does matter but as I said in the café, I love you Robert Brown and I'm okay with things how they are, and like you said hopefully it won't be for much longer."

"Oh God Sam, I love you so much."

They kissed passionately until they were quite breathless, Samantha took robs hand and then him out of the kitchen and up the stairs to her room.

"You're the first boy who's ever been in here."

They fell onto the bed, pulling their T-shirts off, then held each other tightly. Samantha felt quite lightheaded with desire.

"Oh God, Sam you are so beautiful."

Robert moved his hands around her waist then upwards fumbling for her bra strap. Amazingly Samantha didn't feel remotely shy, she trusted Robert completely as he released her breasts. She arched her back as he moved his hands over her hardened nipples, she hadn't experienced anything like this before. She responded by unzipping his trousers and sliding her hand into his groin. He was ready.

"Hang on Sam."

"What?"

"Is it safe? Are you on the pill?"

Samantha lay back.

"No, do you have anything on you?"

"If you mean like Durex, then no."

Robert lay beside her.

"Could you just take it out at the last minute? Isn't that how Catholics do it?"

"Yeah and they all have about 20 kids. We need to be a bit more prepared that's all."

"Rob I really want to make love with you."

"Tell me about it."

"Never mind I can still make you feel nice lie back I'm taking over."

Afterwards they lay in each other's arms talked about Uni, favourite music, films and TV programmes.

"We'd better get dressed, I ought to have a wash, but I don't want to lose the smell of you on my skin."

The Easter holidays seem to drag for both of them, each desperate to see each other. Robert managed to escape for an afternoon and called into the shop to see Samantha . He knew she was working a half day. The weather was glorious so they decided to walk to the park and sit on their bench, forgetting all the schools were off and the park was full of families enjoying the sunshine.

"Shit, it's so busy," exclaimed Samantha .

"I don't mind, we can try and find a quiet bit."

"No, why don't we walk along the river?"

The footpath beside the river was also busy with children paddling and fishing in the shallow water. They kept on walking until they came to the bridge.

"I have an idea," said Samantha , "let's keep walking."

They continued over the bridge and joined another footpath that led them away from the town through fields of grazing cattle.

"This is lovely Sam, where does it come out?"

"Wait and see."

They walked for about half an hour through a kissing gate and out onto a road.

"This is Chewton Keyford, it's a small hamlet, I would love to live here, maybe one day I will."

It was very picturesque, Robert took an interest in the houses and cottages as they walked by.

"Which one shall we buy?"

"I don't mind, as long as it's with you."

They walked to the end of the hamlet, Robert checked his watch.

"I could walk forever, it's such a lovely day especially with you but sadly I think we better head back. I'm supposed to be out buying Easter eggs!"

They walked back hand-in-hand stopping every now and then to kiss until they reached Keyford. Robert bought a couple of Easter eggs for his mum and his sister and a beautiful egg for Samantha which he handed to her.

"I'll see you back at school next Tuesday, have a lovely Easter and thanks for this afternoon."

After Easter the sixth form prepared for their exams. Robert and Samantha struggle to get time together alone. One lunchtime Samantha asked Robert whether he'd managed to buy some condoms. He blushed.

"No every time I try I feel like all those women assistants are watching me. I'm sure they think I'm a shoplifter, then I panic and walk out."

Sam laughed.

"Don't worry I'll get us some."

The following Saturday Samantha was at work. She was sent upstairs to the storeroom with a list of stock items that would need replenishing. She pushed her trolley along the row of shelves checking her list and loading the items into the trolley. She was almost finished when she noticed a shelf containing condoms. Samantha froze, she'd never taking much notice of them before. There were boxes of 3 or 12 and a variety of different types. She stared, then looked around, she was completely alone, quickly she grabbed a pack of three and put them in her pocket. Samantha had never done anything bad in her life. Her heart was pounding and her hands were shaking, what had she done? The storeroom door opened and one of the trainee pharmacists walked in.

"Hi Sam, how are you doing?"

"Oh hi, fine thanks, I better get back or else Mrs Thomas will be after me."

The girl smiled, Samantha quickly pushed her trolley into the lift. Back on the shop floor she started to stock the shelves, the pack of Durex burning a hole in her pocket.

"Samantha Thompson, over here," called Mrs Thomas.

Oh God, thought Samantha , she knew, she would be made to empty her pockets and everyone would see, they'd probably call the police. Samantha felt sick.

"Leave the rest of that stock and go to lunch."

Samantha was overcome with relief.

"Yes Mrs Thomas."

Chapter Fourteen

June had arrived, Robert met Samantha at her house for their last exam.

"I can't believe it Rob, this is our last ever day at school."

"Are you getting your results by post or going in?"

"I'll go in and collect them but probably won't open them until I get home."

"You'll be fine Sam.

"Martin said his parents are hosting a party again at the farm, it was really good last year, will you be able to come?"

"I don't know, I'd really like to."

"It will be no different from being at school, and your mum could go so please ask her."

"I can't imagine she'd want to go."

The exam was finally over. Samantha, Robert and a few friends met in the six form block to discuss the forthcoming party before leaving school for the last time. Samantha held Robert's hand as they walked home to her house.

"Are you coming round tomorrow?"

"Oh yes, but I haven't bought any, you know, Durex."

"You don't need to worry, I've sorted it."

"Really? You're braver than me!"

"We've got about half an hour before you need to leave, do you want to try one out?"

"Samantha Thompson you're a wicked girl, are you that desperate?" he teased.

Samantha blushed.

"Rob!" she squealed, slapping him playfully.

"I don't want our first time to be a quickie, I'll be here tomorrow and we can spend the whole day in bed if you like."

She hugged him.

"I like that idea very much. Let's just hope nothing happens between now and then to mess things up."

Robert stayed a little longer and then it was time to leave.

"I'll see you tomorrow Sam."

"I shall look forward to it Mr Brown."

Robert could barely sleep that night he was so full of anticipation.

At breakfast he tried to play it cool.

"How many more exams do you have left? asked his mother.

"Just a few more, I've almost finished."

"That will be a relief when they're all done, what is it today?"

"Chemistry."

"Oh, I thought that was yesterday"

"It's a tutorial, for next weeks exam."

God he hated lying.

"Bless you, you've worked so hard, Dad will be so proud." At the mention of his father, Robert felt dreadful. He certainly wouldn't be proud if he knew Robert was lying to his mum. He gave his mother a kiss.

"I'd better be off."

"You smell nice, don't forget to brush your teeth," she called as he left the room.

Robert smiled to himself, he definitely would brush his teeth especially after Samantha had told him about Dean's bad breath. Five minutes later he left the house.

"Bye mum see you later."

Mary smiled to herself, he was such a good lad, she thought. They had been in Keyford for just over nine months and he had settled in well with the minimum of fuss, she had received a phone call to say the court case was imminent and soon this nightmare would be over and they could get their lives back. She cleared the breakfast dishes and made a note to phone the school later as she needed to confirm where Robert's results should be sent.

Robert had to stop himself running to Samantha's yet he still arrived way too early and was horrified to see her mum's car in the drive. He decided to retrace his steps almost back to his own house then tried to walk as slow as he could. This time to his relief the driveway was empty, he knocked on the door, Samantha opened it.

"I've been waiting for you."

"I got here about 15 minutes earlier, but your mum's car was on the drive."

"Yeah I thought she'd never go."

Samantha led Robert into the kitchen.

"Would you like a drink or anything?"

For the first time they were both a bit shy with each other.

"A cup of tea would be nice."

Samantha raced around, filling the kettle and tripping over her feet spilling the milk and dropping Robert's mug.

"Wow! Slowdown Sam."

"Sorry, I'm a bit jittery."

Robert took her hands.

"Sam it's okay we don't need to do anything, we could just have a cuddle."

Samantha closed her eyes and took some deep breaths she gave him a squeeze .

"Rob you're amazing. I do want to make love, I'm just a bit nervous."

"I feel the same way Sam, it's my first time too, we just take it slowly, okay?

Samantha nodded, her heart was pounding, she held onto Robert's hand as they climbed the stairs. They slowly undressed each other, both found their hands shaking as they started to explore each other's bodies. It wasn't long before they both relaxed and were completely immersed in their passion, leaving them breathless and hungry for more.

Samantha had put the Durex on the bedside table, she picked one up and handed it to Robert .

"Are you sure?"

"Oh my god yes."

He took it from her and managed to put it on without any mishaps. He felt her guide him in, it was exquisite.

"Oh Sam I love you," he gasped.

She clawed at his back as his thrusts became more urgent. It didn't take long, he rolled away from her.

"Sorry Sam."

"Sorry? For what?"

"I was hoping to last a little longer."

Samantha grinned.

"Robert Brown, it was bloody incredible."

"Really?"

"Really."

They lay exhausted side-by-side on Samantha's bed holding hands and regaining their breath whilst looking at each other.

"I better go to the bathroom and clean up."

"Don't be long my love."

The lovers spent the next couple of hours talking kissing and planning ahead.

"Mum and Dad are away next week at an art exhibition in Birmingham, they'll be back next weekend. I'd really like you to meet them, would that be possible?"

"I'm going to have to tell mum soon. She'll soon realise that my exams are finished and the school holidays aren't too far off."

"What if she won't let you see me."

"She's not an ogre Sam," laughed Rob, "in fact my mum is really lovely. I know you'll like her, once I've explained, she won't stop us seeing each other, but you may have to come over to mine every now and then so we may not get as much time like this together."

"You better make the most of today then," said Samantha running her hands over his body.

Robert groaned.

"Samantha Thompson is that all you want me for?"

Samantha giggled.

"Yes I'm going to keep you here as my slave."

She suddenly jumped up.

"Come with me slave."

Robert followed her out of the bedroom along the landing into her parents room and their ensuite.

"Wow what is this?"

"The new power shower, I think as it's construction stopped us from getting together a couple of weeks ago we need to try it out."

Robert had never seen anything like it, there was no shower tray but a large tiled area of floor with half a partition door and an array of horizontal bars mounted on the walls.

"These are body jets and there is an overhead shower as well but we'll just use the body jets"

Samantha adjusted the taps and soon hot water was spraying across the shower. She took Robert by the hand.

"Come on."

Samantha rubbed soap over Robert's body. It was the most erotic experience he had ever had it wasn't long before his body reacted. They made love more slowly this time, standing up with a water cascading over them. They washed each other's bodies then Samantha grabbed a couple of towels and turned off the water.

"I better turn the immersion on, as there won't be any hot water for Mum and Dad later."

"Do you think they will use it in the same way?"

"Yuck, don't be gross they're so old."

Robert suddenly look horrified.

"Shit Sam."

"What!"

"We just made love without any protection!"

"Bloody hell Rob, but we were in the shower"

"I don't think that makes any difference, I was inside you."

"But we used a condom the first time round, isn't it covered in something to kill the sperm, it wasn't that long ago I'm probably okay."

"You may be right."

Samantha thought for a minute.

"I know, there is this new pill I think it's called the morning after pill. I'll check at work."

Robert relaxed.

"Sam that was probably the most mind blowing experience I've ever had, but next time we must be a bit more careful, agreed?"

"Agreed, I'll get a doctor's appointment next week to go on the pill so no cock ups."

"Very funny."

"Let's get dressed and grab something to eat. I'll swap these towels over for ones in my bathroom so Mum won't know what we've been been up to."

They were now downstairs Samantha had made them some sandwiches.

"Do you think your mum would let you stay over next week?"

Rob nearly choked on his sandwich.

"Bloody hell Sam, I haven't even told her about us yet!"

"I know but I'll be all alone here in my little bed."

Robert laughed.

"Samantha Thompson you're sex mad, but the weekends are going to feel like an eternity"

Samantha cuddled into him.

"Don't forget I'm working tomorrow but I've got the whole of next week free, so we can spend as much time as possible together. When does Ruth finish Uni?"

"Ruth?"

"Your sister dummy."

Robert could've kicked himself.

"Oh yeah Ruth, I think I've lost a few brain cells today. She could be back soon, that will make things easier. I think you and her would get on well."

"Well hopefully we'll get to meet each other soon. Please tell your mum."

Sitting in Samantha's kitchen with her and being surrounded by all the homely clutter, Robert felt anything was possible. Things were definitely looking up but it wasn't long before Robert had to make a move.

"How can the day have gone so quickly?" protested Samantha .

" As they say time flies when you're having fun."

"Rob I think that's been the best fun I've ever had in my entire life."

Rob kissed her..

"Parting is such sweet sorrow."

"Wow Shakespeare now, you are a man of many hidden talents."

"A man?"

"Oh yes, definitely a man."

"Oh Sam I really don't want to go."

They walked to the door.

"Have a good weekend."

"You too, I'll watch 'Howard's Way' on Sunday and think of you Sam."

She returned a smile as Robert gave her a final kiss.

"I'll see you Monday morning my love."

She didn't want to let him go

"Stay another five minutes."
"If I don't go now I'll never leave."
"Suits me!"
She watched him walk down the drive.
"Rob, Rob," she called out.
He swung round.
"What?"
"I love you."
"Good. See you Monday."
Robert walked down Queens Road and into Albert Road along to the High Street it felt like it he was walking on air, life was good. He was so distracted he was completely unaware he was being followed.

His school bag was slung over his shoulder, he decided to come clean with his mum and tell her his exams were over and he had a girlfriend. He wanted her to meet Samantha .
He was still smiling as he turned into the drive, oblivious to the two white vans parked near the house in the quiet cul-de-sac.

He opened the back door and stepped into the house, unaware of the drama that was about to unfold.

Chapter Fifteen

Adeline arrived home from her studio and noticed a change in her daughter. Samantha had always been a glass half full girl but her glass seem to be overflowing.
That evening she sat on Samantha's bed.
"So, tell me about him."
"Who?"
"Well It's a either a boy or you've won the football pools."
Samantha grinned.
"He is called Robert, oh mum he really is the one."
"So have you.." she trailed off.
Samantha blushed.
"Mum don't be so embarrassing."
Adeline smiled.
"So you have. I hope you were careful."

Samantha went to work the next day, Mrs Thomas wondered whether she had a new skin regime, she seemed to be glowing. After her coffee break Samantha looked across the shop floor to the pharmacy.
Miss Green the pharmacist was speaking to a customer discussing his prescription. Samantha had planned to speak to Miss Green about the morning after pill, but now she wasn't feeling so confident and knew if she said it was for a friend, Miss Green would see right through her. Anyway she thought, it's not as if she needed it, nobody got pregnant the first time they had sex, did they? She would make a doctor's appointment on Monday.
"Samantha stop dreaming."
"Oh sorry Miss Thomas," replied Samantha having her thoughts interrupted.
She forgot about her dilemma and was kept busy with a steady flow of customers. That evening she would see Megan and tell her about Robert.
"I knew there was something going on with you two, so we're just friends," mocked Megan.

"Sorry Megs we didn't tell anyone, we didn't want to jinx it. I know I've been a bit antisocial lately, but things have been quite intense between us."

"Bloody hell Sam, don't tell me you've done it," she shrieked.

"Shush keep your voice down."

"Oh my God, you have, haven't you?"

Samantha blushed and nodded.

"Well are you going to give me the details?"

"No!"

Megan laughed,

"How many times?"

"Twice, the first time here in the bedroom..."

"And the second?"

Samantha grinned and whispered.

"In Mum and Dad's new shower."

"In the shower!"

"Hells bells Meg, shut up".

Megan grinned.

"Tim and I have never done it in the shower, what was it like?"

"Wet!"

Both girls burst into laughter.

"Samantha Thompson you're a dark horse."

Samantha explained to Megan they probably wouldn't see much of each other the following week as her parents would be away and she was hoping Robert would spend most of the week with her. Megan wasn't worried as she still had a couple more exams to occupy her time.

Adeline and David were up early on the Monday and had hired a van to transport Adeline's paintings and sculptures. Samantha loved her parents but was desperate for them to leave.

"Now, I've written the name of the hotel and it's phone number on the pin board, you can reach us there, but we won't be there until the evening so you'll have to leave a message. Nan's number is there as well and Mrs Hill knows you're on your own if there is an emergency."

"Mum you've already told me," interrupted Samantha .

"Sorry love, but I hate leaving you alone."

"I'll be fine, Megan may stay over."

"Are you sure you won't come with us?"

"No thanks, I don't want to spend my first week of freedom at some art gallery."

"Just phone if you need us."

"Mum go!"

At last Samantha waved her parents off. She checked her watch, only another hour and Robert would be there. She wandered back into the house and made some toast checking her watch every five minutes. She cleared the kitchen and brushed her teeth and hair and checked her watch again, he was late. By 11 o'clock she was getting agitated. Where can he be she thought, perhaps he was ill or maybe he told his mum and she'd locked him in his room. Samantha paced the house, she didn't want to go out in case he turned up. By 4 pm she knew he wasn't going to come, he must be ill, there was no way he'd let her down. Hopefully he would arrive tomorrow full of apologies.

The next couple of days were no different. Samantha was becoming more and more distressed. She didn't want to worry her parents, so pretended everything was okay when she spoke to them on the phone that evening. By Wednesday evening Samantha was a wreck, she phoned Megan but couldn't speak for crying. In no time Megan had turned up with an overnight bag.

"Sam what on earth's happened you look terrible."

Samantha sobbed on her friends shoulder and eventually managed to tell her about Robert's no-show.

"Oh Megs, I can't sleep, I can't eat. I feel like shit. Why do you think he's done it?"

"Like you said he may be ill. Have you called him or been round to his house?"

"They don't have a phone and I don't even know where he lives!"

"Who doesn't have a phone in this day and age? Right we need a plan, get showered and freshen up you will feel a lot better and while you're doing that I will find us something to eat."

Samantha looked and felt better when she returned to the kitchen. In front of her Megan placed a plate of scrambled egg on toast. Samantha thought to herself, a problem shared was definitely a problem halved especially with your best friend.

"I've been thinking Sam, tomorrow morning phone the school and ask for his address."

"Will they give it to me?"

Megan thought.

"I know, say you lent him some books and you want them back. If it's Mrs Bishop on reception it'll be okay, she is a complete pushover."

"Megs you're a star. Do you need to go to school tomorrow?"

"No I have a private Italian lesson, I'll just call in sick."

"You can't do that, I'll never forgive myself if you failed your exam."

Megan rolled her eyes.

"Sam please, my Italian is better than the tutors, my parents are mad paying for them."

Samantha hugged her.

"Thank you Megs."

By the evening Samantha was exhausted and for the first time since her parents had left she slept well.

Samantha woke and looked at the clock it had gone 9.30. Megan appeared with a cup of tea.

"Morning, did you know you snore really loud!"

"I do not you cheeky bugger."

Megan was glad to see her friend looking more like her old self.

"I've cancelled my Italian, now you need to call the school."

After breakfast and armed with a pen and paper Samantha dialled The school. She felt nervous, but Megan was there for moral support.

"Good morning, Oldway school, how can I help you?"

Samantha relaxed a little, it was Mrs Bishop.

"Oh hi Mrs Bishop it's Samantha Thompson here."

"Samantha, how lovely to talk to you, have you finished your exams?"

Samantha made a face at Megan, this was going to take some time. She and Mrs Bishop chatted for a little while.

"The reason I'm phoning is Mr Quilter partnered up some of his students for revision. I worked with Robert Brown and lent him some of my books. We've both now finished, and I'd like my books back, but realise I don't have his address.

"Well, we don't usually give out students details over the phone dear"

Samantha looked downhearted, Megan made encouraging gestures with her hands.

"I appreciate that Mrs Bishop, and I certainly don't want to get you into trouble, but I didn't tell my mum and dad I'd loaned the books to him as they were quite expensive."

"Oh dear, wait a moment."

"What's happening?" whispered Megan.

Samantha shrugged.

"She's disappeared."

"Samantha, here you go, do you have a pen?"

"Yes."

The receptionist rattled off the address.

"Thank you so much Mrs Bishop."

"Wouldn't it be easier to phone."

"Well..."

"Would you like his number?"

"Oh, uh, please."

Mrs Bishop gave the number and Samantha wrote it down, her face was like thunder. Megan watched on intrigued, Samantha thanked her again and put the phone down.

"Well, what's wrong?"

"She gave me his phone number!"

"Brilliant, let's give him a call."

"Meg, he told me they didn't have a phone, he lied to me Meg, the bastard lied."

Megan didn't know what to say, she put her arms around her friend .

"Maybe they've not long had a phone."

Samantha took a couple of deep breaths, then dialled the number it rang and rang.

"Is it the right number?"

Samantha checked her notepad.

"Well it's what she gave me."

"Come on, let's go and find his house."

The girls checked the address and set off across town. They wandered around for some time until Megan had a brainwave and asked a passing postman. They quickly found Milward road, it was actually a cul-de-sac. Number 12 was quite a way along on the right hand side, Sam checked the house number, it was so quiet and no sign of life.

"It's a bit spooky it's as if no one lives here."

"Don't forget most kids are still at school and people are out at work."

They stood outside for a moment.

"What do you think Megan front or back door? I'll try the front first."

They walked up the drive and up the steps to the front door, Samantha rang the bell stood back and waited. She rang it again, nothing.

"Back door then."

They made their way around the side of the house to the back door. Samantha knocked, no one answered. Megan had passed her and was looking through the kitchen window.

"It's empty!"

"Yeah, no one is home," responded Samantha .

"No I mean it's really empty, look!

Samantha peered in. The kitchen looked as if it hadn't been used, with the exception of a lonely kettle tucked away in one corner of the empty worktops. Samantha remembered how clutter free Dean's family kitchen had been, but this looked different. She could see a pin board on the wall but there was nothing on it, Megan had already moved along and was looking through the patio doors into the sitting room. Samantha joined her, there was a leather sofa, coffee table and a TV, beyond that a small dining table and a couple of chairs but absolutely no ornaments, personal effects, or photos. Samantha and Megan exchanged puzzled looks.

"Do you think Mrs Bishop gave you the right address?"

Samantha felt confused, what an earth was going on here.

"Megs I need to get inside."

"What!"

Samantha looked around.

"Perhaps there's a spare key under a stone or something."

They searched but found nothing.

"Sam, this must be the wrong house."

Samantha wasn't going to give up that easily, she walked up the garden to look back at the house. A small window in what must've been the bathroom didn't look as if it was closed properly, a porch covered the back door. If she could climb on that, then maybe she could get inside.

"Sam, what are you planning?"

Samantha was looking around for something climb on.

"Could you give me a lift up onto the porch?"

"Sam have you lost your mind?"

"I have to know whether he was here."

"Sam, no one is living here, what if someone comes? What do I say?"

Samantha shrugged "Just say you're looking for Robert Brown and school gave you this address, which is actually true."

"But how will I warn you if you're inside? Sam this is mad you're planning on breaking into someone's house."

Samantha wouldn't be put off. Megan grabbed the dustbin and dragged it nearer to the porch, helping Samantha climb onto the bin and then she was able to pull herself up. Samantha tried the window, she was right it wasn't closed tightly, using her nails she managed to prize the window open and looked inside. The bathroom was empty no towels, toothbrushes or any visible signs of occupancy. With difficulty Samantha climbed through the window, she caught her reflection in the mirror and grinned, she had never done anything like this before! Her heart was pounding as she slowly opened the bathroom door and listened, not a sound. She crept downstairs at the bottom sat the phone on a small table, Samantha checked the number, it was definitely the same as school had given her, bloody bastard she thought. Samantha looked around and channelled her inner Miss Marple, scanning the hallway she noted there was no mail, which meant someone must have been there fairly recently. The living room was also completely devoid of any personal possessions, just the basic furniture she had seen through the window.

Megan was looking in at her and gestured for her to hurry up. Samantha walked into the kitchen, again nothing, no signs of life opening cupboards and drawers nothing. Returning upstairs Samantha looked into the bedrooms and noted each had a bed and a wardrobe and chest of drawers, but there was no bedding or clothes in them. She remembered Robert telling her he had the back bedroom, she walked in, if this was his where the hell was he. She checked the drawers and wardrobe, nothing. She sat on the bed feeling fed up, this had to be the right house. Looking around a bit of paper caught her eye, she picked it up turned it over and recognised it was a small piece of the wrapping paper she'd used for Robert's Christmas present. She had proof, he had been here. She slipped the scrap of paper into her pocket and with great difficulty climbed back out of the window and jumped down to an anxious Megan.

"Well, anything?"

Samantha proudly produce the scrap of paper.

"And that means what?"

"He was here!"

"Sam it's a bit of Christmas wrapping paper."

"I know, and I chose it especially for him."

Megan looked doubtful.

"Anyone could've brought the same paper, it's just a coincidence."

"Megs, this is the address the school had for him."

"Okay, so you're right, but there is definitely no one living here now!"

Samantha felt beaten.

"I know, I just don't understand why."

"How about we go and have something to eat at the teashop I'm sure a nice chocolate eclair will clear our heads."

Samantha took a final look around the garden and the empty shed and conceded there was no one living there. As they walked back along the road, a man in one of the houses opposite cleared away the last bit of surveillance equipment and hoped he wouldn't have to wait too long to be picked up, completely oblivious to the breaking and entry taking place on the house he'd been watching.   The girls walked back through the High Street towards the Tea shop where they found a couple of their school friends full of excitement discussing the leaving party at Martin's parents farm.

Samantha really wasn't interested in the party although she and Robert had talked about it. Maybe he would be there.

The girls sat and Savannah came across to serve them. She announced she would be going with Dean although she was hoping Mr Johnson would be there as well. The afternoon rolled on, Samantha was suffering a headache and couldn't wait to get away from the chatter. Megan offered to stay over again as she had no lessons or exams on the Friday and Samantha's parents wouldn't be home until the following morning.

That evening the girls watched Top of the Pops together. Megan was desperately trying to distract Samantha as she had become more and more miserable since their morning adventure.

"Is there no one else he ever mentioned to you?"

Samantha jumped out of her seat.

"Hells bells I really must be thick, we went to visit his grandmother a couple of times, she lives in an old peoples home near Bristol. How could I forgotten about her?"

"Do you remember where it is?"

"Yep. I'll go tomorrow and see if she can tell me where they are."

"I'll go with you Sam."

"Megs you are the best friend anyone could wish for."

Megan grinned at her, she was glad to see her friend looking more positive again now they had another plan.

Samantha slept well again and felt positively energetic the next morning. They walked down to the High Street and caught the bus into Bristol and then onto the nursing home.

They entered the vestibule and Samantha lead Megan across to the visitors book.

"We have to sign in and out."

She stopped and looked at Megan.

"Shit you have to write down who you're visiting and I don't know her name."

"Flick through the book and see if you recognise it."

"I haven't a clue, Robert signed in for us and he just called her Nan."

"When were you here last?"

"Way back before Easter."

"Do you remember the date?"

Samantha thumbed through the book and suddenly spotted her name in Robert's familiar handwriting.

"Meg you've done it again, there she is, Stella Jack."

Samantha turn the pages back and made the entry. Megan looked on puzzled.

"What?" Samantha chirped.

"Just go back again."

Samantha found the page.

"He's spelt my surname wrong he's put Timpson."

"That's not the only thing, where's his name?"

Megan was right, Robert's name wasn't there. She turned the pages further back to their first visit. Sam Timpson but no Robert , she looked at Megan.

"What the hell is going on?"

Megan shrugged her shoulders.

"Let's go see Stella and see if she can help."

The girls walked to Stella's room, Samantha knocked on the door as they entered. Robert's grandmother was sitting in her usual chair humming to herself.

"Hello, do you remember me?" announced Samantha

Stella looked at her and broke into a smile.

"Of course I do, have you bought the baby?"

Megan looked surprised.

"She always says that," whispered Sam.

"Not today, this is my friend Megan."

"Megan, what a lovely name are you Welsh."

Megan smiled.

"No, believe it or not I'm part Italian."

"Oh, how lovely."

Samantha sat down and took Stella's hand.

"Do you remember when I was here last time with your grandson Robert?"

Stella looked puzzled.

"Robert?"

"Yes we've been a couple of times to visit."

"Robert?" she repeated.

"Yes."

Megan broke the stalemate.

"Should I have a little look around for clues?"

"Like what, Miss Marple?"

"I don't know, any photos?"

Samantha looked up.

"There's one by the bed and a couple on the chest of drawers."

Megan walked around the room, the picture by the bed was a sepia photo of a couple on their wedding day.

"Who is this?"

Stella looked at the photo carefully.

"That's Brian on his wedding day. He is so handsome with such dark eyes."

"And the bride?"

"Oh she looks lovely doesn't she, so happy."

Megan and Samantha exchanged looks. They showed Stella some other photos but she didn't seem to recognise anyone, even though they were obviously of herself. Megan put the photos back.

"Megan, this is hopeless, it's if he never existed."

Megan brought across a large book. Stella clapped her hands in joy.

"Oh my bible."

She took it from Megan and carefully opened it. On the inside cover was a list of names and dates.

"I've heard about this," said Samantha, "people wrote in the family bible, all the family births, marriages and deaths."

Megan and Samantha looked over Stella's shoulder. The first few lines were faded and not very clear the onlookers were fascinated, Samantha read down down the list of names.

"Stella, there you are born to Malcolm and Rachel married to Brian, you have a daughter Rebecca."

"Who did she marry?" asked Megan.

Stella moved her hand so they could see, but something had been spilled and smudged the writing, it was illegible.

"Can you make out anything."

Samantha shook her head.

"She married, that may say Adrian."

"Or Andrew."

"Andrew?"

"Possibly."

"Stella, did she marry Andrew? You were worried about him, he was missing."

Stella looked at her.

"Did you find him?" she quizzed."

"What are you two talking about?"

Samantha explained what happened the last time and how Robert had reacted. Megan looked at the names again.

"It could be Andrew and I reckon they had two children, but couldn't say what their names are, it's too badly smudged."

Megan stood up and put the bible back. Stella instructed her to bring the jewellery box that was on the chest of drawers, then proceeded to pull out the contents until she found the small box which contained the locket. She carefully took it out and handed it to Samantha .

"You must take this, it's yours, for the baby."

Samantha inspected the locket and whispered to Megan.

"She keeps doing this as well. In a minute you distract her and I'll put it back."

A short while later there was a knock at the door and a young girl came in.

"Oh sorry, I didn't know you had visitors, I've come to see if you'd like to come down to lunch Stella?"

Stella smiled.

"Oh yes please."

"I'll go get a wheelchair."

"I suppose we better go," suggested Megan.

Samantha was reluctant to leave, despite the lack of information Stella was her only link to Robert. The young carer returned with the wheelchair.

"I just wondered if any of Stella's family had visited recently?" enquired Samantha .

"I don't think she's got any family."

"Oh she has, I visited her before with her grandson Robert ."

"Matron will be surprised, as far as I know she doesn't get any visitors, that's why you took me by surprise."

Megan and Sam said their goodbyes and left. Samantha in particular was feeling despondent.

"I don't understand it Meg. It's like he's completely disappeared!"

"How about going to school on Monday and tell them the same story about the books, say you've been to the house and they've obviously given you the wrong address and see what happens."

Samantha nodded in agreement.

"I just have to get through the weekend and I can't face going to work. I'll have to phone in sick, I still can't believe he's lied about the phone why would he do that?"

Megan left on the Saturday morning. Samantha felt quite jittery, she wasn't sure whether to tell her parents about Robert. She decided against it, she couldn't face the barrage of questions from her mum. Just before lunch Samantha heard the van pull onto the drive. Okay she thought, take a deep breath and smile.

"Hello, we're home," called Adeline as she walked into the kitchen. "I wondered whether you'd take the day off love."

Samantha stayed frozen to the spot smiling.

"What on earth is wrong?"

With that the floodgates opened, Samantha sobbed uncontrollably. Her mother held her stroking her hair.

"What the devil has happened love? Come on calm down."

David walked in with the suitcases, took one look and decided it was a mother and daughter moment.

Samantha eventually stopped crying and was able to tell her mum all that had happened, omitting the housebreaking incident.

"Oh my poor angel, why didn't you say something on the phone?"

"I didn't want to spoil your week by worrying you."

"You know we wouldn't have minded, Birmingham isn't all that far away, we could easily have come back."

"But mum, what do you think happened to him?"

Adeline thought about it as she filled the kettle.

"Did you say it was just him and his mum?"

"And a sister, although supposedly she's at Uni, but I don't even know if that's true."

"Well, maybe his dad is abusive or something and they had to keep moving so he doesn't find them. Some men are like that love."

Sam frowned.

"I suppose, but he said he really misses his dad."

"I'm no expert, but just because a man can be abusive, maybe even violent, although I'm not saying his dad is, their wives and children often still love them."

"I guess that sort of makes sense," said Samantha reluctantly, "and if his dad went to visit Stella, he wouldn't know Robert had even been there because he didn't write his name in the visitors book."

The thought that Robert had may have been hiding from his dad consoled Samantha a little, and it explained a lot of his behaviour and why his mum worried about him being away from the house. That said, she wished he would make contact with her, just to let her know he was okay and to help heal the gaping hole in her heart.

Chapter Sixteen

The days rolled into weeks, Samantha heard nothing from Robert. She spent her evenings listening to the cassette he had made her. Wallowing in self pity, anger at the lies he had told and the way he had treated her, slowly replacing the heart ache. She visited Stella again and tried to talk about Andrew but the old lady seem to have forgotten about him completely and was becoming more confused. Again she insisted Samantha took the locket, this time Samantha had to give it to the young carer she had met before explaining it needed to go back into Stella's jewellery box.

Reluctantly Samantha went to the end of school party at Martin's parents farm desperately hoping Robert would turn up.Only Megan new about their romance, Samantha hadn't confided in any of her other friends.

Martin's parents had really made an effort, with a barbecue and a local band, much to the school leavers delight. Dean arrived arm in arm with Savannah, he'd tried to recreate the Tom Cruise look from 'Top gun' while Savannah wore a lycra mini skirt and a crop top which made her look extremely top-heavy.

"She looks like a prostitute!" exclaimed Martin.

"Well that should suit Dean down to the ground," laughed Samantha .

Megan grabbed Samantha's arm and gave it a squeeze.

"I don't think he's coming Sam."

"I know, I just keep hoping."

Later that evening Martin approached Samantha .

"Any news from Rob, I know you two got on well, it's like he's disappeared, I wondered whether you'd heard from him?"

Samantha wanted to cry, luckily it was fairly dark so he couldn't see her face.

"Rob? No we hadn't made any plans to keep in touch. So you haven't heard from him either?" said Samantha trying to sound disinterested.

"No, I never saw him outside school, you?"

"Oh only just for revision."

"I think he really fancied you, I caught him watching you walk across school from our form room a couple of times."

Samantha just grunted a response.

"Yeah I told him, he didn't have a chance."

Samantha couldn't keep up the pretence for much longer, she wandered away to find Megan.

"How are you doing?" Megan asked.

"I know I'm being pathetic Megs, but I miss him so much."

Savannah suddenly appeared, obviously very drunk.

"Sam, where is your boyfriend? Has he dumped you as well for being frigid?"

"Ignore her Sam she's pissed let's get drunk ourselves."

"Don't worry Megs. I'm not going to kill her," she paused, "yet!"

Samantha declined the drink, she really wasn't in the mood. She was dreading Megan going away for her summer trip to Italy. She was the only friend who knew about her broken heart.

Samantha decided to write Robert a letter asking him what had happened. It wasn't easy, she didn't want to sound too pathetic or too angry, she just needed some answers. After a number of attempts she was finally satisfied. There had been a Madonna song in her head for a couple of weeks, should she quote some lyrics? Would he get the message? After some indecision she decided to risk it. She wrote his name on the envelope, but had no address, what should she do? School had finished for the summer so there was no help from that quarter. The following day Samantha walked back to the house in Millward Road but it was still empty. Her only hope was Stella.

On arrival at the nursing home she signed in and went to Stella's room. The old lady was in bed and looked very frail. Samantha chatted to her for a while and took her hand. While she sat, Samantha looked around the room. Where could she leave it so it wouldn't get lost or even worse opened by his dad. If she left it on the dressing table someone could move it, or just think it had been left there by mistake and throw it away.

Samantha looked in Stella's handbag it seemed pretty empty, what if they decided to chuck it away.

The large family Bible lay on the bedside table it had obviously been in Robert's mums family for a number of generations, surely that was something to be treasured. She slipped the envelope inside the front cover but worried it could fall out if the Bible was knocked or dropped so she placed it between the centre pages hoping it would be found by Robert.

Julie the tea girl popped in, she and Samantha had become quite friendly.

"Hi Sam, oh bless she's asleep again."

"Yes she's certainly not herself today."

" To be honest I think she is fading away, she hardly says anything," whispered Julie.

"That's sad. Does the family know?"

"Like I said before, I didn't think she had any family, I tried to ask Matron but she told me it wasn't my business."

"What usually happens in this situation?"

"Well if they have family, they're called in before it's too late."

"Julie, if I give you my phone number could you ring me if that happens?"

Julie looked anxious.

"I really don't think I should, I could get into a lot of trouble with Matron."

" I wouldn't want you to get into trouble but, Julie I'm desperate."

With that Samantha told Julie about Robert and how he was the love of her life, but his disappearance had left her brokenhearted, and how she'd written him a love letter. Julie was completely spellbound, it was the most romantic story she'd ever heard. She made a note of Samantha's phone number and promised she would do her best to contact her if any family were called.

Samantha said goodbye to Stella and hoped she would see her again, Stella just gave her a weak smile and patted her hand. Samantha had grown very fond of her.

Work kept Samantha busy for the next few weeks. Megan at last arrived home from Italy and the girls spent as much time as possible together before they went off to their university's.

They had been sitting in the garden chatting when Adeline came out to tell Samantha she was wanted on the phone.

"I think she said her name was Julie, she's in a phone box so hurry."

Samantha leapt out of the deckchair and ran to the phone.

"Julie?"

"Hi Sam, um, I didn't know if you knew, but I'm really sorry Stella passed away last week.

Samantha wanted to scream at her.

"Last week!"

Why hadn't she called, thought Samantha .

"Yes sorry, I've been on holiday, came back today and the room has been cleared."

Samantha couldn't believe it, she closed her eyes and took a deep breath.

"Sam, Sam, are you still there? Hang on."

Samantha could hear Julie putting more money into the phone box.

"Thanks Julie, did the family come?"

"I think so, one of the nurses who is quite friendly said a lady came, I think her daughter, but apparently she looked really ill."

"No one else?"

"I don't think so, but she boxed up all of Stella's possessions and took them away. I'm sorry I wasn't here Sam."

Samantha felt disappointed, it had been her last hope.

"Thanks for phoning Julie, hopefully she'll find my letter to Rob."

"Okay, I better go now before I get told off."

"Bye Julie."

Samantha went back into the garden and told Megan all about the phone call.

"At least there's a chance he'll get your letter now." enthused Megan.

Samantha didn't share her optimism.

"Yeah, I guess, but if I don't hear anything then I'll know it didn't really mean anything to him."

Chapter Seventeen

Although Robert had gained straight A's for his A-levels it did little to help the terrible feelings of shock, grief, anger and guilt that he had following the trial. He had deferred his place at Oxford to read physics for a year.

Despite their ages, social services had come forward to support the family with Robert and Ruth receiving counselling. Their mother had shrunk into herself, she was also offered help but had declined.

The three of them were living in a safe house in North Wales and were advised to avoid contact with any of their old friends. Robert found it particularly hard as there was no one of his age locally. He was pleased to get his bike back and spent a lot of time cycling alone in the beautiful countryside trying to make sense of everything that had happened.

Three times a week Mrs Jones their 'Counsellor' came to the house to talk to them. Robert felt the sessions were a waste of time and found Mrs Jones extremely patronising.

"So Robert, how does that make you feel?"

That had been the fifth time Mrs Jones had asked that question. Robert wanted to smack her, he leapt up knocking the coffee table over.

"My fucking name is not Robert Brown, it's fucking William Layton and I've had too much of your mindless fucking questions while you sit there writing in that fucking notebook. I feel fucking crap okay!"

With that he ran out of the room slamming the door, passing his mother and sister who had heard the shouting, then left the house. Mary opened the sitting room door.

"Is everything alright?"

"Oh yes, I think we're making good progress," replied Mrs Jones.

"I'll go after him," offered Ruth.

"No need, he just needs to let off a little steam."

Ruth and Mary looked at each other.

"Well Ruth, I think we may as well carry on as Robert has left us." announced Mrs Jones.

Ruth glared at her.

"As my brother would say, I'm not fucking Ruth Brown, I'm fucking Katherine Layton and that makes me feel fucking marvellous."

"Excellent," replied an undeterred Mrs Jones, "why don't you sit down and we'll carry on."

"No thanks" snapped Katie as she walked out of the room.

Later that evening Mary, William and Katie sat at the kitchen table eating supper. William had returned but had been sullen and reluctant to speak.

"Shit!" blurted William putting his hand to his mouth. Blood on his fingers confirmed he had bitten his lip. Katie looked up.

"Tell me Robert how does that make you feel?"

William glared at her.

"It's fucking Will, how does that make you feel Ruth?"

Katie grinned at him.

"It's fucking Katie and I feel fucking brilliant!"

William grinned back. Mary was looking silently at her plate, Katie looked at William and raised her eyebrows, had they pushed it too far?

"Mum, will you change your name back?"

Mary looked up and squared her shoulders.

"No I'm going to stay with fucking Mary!"

Her children looked at her in horror. They had never heard her swear before, let alone the 'f' word.

"I think we're making very good progress" mocked Mary impersonating Mrs Jones.

Katie and William leapt out of their seats and hugged her. She held them tightly.

"I don't know what I would do without you two."

"As Gloria would say," piped Katie, "'We will survive'."

"No, that's cheating," protested William, " it's 'I will survive'."

"Yeah, well she was being a bit selfish, I'm sure she meant 'we will'."

Mary smiled, she loved to hear them bickering over the song lyric.

At the end of the holidays, Katie asked to go back to University as her desire to become a lawyer was even stronger after the events of the summer, William got a part-time job in the local supermarket. As time went on he learnt not to mention his father, as his mum would become increasingly agitated. The family home in Derby was sold, property prices had increased, so although now in rented accommodation Mary had over £80,000 in savings.

At Christmas Katie was home for the holidays, it was a very quiet affair, Katie cooked a roast dinner and brought some crackers but nobody felt like celebrating. They exchanged a few presents, when Katie announced she had some news. She was gay and in love with Sarah, the police woman who had been allocated to support her before and during the trial. William wasn't surprised, Mary wasn't bothered which was sad, nothing interested her at all since the trial, closely followed by the death of her mother Stella.

Katie suggested that William and Mary should move from their remote cottage as she had a couple more years at University and felt William especially, needed some younger company. She had been looking at properties in Cardiff and found a nice partly furnished flat near the centre not far from the University. She suggested William could join her for various events and concerts. William showed an interest and surprisingly Mary accepted the idea.

By the end of January Mary and William were relocated to Cardiff. Moving to the city really helped William, he began to socialise a little and got a job in a clothes shop which provoked him into take an interest in his appearance. He got rid of his brace and his glasses, but kept his fringe and long hair as he still felt vulnerable.

Katie introduced them to Sarah, who became another sister for William. She had been on the peripheries of the events that summer, so was able to empathise without getting emotionally involved. This helped William as he could talk to her about his feelings.

Spring turned into summer, William was feeling stronger regaining some of his old confidence, and had stopped looking over his shoulder. At last September came and he left for Oxford to start his further education. Oxford was wonderful, no one knew his personal history. Many of his new friends had single parents, so he felt no different, and much to his surprise the fact his sister was gay gave him a certain amount of kudos, he started dating, nothing serious but he was beginning to enjoy life again. Christmas holidays came around so quickly, William didn't really want to go back home, but all his friends were returning to theirs. He was pleasantly surprised to find a Christmas tree with lights and decorations in the living room, however it was all done by Katie and Sarah, Mary remained as lacklustre as ever. Katie and Sarah had turned up on Christmas morning and prepared a wonderful meal, they were full of fun lifting the whole day.

Sarah had to return to work in Bath on Boxing Day, Katie spent the next few days with William and Mary asking him about University, playing Trivial Pursuit and scrabble which seemed to lift Mary's spirits if only for a short while. Sarah was back for New Year's Eve and joined Katie and William on a pub crawl around Cardiff.

William sailed through University, he realised physics was his thing. Most of his friends left after graduation but William decided to stay on and do his Masters, once achieving that he continued his studies to get his Doctorate. He was being headhunted by pharmaceutical companies but decided he loved the academic life and felt at home in Oxford where he had digs in the city and was able to cycle to the University each day. He went back to his mothers home less and less spending much of the summer holidays doing research and volunteering to teach foreign students English and maths, discovering he really enjoyed teaching. All his hard work was rewarded when the faculty approached him to stay on as a paid tutor, teaching physics and chemistry.

Chapter Eighteen

1995

William became a minor celebrity, having successfully made a breakthrough in a joint project with a team from NASA. The local newspaper sent a young journalist to interview him. Her name was Hannah Nelson, she was bright and very ambitious and was instantly attracted to the tall modest, good looking professor. He was so different from the usual toe rags she dated, William was quiet, gentle and polite. Hannah however usually spent the evening in the pub, drunk with the lads. She discovered he was single, owned his own modest home, while she was living in a bedsit that she could ill afford. She chased him determined to hook herself a man with potential. Once they started dating she worked on his appearance, he was most comfortable in shorts and T-shirt yet she persuaded him to cut his hair into the latest style wore white shirts with designer jeans. William was happy to go along with Hannah's suggestions because he wanted a quiet life.

Katie had completed her law degree and managed to get a position with a firm in Bath. Sarah and Katie had been able to buy a house together as they were both working. Katie had persuaded Mary to move to Bath to be nearer them, initially she'd been reluctant to move but then realised there was nothing to keep her in Cardiff.

Katie had found her mother a place to rent whilst they went house hunting for something more permanent. Mary's savings had grown over time and she was able to buy a bungalow outright and still have some money left over. She had kept a few basic pieces of furniture from the family home in Derby and the remainder of the house contents had been put into storage. Now she had her own home Mary was able to be reunited with them.

Some weeks into their relationship William asked Hannah to accompany him to Bath to visit his mother. He decided on the drive down not to tell her about his family's tragedy, he thought correctly that Hannah would see it as a story to be sold.

Instead he explained his mum suffered from depression, his dad was dead and wasn't talked about as it upset his mother so much. Hannah didn't appear terribly interested.

"Is your sister going to be there?"

"I don't know, she knows were coming down so she may call in."

"Oh."

"Is that a problem?"

"Look, I've nothing against lesbians, but what if she starts flirting with me?"

William laughed.

"Don't be silly, she may even bring Sarah."

"Oh," Hannah sighed, "Do they, you know, kiss and that in front of you."

"No, why would they do that, we don't do it in public!"

This bothered William a little, Hannah never liked to show affection if anyone was around.

"I just find it all a bit weird. Why would your sister fancy another girl."

"Well I fancy girls!"

She gave him a playful slap on the arm.

"Idiot," she laughed.

The journey hadn't taken long, Hannah had never been to Bath so William did a little detour around the city to show her the Royal Crescent and the circus.

"It's quite nice, but I prefer Oxford."

William disagreed.

"Wait until you see the Roman baths and the pump room. Bath and Oxford are really quite different."

They arrived at the bungalow and parked in the drive.

"Look Hannah, depending on what sort of day mum is having will make a difference to what to expect, okay?

"Don't worry. You know me I'll go with the flow."

William shouldn't have worried, Hannah was the first girl he had ever brought home to meet his mum and she'd made a real effort. The dining table was laid with a pretty cloth and his mother had made sandwiches, scones and a sponge. William felt moved to see what was in front of him.

"Thanks Mum."

He knew what an effort it had been for her. Hannah breezed in, full of confidence.

"Oh that's nice, shame William and I are watching our figures, so just a sandwich thanks."

William could've kicked her.

"Don't worry Mum I'm actually very hungry! I can just eat less tomorrow."

"I'll pop the kettle on, what do you prefer Hannah, tea or coffee?"

"Have you any herbal tea, I'm off caffeine. I've been doing an article for a magazine... Do you know its so bad for you."

"I'll have tea please Mum."

While Mary had gone to the kitchen William turned to Hannah.

"Please have something Hannah, Mum has really worked hard to give us a nice tea."

Hannah didn't look very impressed and before she could reply they heard voices in the kitchen. William stood up.

"Excellent, Katie is here!"

Hannah groaned inwardly and thought bloody lesbians! Katie came through into the room.

"Wow Mum what a spread, can I stay for tea?"

Mary looked so proud.

"Of course love."

William introduced Hannah to Katie.

"Is Sarah with you?"

"No, she is working but sends her love. Nice to meet you Hannah."

"Likewise."

Hannah looked Katie up and down critically, noticing her cropped hair, faded jeans, T-shirt and trade mark Dr Martens. Hannah herself was dressed in a designer skirt, blouse and heels.Which William secretly thought was far too short and tight. Katie tried to engage Hannah in conversation but discovered they didn't share the same interests.

William got on so well with Katie they chatted about work, home and Sarah. Hannah watched enviously, she had two sisters and a brother. Her parents were divorced and none of the family got along with each other so watching William with his sister made her feel jealous and left out. In fact she thought Katie and William were being bloody rude, with that she stood up and looked at her watch.

"William it's time we left, I have a deadline to catch. Nice to meet you Katie."

William looked up.

"We've not been here long!"

Hannah glared at him.

"Well I have work to do."

William stood.

"Okay, sorry guys lovely to see you both, and thanks Mum for doing such a lovely spread, we really appreciated it, didn't we Hannah."

Hannah smiled with her teeth. Mary looked at the table and the unfinished sandwich on Hannah's plate.

"There is so much left love, I'll wrap them up and you can take them home."

"Thanks Mum that would be great."

Hannah started to walk out of the door.

"I'll wait in the car."

William gave Katie a big hug.

"Love to Sarah."

Mary reappeared with a Tupperware full of cakes and sandwiches. William bent forward and kissed her on the cheek.

"Thanks Mum see you soon."

Hannah was waiting by the car arms folded, William appeared.

"You took your time!"

Katie and Mary watched from the window and waved them off.

"Bloody hell Mum she's a right moody bitch."

"Katie, watch your language, if William is happy that's all that matters."

"Mum she's awful I bet they're having a right old barney now. If I was William I tell her to take a hike."

That moment another car drove up and out jumped Sarah. She had come straight from work and was wearing her customary navy trousers and a plain blouse, her strawberry blonde hair tied up in a ponytail . She bounced into the house.

"Hi you two, William not arrived yet?"

"Been and gone with the ice queen."
"What, I've missed them!"
"Yes, William sends his love."
"Oh, is that cake I see?"
"Go on sit down I'll put the kettle on."
"Thanks Mary."
Sarah gave Katie a hug.
"Good day?"
"Not bad and I managed to take some time back, hence why I'm here now I was really hoping to see William and meet Hannah. What is she like?"

"In looks, quite pleasant, shoulder length brown hair and eyes to match, nice if she smiled, but she's got one of those mouths which seem to be turned down the whole time. Personality, bloody awful, abrupt, rude, all I can say she must be good in bed to have Will so hooked."

Mary walked in with tea.

"Katie really, behave yourself."

"Sorry Mum, but she was dreadful, neither of us could get her to talk about anything, I felt she was looking down her nose at us and then she suddenly announced they had to leave. They were only here five minutes. Mums made an amazing tea as you can see, Will
was loving it and the little madam just nibbled the edge of a sandwich. All I can say is be very careful William!"

There was an atmosphere in the car. Hannah sat with her arms folded and looked out the window, William drove wondering what he had done wrong now. He broke the silence

"Sorry Hannah I hadn't realised you had work to do, where do you want me to take you when we get back to Oxford? The office or your place?"

"Neither," she huffed "where shall we eat?"

"Eat! I've just had sandwiches and cakes if you're hungry there's plenty in the back you can take with you."

Hannah huffed again.

"I don't want sandwiches and cakes I would've thought even you could see that!"

William raised his eyebrows, what was her problem? They drove on in silence again the atmosphere in the car returned. On arrival in Oxford Hannah spoke.

"Drop me at my digs I'll call you tomorrow."

She got out and slammed the door. William look at her retreating back and wondered why he bothered.

William would have definitely called it a day if he'd seen and heard her later that evening. Hannah was in one of the rough pubs in town with a few of her mates. She's been telling them about her 'afternoon tea'.

"Bloody hell you should've seen it, a pretty tablecloth with sandwiches and cakes it was something out of the 1950s."

Kev, a man in his late 20s with more tattoos and facial piercings then anybody would need, spoke.

"I like afternoon tea."

"Fuck off Kev, you should've been there, then there was his mum."

Cass, another friend piped in.

"What was she like?"

"A fucking frumpy mouse. I can see now where he gets his lack of backbone from."

"Was the Dyke there?"

"Fucking yes she was dressed like a bloke, although could be quite good-looking if she made an effort."

Kev raised an eyebrow.

"Fuck, Hannah did you fancy her then?"

The others laughed.

"Fuck off Kev, but she was like a bloke I didn't see the girlfriend but she may as well go out with a bloke."

"But they don't like cock Hannah, unlike yourself, wanna come back to mine tonight?"

"Yeah okay I could do with some fun, got anything to smoke?"

"Always."

Hannah spent the next couple of days in Kev's bed.

"Why are you with him then?"

"Who?"

"The spineless wonder."

"He is my ticket out of here. I'm planning on getting married quickly, move in then get him to divorce me."

"How are you going to do that?"

"Simple I'll get you lot over a couple of times a week, it will drive him insane. Then I'll get him to give me the house."

"Can't see that happening."

"Do you know my friend Ray."

"No."

"Course you do, anyway we went to school together. He works at the estate agents. When we get divorced if William wants to keep the house Ray will do a high value so I get more money. If William agrees to move out Ray will do a low value, then I'll sell a bit later for a lot more."

"Cool but how are you going to buy the man off, you ain't got any money."

"All sorted, Ray says he can sort me out a mortgage for my half as there is no mortgage on the house, Will paid cash for it."

"Fuck, he must be loaded. Hey, are you shagging that Ray?"

"Don't get jealous I have to keep in touch with him. Once I've sold the house you and me can get together again."

"Cool, do you wanna smoke?"

"No I better get off I haven't spoken to Will for a few days. I'll give him a ring and apologise, blame it on work, yeah that will do it, he's putty in my hands. I'm off Kev, see you around."

Kev was already out of it. Hannah had a quick freshen up in his disgusting bathroom. God she looked dreadful, mind you it could have been the dirty mirror. Searching for her shoes she had a look round the room, what a dump, there was some dirty plates and mugs under the bed. Kev was okay for a bit of fun but bloody hell what a loser. She walked out into the drizzle and made her way home back to her bedsit, it wasn't much bigger than Kev's but at least it was clean. Hannah thought to herself she needed to get married soon, operation 'William'.

Chapter Nineteen

William had been thoroughly fed up after his return to Oxford. He was grumpy, suffering a backache after the long drive and vowed that he would tell Hannah to sling her hook. He had been so pleased his mum had made such an effort knowing how difficult she found it. He put the kettle on and gave her a call.

"Hi Mum."

"Hi love you're back safely then."

"Yes. Hannah wanted me to apologise for her, her editor had called her just as we arrived and that's why she couldn't settle."

"It's alright love, it was nice to meet her. Sarah turned up just after you left and was sorry she missed you. They stayed and managed to eat most of the food, for two slim women they can certainly eat!"

"Oh that's good Mum. I'm sorry Hannah didn't get to meet Sarah, I'll give them a call."

"Alright love it was lovely to see you."

"Take care Mum."

"Love you son."

"And me you."

William ended the call. He immediately phoned his sister, she wasn't quite so kind about Hannah after he'd given her the same apology.

"Rubbish Will, I'm sorry but I thought she was extremely rude."

William knew there was no fooling Katie. She continued her rant.

"Mum had actually been really excited about meeting her, I just felt so sorry after she worked so hard."

"I spoke to Mum and apologised, don't make me feel any worse than I already do."

They were both silent for a while. William thought he could hear Sarah whispering in the background.

"Sorry Will, forget what I said."

"It's okay sis I know you're right, that's what makes it worse."

They parted on good terms and William promised to visit again soon.

Work had been busy for William. He spent the evenings marking coursework and listening to music, he hadn't missed Hannah at all, so decided that on Tuesday evening he needed to end the relationship. It hadn't gone as planned as he received a call from Hannah that morning which made him feel bad, so he thought he would see how the following week went, he hated any confrontation. That evening Hannah appeared on his doorstep freshly showered and with a takeaway in her hand. She was on her best behaviour chatty and friendly even feigning interest in his music, it really wasn't her taste. They had a nice evening and with that Hannah stayed over.

The week passed in a blur. Hannah had stayed every night and returned to work on the Thursday and the Friday, although her editor told her she really needed to buck her ideas up or she would be out of a job.

At the weekend Hannah and William went out for a long walk finishing at a pub for lunch. William was really enjoying himself, this is how a relationship works, both appreciating the simple things in life. Hannah was making a real effort, once she nabbed him she wasn't going to walk anywhere ever again, the lunch was okay, but the pub was very quiet and dull, again not her idea of a good time but she kept smiling. Hannah thought to herself 'I deserve a bloody Oscar!'

The following weeks passed in the same vein. Hannah stayed most nights although William had a couple of late lectures and stayed in his rooms at the University. He went down to Bath to visit his mum and sister for the weekend, Hannah declined saying she had work to do. William realised although he and Hannah were getting on well, he was glad to be driving down alone. He gave Hannah's apologies to Katie who didn't mention her again and this complimented a lovely day staying at the bungalow. On the Sunday they persuaded Mary to go out for lunch. She seem quieter than usual and had barely ate her food, for now was the time for her to drop her bombshell.

That evening in the pub over a couple of drinks with her friend Cass, Hannah explained her plan.

"Do you really dislike him that much? I saw you two out together last Friday evening, I can't believe it after what you said about him I thought he looked well fit."

" Actually you're right he is bloody good-looking with a great body and he treats me dead nice. He does this weird thing by quoting song lyrics."

"Why?"

"I don't know I've never heard half of them, but..."

"But what..."

"But, I don't know I'm used to real men. Will is a bit soft."

Cass laughed.

"What real men, like Kev!"

Hannah snorted.

"Oh I don't know, Will he's too kind, too bloody polite. We were out for lunch the other day and they got his order wrong. The waitress got all flustered and Will just said it wasn't a problem, he was quite happy with what she'd given him. Well I'm telling you Cass if I hadn't been on my best behaviour I'd of gone ape shit and demanded the food I ordered or a free meal. He never loses his rag, like when we went to visit his mum that time, I behaved probably worse than normal just to get a fucking reaction from him. He's a bit like an overgrown puppy, he wakes up in the morning smiling and raring to go, well you know what I'm like in the mornings. I'm bloody knackered from faking it."

"What, orgasms."

"No stupid, faking Mrs Jolly, it's so not me."

"Doesn't it make you feel a bit bad planning to take his money?"

Cass wondered whether she should leave William an anonymous note to warn him. It didn't seem fair Hannah had snapped a good looking kind rich bloke, while she was dating an unemployed, overweight loser.

"To be honest no, but if he only suggested we do something like, I don't know, go to America or Dubai or somewhere, which we could do as he's really brainy."

"Can't drink in Dubai."

"What? America then, I'll try and behave a bit longer I'd love to go to America."

"So, have you told him you're pregnant yet?"

"No I'm just waiting for the right moment. I don't know whether to pretend I've got morning sickness and see if he notices."

"They'll be no drinking for you then if you were really pregnant. My sister Fran couldn't even bear the smell of it, although she was okay with vodka."

"Shit I forgot about that. I'll just have to stay at mine a bit more, I can't not drink plus I bet he'd be a bit weird about a pregnant woman drinking."

"Not to mention the fags!"

"He doesn't know I smoke."

"What! How do you get away with it."

"Just chain-smoke when he's not around, say I've been in a smoky room if he smells it."

Class laughed.

"You're insane I don't know how you do it. How's work? Your boss still hassling you?"

"God I didn't tell you, because of being so well-behaved with Will I'm not been getting pissed, I go to bed and get a good nights sleep. I've been getting to work on time. Derek called me into his office and said he was so pleased that I was obviously taking my work seriously and the last couple of pieces had been very good, in fact he gave me a fucking bonus!"

"Bloody hell, you sleeping with him as well?"

"Oh God no, he is seriously overweight and with the worst B O you've ever smelt. I'd have to be paid at least a couple of million, absolutely gross."

The two women were interrupted with the arrival of Kev, Nelson and Fraser. They had been watching football at Fraser's parents house with his dad. They were in fine spirits as their team had won, Frasers dad had supplied them with beer, they were now loud and rowdy. This is what I love thought Hannah, real men, getting pissed and trying to grope her under the table. A couple more friends turned up and joined them, they all got completely wasted.

Hannah went home with Kev spending most of the Sunday in bed, leaving for home in the afternoon so she could freshen up and meet William that evening.

William, Sarah, Katie and Mary had driven back from the restaurant to Mary's bungalow.

"Anyone fancy a cuppa? I'll put the kettle on"

"Yes please," replied William and Katie in unison.

"How about you Mary?"

"Oh, I'm fine, I feel so full after that lovely lunch".

William and Katie looked at each other, she had barely eaten a thing. Sarah returned with two coffees and a tea.

"You sure Mary?"

"I'm fine love, thanks."

Katie looked at her mum, she'd definitely lost weight. Mary had worn a dress to the restaurant, something she hadn't done for awhile, but looking at her now Katie realised the dress looked too big.

"Is everything okay Mum?"

Mary smiled.

"I've not been feeling too well lately, so I went to see my GP. I hadn't been there for a while, there is a new lady, very nice, Dr Moss. Well the long and the short of it is I've got....," she paused. "cancer."

The four of them sat in silence, not knowing what to say, then Katie approached her mother and held her.

"Oh mum why didn't you say anything? How long have you known? You know we're all here for you."

William and Sarah both came across and hugged Mary in turn.

"Mum just let us know if you need any help, anything at all, whatever you need."

"Do you know where the cancer is?"

"Yes Katie, in my left breast which is annoying."

"Annoying? It's not bloody fair mum."

"Don't make a fuss, I know it's a shock for you but they've offered me surgery and chemotherapy ."

"That's good, when can you start?"

"I don't know if I want to go through with it."

"What! Mum you can't give up like that, We'll look after you."

"Katie love, I don't know if I can cope with it all and what have I got to look forward to?"

"Mum you've got us we need you and love you."

The three of them were now kneeling around her feet.

"My beautiful children and you're one of them Sarah, you have your own lives to live. I can't expect you to look after me for the rest of my life."

"You could live with me," announced William.

"Or us!"

Mary smiled.

"Thank you, I'll promise I'll consider all the options. If I need a lift to the hospital I will ask, but only if it's convenient."

"Mum, don't think you're a burden to us. After supporting us we will help you in any way we can please don't give up."

Mary smiled.

"Right, come on drink up. I didn't mean to put a damper on the day and Katie stop looking at me as if I'm about to keel over."

Katie was too choked to speak, but kept hold of her mother's hand.

"William, see if you can find the scrabble. I think it's in the sideboard in the dining room, let's have a game."

William went into the dining room and stood for a minute he couldn't see for the tears that threatened. He took some deep breaths. His mother needed them to be strong, they could get through this together, perhaps he could take some time off. Sarah appeared in the doorway.

"Mary sent me in, she said you were always rubbish at finding anything."

"Oh Sarah," said William hugging her.

"Come on Will, we can do this, between us."

"Yes you're right."

They found the scrabble and spent the rest of the afternoon playing. At first they played in relative silence, then slowly started to relax and argue over words, William being sent back into the dining room to find the dictionary to check some of the spellings. By the time William announced he needed to make a move the atmosphere was back to normal with everybody chatting as usual.

"Right, I better be off, I'll give you a ring when I get back."

"That will be lovely, have a safe journey and bring Hannah with you next time."

"I will mum, she'd hoped to come but didn't want to have to rush off again."

He collected his overnight bag from the spare room.

"Did you want me to strip the bed mum."

Mary looked at Katie.

"Save me shouting, tell him to leave it, he was only in it for one night I've got no one else coming to stay."

Katie found William in the bedroom.

"Mum says to leave it," she hugged him."Why do some people have such shit lives?"

"I know, but we're going to make everything as good as we can for her, whatever she decides to do, and Katie, it's her decision."

"Okay."

William popped back into the lounge and gave his mum and Sarah a hug and a kiss.

"See you all soon."

William drove back to Oxford in a sombre mood, even his music didn't help. What more shit could life throw at him? He was feeling guilty for the years he had avoided spending his free time with his mother, he promised himself that would change and he would make a real effort to show her how much he loved her. He estimated he would arrive in Oxford about 7 pm but wasn't sure if he could face Hannah. She hadn't phoned, he assumed she was busy with work, all he needed peace and quiet and a stiff drink.

When he arrived back he noticed he had three missed calls from Hannah, he hoped she wasn't going to be pissy with him as he really didn't need it right now. He called her and before she could say anything he apologised and explained why he hadn't been in contact and that he needed some time to himself. Hannah said she completely understood and would see him the following day. Well thought William that had gone surprisingly well, he would really try and persuade her to go with him next time.

"Yes!" exclaimed Hannah as she put the phone down.

Immediately she picked up the receiver again and dialled Cass.

"Ring Of bells in half an hour?"

"Yeah? Thought you were seeing loverboy!"

"Not anymore, I can come out to play."

Hannah had stayed over with William a couple of times that week, but found his concern for his mum a bit over the top. The nights she didn't see him she spent at Kev's and predictably her work suffered. Derek called her into his office on the Friday morning.

"Hannah, last month you really worked hard and produced some good pieces, I gave you a bonus to show what happens when you work well, but this week you've been dreadful, getting in late, half asleep most of the time, you need to watch your step. This is the second time I've had to tell you, once more and you're out, understand?"

Hannah had to bite her lip, her fists were clenched tightly in her lap. Deep breath Hannah she thought, don't lose it and tell him where he could stuff his job, you need the money.

"Sorry Derek. I've had a difficult time, William's mum told us on Sunday she has inoperable cancer. As you can imagine it's been a terrible shock, she's been like a mum to me. We've been travelling backwards and forwards to Bath, that's why I've been late and so tired."

Bloody hell she was good, even managed a tear. Derek the fat tosser fell for it completely.

"Hannah I'm sorry you should've told me, do you need some time off?"

"I think it will be okay. Maybe if I could leave a bit early today so we can go to Bath for the weekend."

"Of course, look, what have you got left to do today? Could Phyllis finish it for you?"

"I was doing that article about abandoned dogs, so if she could visit the dogs home?"

Bloody excellent she thought, she couldn't bear Phyllis and she hated dogs.

Later that day William called Hannah. He said he would go to Bath on Saturday and stay over and would she like to go.

Hannah declined and although she told Derek about Williams mother and he had been sympathetic, she had to work. William said not to worry her job was important.

Hannah knew she had to tell him her 'news'. That evening armed with a Chinese takeaway and no alcohol she sat him down.

"Will, I have some news."

Thinking he didn't need any more bad news.

"Yes, good or bad?"

"I hope you think it's good news," she paused this was it, "I'm pregnant!"

"Pregnant! Really?"

She smiled and nodded.

"Its early days, but I wanted you to know as soon as I was sure."

"Pregnant! Oh Hannah are you okay with that?"

"Of course are you?"

"Of course I am, it's just a bit of a shock, can I tell Mum? It will give her something to look forward to, a grandchild."

Shit, thought Hannah she hadn't thought of that, oh well in for a penny.

"Yes that would be lovely, how about going the whole hog and we get married while your mum is able to enjoy it."

"Wow, okay. I think we need a drink."

"No, not for me!"

"Of course not, bloody hell, a baby she'll be thrilled, and a wedding!"

Hannah thought that had been a lot easier than she had imagined.

William and Hannah travelled to Bath the following weekend to announce their engagement. Hannah had insisted on choosing her own ring and it was the biggest one the shop had to offer. Mary was delighted for them, although felt they needn't rush to get married so quickly. Hannah again insisted it would be better to organise everything as soon as possible.

Chapter Twenty

Within a month the wedding was planned. Hannah invited her friend Cass, her sister Gemma, the only member of her family she was speaking to, a couple of work colleagues and Derek her boss. On Williams side was his mother, Katie, Sarah and a couple of his work colleagues it was all very low-key.

All brides look beautiful and Hannah was no exception. She wore a cream ankle length dress with a large split up one side and her usual killer heels. She'd had her hair done professionally, Williams mother gave her a silver locket to wear, which Hannah didn't like, it was so old fashioned. Cass pointed out it was, 'something old', so she relented. William wore a navy designer suit and looked very handsome, he walked tall and gazed proudly at his new wife. After the ceremony the small group went to a local pub and had the reception in a room at the rear where they had a light buffet lunch and of course champagne.

Mary had undergone more tests and had finally agreed to a mastectomy. This was the first outing she'd made and looked very pale and frail. Derek made a big fuss of her, telling William, after a few drinks, it was lovely to meet her and he was so sorry to hear about her cancer.

"Between you and me, I thought young Hannah was pulling a fast one when she said she needed all that time off to spend with you and your mum. You're certainly a positive influence on her, her work has improved as she hasn't come in stinking of booze for some weeks, it was getting so bad I thought I had to get rid of her!"

William had had a few drinks himself, he just nodded and smiled not really absorbing what Derek was saying.

Meanwhile Cass was getting on really well with Sarah and Katie. She decided being a lesbian wasn't so bad, it was like having your best mate with you all the time, although she wouldn't like the sex.

As things were winding down she found herself alone with Sarah, she'd had a fair bit to drink.

"Sarah, Katie and you are really cool, and Williams mum is lovely, so is Will, and he's so good looking."

Sarah who was sober, laughed.

"I feel there is a bit more to come."

"Oh, I just feel so bad."

"About what?"

"All the lies Hannah has told, I wish she hadn't told me."

"Lies?"

"You know, not really being pregnant, and the fact she smokes and she likes to get completely wasted and of course, Kev."

"Whose Kev?"

"Her boyfriend. Thanks Sarah for listening I feel better now I've told someone."

"I wish you'd told me earlier."

Sarah was not happy, as Cass said she wished she didn't know. What should she do? The happy couple were just about to leave, Sarah gave them both a hug, she held William tight and whispered to him.

"William I love you, don't trust her."

He jerked his head back.

"What?"

Sarah was elbowed out of the way by Katie as she said her goodbyes to William.

A taxi arrived for the newlyweds to take them for their honeymoon in Paris. As William got into the taxi he looked for Sarah and catching her eye mouthed the word 'Why?'

Sarah just shook her head and looked sad.

William and Hannah had a lovely weekend. Hannah loved Paris, William spoilt her with a new wardrobe of designer clothes and romantic meals out. They behaved like tourists, visiting the Eiffel Tower and the Louvre, although Hannah was rather underwhelmed by the Mona Lisa. They arrived back home the following Wednesday to pouring rain. Dumping their bags in the hallway William looked at his new wife.

"How are you feeling Hannah? Your morning sickness seems to have stopped that must be a relief."

Bugger she'd forgotten, she'd been having such a good time. They had moved into the kitchen where Hannah filled the kettle to make a drink.

"It's like this William, with all the wedding planning and everything I didn't like to tell you but," she paused "well, I've had a miscarriage"

William looked shocked.

"My god Hannah are you okay." He jumped up and held her.

"You poor thing, Coping with that on your own, how are feeling?"

Hannah thought, this was like taking candy from a baby. They hadn't made love on their honeymoon as he thought she'd been worried about the pregnancy, he understood now why she hadn't been interested.

"Come and sit down, when did it happen? Was it when you stayed at the flat? Why didn't you tell me, you must have known on our honeymoon."

"Will I'm fine honestly, I didn't want to spoil our honeymoon, the doctor just said no sex for a while."

What she really wanted to say was bloody hell Will stop fucking fussing, especially as it wasn't true.

"Right Hannah you sit there I'll sort out supper."

Maybe she should let him fuss, nice to be spoiled. She thought, all going to plan, married tick, not pregnant tick, now work towards America or divorce.

William was blissfully unaware of her plans, as he prepared supper. He brought out a bottle of wine.

"I suppose you can have a drink now, would you like one?"

Hannah looked up.

"To be honest Will I hate wine, I'd love a cider though."

"Cider? We haven't got any I can pop to the shops and get some."

It was still raining as Will left for the shops on his bike. Hannah smiled, she was loving this.

As the weeks rolled by William and Hannah settled into married life, although she hadn't realised how boring life could be especially in the evenings when William worked late. She started meeting up with some of her mates again.

"How is married life then."

"Fucking boring Cass, we don't do anything. He is usually too knackered, I have to get my nicotine fix at work, Derek moans like mad he hates smoking. Then to top it all William wants us to visit his mum this weekend."

"His mum was really nice, how is she?"

"I really don't know or care, we had such a good time in Paris, I want to go back there. This weekend would be good but no, he wants to see his mummy."

"Well she's probably hasn't got long to live.

"Cass I don't give a flying fuck, he's boring, she's boring. I tried to talk about us going to America, he could get a job in one of those Unis or with bloody NASA, I could work on Wall Street imagine that."

"What did he say to that then?"

"Couldn't think about it while his mummy was so poorly. Anyway I don't wanna talk about him I wanna get pissed, Kev! Over here, I've missed you."

The following weekend Hannah feigned work again so William went to visit his mother . Saturday night Hannah had invited Cass, Kev and a few others over, they had pizza, booze and fags, quite a party. Kev Slept with Hannah in their bed, Cass was starting to feel more and more uncomfortable with Hannah's behaviour, early next morning she decided to go home and not come back again unless William was there.

Sunday Hannah woke to the sound of the phone. Her head was pounding, God what time was it, only 10:30 she let it ring. Her friends left about midday and she made a small effort to tidy up, she didn't think he'd notice.

Chapter Twenty One

As Mary improved, William had suggested inviting his family down on a number of occasions. Hannah always used work as an excuse to avoid seeing them. However on one such occasion Hannah was 'away' following a story, when William received a bereavement card from Derek. It read 'Sorry to hear about your loss, I thought your mother was a lovely lady'. William was confused why the hell did he think his mother had died, he decided to phone Derek.

"Derek, it's William, Hannah's other half."

"Will, nice to hear from you especially at this time."

"I think there's been some mistake. Mum is actually been responding well to the treatment, she is very much alive and kicking."

There was an awkward silence.

"William I feel such a fool, why would Hannah tell me otherwise? Let me speak to her."

"Derek, she's not here, she's away for a few days in her words chasing a story."

"What story?"

"I don't know, she said you'd assigned her something. I've been rather busy with work so I didn't pay much attention."

Derek swore under his breath.

"I hope you're right William, you've been such a good influence, I just hope she hasn't gone back to her old ways!"

"Old ways?"

"You know."

"No, please elaborate."

Derek felt awkward in his response ..

"This is all a bit embarrassing, when she first started here she was a good reporter. I'd say she had a lot of potential but," he hesitated, "well she has, or rather had a real drink problem."

Derek didn't like to mention her drug habit.

"Drink problem! Hannah, I don't think I've ever seen her tipsy let alone drunk."

"No, well she can put away a fair amount before it shows. She then can't work for a day or two because she's so hung over. I've tried to support her over the last 18 months. But I've had to give her two formal warnings, and tell her she really had to buck her ideas up."

"So you've got no idea where she is?"

"No sorry William, but when she gets back let her know I'll be wanting a word."

William said goodbye and looked at the phone, he wasn't a bad person he didn't like confrontation but he also didn't like being taken for a fool. Where in the hell was she.

At that moment she was in bed with Kev smoking a joint.

"See I told you nothing would change just because I got married!"

Kevin grinned.

Over the last six months William had discovered Hannah didn't do any cooking, shopping or housework of any sort but got quite touchy if the house was a mess, no clothes to wear, and nothing to eat. William had taken on the household chores on top of his work and a number of times he had come home to find her having a few drinks with her work colleagues, although he was sure no one would employ a man with such excessive facial piercings.

That evening Hannah arrived home with her story planned. Feeling tired she didn't fancy sex, in fact she was a bit sore and hoped she hadn't caught anything from Kev. She had had a good couple of days although she always felt grubby after spending time at Kev's, she just needed a shower and a hair of the dog, cider.

"Will, I'm back!"

They had their first major row and if William thought Hannah would be full of apologies he was very much mistaken.

"What the fuck did you phone Derek for? It's none of his fucking business."

"Hannah, he sent me a bereavement card, my mum is not dead!"

"Yet," she replied viciously.

"What did you say?"

"Oh for fuck's sake Will, she ain't gonna last much longer."

William was speechless. Hannah went on.

"If I've lost my job because of you, I'm going to be well and truly pissed off."

William couldn't believe it. He made his way to the door.

"I'm off."

He left and drove to the university and spent the next couple of nights there.

William and Hannah slowly recovered from that fight, but there were many more to come. Hannah had been hassling William to think about moving abroad, she increasingly went out and got drunk and then William was faced with her hangover which would last a couple of days. After a further eight months of continuing unsettled behaviour William sat down with Hannah.

"Hannah, we can't go on like this. We have no relationship to speak off, we certainly don't have a physical one."

Hannah smirked. It was just what she wanted although it had taken longer than she anticipated.

"I think we need to discuss our future."

"Divorce?"

"What!"

"Come on Will, we are so unsuited. I'm bored witless, you won't consider leaving UK while your mum is alive. We never do anything, you don't like what I like, so let's get on with it."

"Blimey! I thought we might get some sort of marriage guidance."

"Waste of time, we don't love each other, as I said let's get on with it."

Although rocked by the unfolding situation William kept calm.

"Wow, what do we do about the house? Possessions?"

"I'll get it valued and buy you out."

"Can you afford that?"

"Don't know I'll see how much the house is worth."

"Hannah, I'm sorry its come to this I think perhaps we should've waited and not jumped into marriage so quickly, we barely knew each other."

"Not a problem Will, we'll get a quickie divorce and move on with our lives no harm done, I'd just like the security of a home."

"Look I'll move to the University accommodation, you stay here, we'll get a solicitor each and if you need any help, you know, financially let me know."

William got up and started to pack.

"I'll pop in and out to collect my clothes and things over the next week."

"Okay no rush I'll contact an estate agent."

William had packed his usual overnight bag.

"I think I'll go to Bath for the weekend. Keep in touch."

He couldn't believe the sense of relief as he got in the car. In the living room Hannah was enjoying the moment 'great I'll move out', she mimicked, he was so fucking pathetic, a real man would've put up a fight, but William just lay down and begged you to walk all over him. He deserved all he got. She quickly phoned her friend Ray.

"Hey handsome, plan 'let's get Hannah a house' is going well, when can you come and do the valuation? Not today better make it look official put it in your diary or whatever you do then give me a call."

Katie heaved a sigh of relief.

"Thank God for that."

Sarah was also relieved as she had carried Cass's secret since the wedding, not even telling Katie. Mary was sad things hadn't worked out for William and Hannah but was glad they had made an amicable decision and no children were involved. Katie asked about the house, William explained the plan.

"Oh Will your lovely little house, you were so excited when you got it."

William smiled.

"Katie if there's one thing I've learnt it's just bricks and mortar, possessions are just stuff you can take with you."

Mary looked up.

"Make sure you get Nanna's locket. I know Hannah wore it on her wedding day, but I'd like it to stay in the family."

"Don't worry Mum I'll ask her for it."

The following week William called into the house to collect some of his possessions to take to his accommodation at the University, which would be his home for the next few months while the divorce was going through. He was surprised to see Hannah and a man in a suit drinking coffee.

"This is my husband Will, this is Mr Gregory the estate agent I told you about, he's just finished measuring up." William shook his hand.

"I'll get back to the office and sort out the valuation, I know you need it for Hannah to arrange a mortgage. Thanks for the coffee. Do you want me to post it or will you pop into the office?"

"I'll pop into the office, thanks again."
Hannah turned to William.

William collected what he hoped would be the last of his possessions.

Hannah turned to him " Have you got everything now?"

"Pretty much, do you mind if I hang onto the key for now in case I think of anything."

William looked around the place it was a tip, Hannah had obviously had some friends around. Not the best idea as she was getting a valuation, he thought.

"Just to let you know Mum's not been too well. She has undergone more tests and they now think she has secondaries in her bones."

Hannah appeared sympathetic, she really wanted to say 'I told you she didn't have long to live' but refrained. As soon as she had the house she could drop the act.

"I'm so sorry Will."

William made his way into the garden and collected his bike from the shed. The garden was only small but was taking on the appearance of a jungle, not his problem he told himself, don't offer to help.

Chapter Twenty Two

Mary's health deteriorated, she decided this time to decline any more treatment but would have palliative care. She visited the local hospice where they talked through all the available options for care and pain relief. Once she felt unable to care for herself at home she would move to the hospice. Katie had accompanied her and found her mothers calm acceptance very humbling. Together with help from social services Katie and William kitted out Mary's bungalow with aids to make her life easier, Katie and Sarah called in frequently providing food and taking her washing while William would stay most weekends depending on his work schedule.

The time had come for Mary to move into the hospice. The staff were pleasant and welcoming, again Katie had accompanied her mother. Sister Bell the senior nurse helped settle Mary into her room and spent some time with her and Katie explaining visiting arrangements, pain management and general care. She also mentioned the hospice currently had two Duke of Edinburgh award students doing their voluntary work, both female, and they would spend their time visiting the residents to chat and read to them. Mary was happy that she would be added to the list.

On the Wednesday the two Duke of Edinburgh award students, Becky and Nadia, arrived at the hospice. They had a chat with the nurse in charge to check if there was anyone they shouldn't visit, any new arrivals or if anyone had passed away. Both girls were mature and pleasant, Sister Bell really appreciated their visits. Becky and Nadia discovered it was easier to keep to the same few residents each as they and sometimes their families got to know them. Becky was allocated Mary.

Mary was sleeping as Becky walked into her room. On her bedside locker were a number of family photos, Becky was studying them when Mary spoke.
"Hello."

Becky smiled.

"Hello my name is Becky I'm a student doing my Duke of Edinburgh."

"Oh yes, Sister Bell told me about you and your friend."

"I thought you were sleeping, I didn't want to disturb you."

"It's fine my dear."

Becky and Mary chatted briefly until Mary said she felt tired again.

"I think it's the painkillers they give me, they're very strong.

"I'll leave you in peace, I come again on Friday, then next Monday, would you like me to visit you again?"

"That would be lovely."

Becky continued to visit Mary after school, she grew very fond of the old lady. She told Mary about her home, school, how she was learning the guitar and how her mum and herself were having piano lessons although they didn't have a piano, just a keyboard. Mary was very interested and mentioned that she had been a music teacher and would love to hear Becky playing her guitar. Mary had become Becky's favourite resident and three weeks after Mary had arrived Sister Bell asked Becky into the office.

"Well Becky, you've be coming here two months now, I know the patients really enjoy you and Nadia's visits, how are you finding it?

"Fine thank you, I thought it would be really sad, but it's not at all."

"I've noticed you and Mary have formed quite a bond."

"Yes she is so lovely."

"I'm sure it's doing Mary the world of good."

Becky smiled.

"I hope so sister."

"The thing that worries me though is." she paused, "you know we care for people who have a very limited life expectancy, Mary is slowly deteriorating and at some point in the not too distant future she will pass away."

Becky's eyes filled with tears she couldn't speak. Sister Bell sat down next to her.

"Come on let's go make you a drink." They walked to the staffroom Becky with her head down trying to stop herself from crying. The sister found a box of tissues and made her a cup of tea.

"I know it's hard, especially for someone as young as you, death seems a long way off but this is why we are here, to care for those people and their families."

Becky wiped her eyes and blew her nose.

"Sorry sister."

"Don't be sorry, do you think you'll be okay now to see her?"

Becky nodded.

"Good girl, because I know it means a lot to her. Her daughter and son come as often as they can, but they both work so it's difficult."

Becky took a deep breath.

"Thank you."

They walked out of the staffroom together. Becky decided to visit some of the other patients first and leave Mary to last, as she didn't want to get upset in front of her.

That evening Becky's mother came to the hospice to pick her and Nadia up. After dropping her friend off Becky looked at her mother and broke down,

"Are you sure you want to carry on going there?" Asked her concerned mother.

"They're all so lovely, especially Mary. I'd feel like I was letting her down, she's so nice I wish you could meet her!"

"As sister says, she has her own family and you don't want to see her upset, so you must try to be brave. You told me she likes music why not take your guitar with you and play something for her."

"That's a nice idea Mum, but you mustn't tell anyone about what I told you, Sister Bell tells us how important confidentiality is."

"Don't worry lovely I have to do the same with my work."

Becky decided to take her guitar on the next visit, she checked in with Sister when she and Nadia arrived. Sister Bell thought it was a lovely idea, but she must ask Mary first. Mary was delighted.

"What are you going to play?"

"I've learnt a few that I can play and sing, but I thought you may recognise this, it is quite an old one. John Denver have you heard of him."

Mary smiled.

"Yes I have."

"It's called 'Perhaps love,', my mum used to sing it to me when I was little."

"I know it well I used to sing it to my children."

Becky grinned.

"You can sing along then."

Becky had practised over the weekend, she had a lovely pure voice and Mary was glad to hear she wasn't trying to put on an American accent. As Becky sang Mary gently joined in. When they finished they were given a round of applause by some one standing in the doorway.

Becky swung round, it was Mary's daughter Katie. Becky stood up.

"Hello."

Katie had tears streaming down her face she went to Becky and gave her a hug the guitar between them.

"Thank you so much."

Now Becky was getting emotional.

"You two behave, I don't want any tears."

Becky managed to distract herself with putting the guitar back in its case. Katie blew her nose and gave her mum a big hug.

"Sorry mum but hearing you sing brought so many lovely memories back."

Becky was standing by the door.

"I'll be off, see you Wednesday."

"Not so quick, come over here. Mums told us so much about you, you really brighten her day."

Becky smiled.

"She's my little ray of sunshine," added Mary.

"Thank you."

She looked at Mary who now had her eyes closed.

"I hope I haven't tired her out too much especially as you're here now."

"Don't worry, I don't mind if she sleeps for the whole visit, after hearing her sing it was wonderful, my brother won't believe me when I tell him."

"I actually do need to go now, my mum will be waiting for Nadia and me. It was nice to meet you."

"And you, make sure you bring your guitar again."

Becky nodded, she gently touched Mary's hand and said goodbye.

Mary slept for most of Katie's visit, she didn't mind she sat there and held her mums hand, the words of the song echoing in her head. William wouldn't believe it.

Mary continued to gently fade, the morphine was increased and she spent more time drifting between wake and sleep. Becky continued to visit, but often found Mary too tired to talk, she would sit and hold her hand. Becky made a recording of the John Denver song onto a cassette, but didn't know whether there was a cassette player Mary could use so she decided to put it in an envelope with a message on it and left it in Mary's locker.

The dreaded day arrived. Becky and Nadia walked into the Sister's office for the usual meeting about whom they could and couldn't visit. They got up to leave, the Sister called Becky back.

"Sit down. I need to let you know we have just called Mary's family to come in. I'm afraid she hasn't much time left."

Becky's heart was pounding so hard and although she had braced herself for this moment she wanted to sob and scream. This was so unfair, Mary was so lovely.

"So I think it would be inappropriate for you to see her."

Becky didn't trust herself to speak, she just nodded her understanding.

"I suggest you go off to the staffroom and have a drink and gather your thoughts. If you don't want to stay I quite understand."

"I'm okay"

"Good girl take your time."

Becky stood up praying her legs wouldn't let her down. She would get a drink and then maybe chat to Mr Harrison, an elderly man with Parkinson. She felt a little calmer after a drink and took a deep breath.

Come on, Mr Harrison will be needing a visit she said to herself. She walked along the corridor passing Mary's door. She stopped, she had to say goodbye. No one was around so she went to Mary calling her name softly and took her hand. Mary opened her eyes.

"William," she murmured.

"No it's me, Becky!"

Mary whispered.

"Yes, yes I know you now."

Becky replied softly.

"Yes, you know me, I'm Becky I sing to you."

"It's your eyes, I know who you are, you must have the locket. Its yours, oh thank you, thank you my angel."

Her eyes were closed again. The door opened, Katie and her partner Sarah walked in with one of the nurses. Becky still holding Mary's hand now had with tears running down her face.

"Becky you're not supposed to be here," said the nurse.

"I'm so sorry."

She apologised to Katie and Sarah.

"Please it's not a problem Becky, you've become one of the family."

"Becky you need to leave now and give Mary's daughter some time with her mother."

Tears still streaming down her face Becky gave Mary a kiss on the cheek, she was unable to speak.

"It's okay, mum loved you visiting," assured a Katie.

"She opened her eyes just now, but I think she's a bit muddled, she called me William."

Katie smiled.

"Would you like to stay?"

"No, I just wanted to say goodbye."

The nurse took Becky out and along to the staffroom where Becky broke down. The nurse found Nadia and the pair of them sat and waited for Becky's mum to collect them.

William arrived as Becky and Nadia were walking across the car park. William had a weird sense of déjà vu he couldn't quite put his finger on, it was something about the way one of the girls had turned and looked at him as she got into a waiting car. He shook his head, he needed to get to his mother.

William walked into the room to be greeted by Katie and Sarah. He hugged them both.

"How is she?"

Katie shook her head.

"Not good. She opened her eyes a couple of times and asked for you. You need to get really close to hear what she's saying."

William went to his mother, bending down he took her hand.

"Mum, it's Will, I'm here."

She opened her eyes and kissed his hand.

"I thought she was you."

William didn't understand.

"Okay."

"It was the eyes."

"Okay Mum don't worry now."

William turned to Katie.

"What's she on about?"

"I've no idea!"

Mary's eyes were closed again she murmured.

"Will, Will.."

"I'm here mum, I'm holding your hand."

"The locket, she must have the locket."

"Who mum?"

"Your daughter."

"Okay she will."

That seem to satisfy Mary as she relaxed and went to sleep again.

William, Katie and Sarah sat around Mary's bed and talked quietly. Mary had opened her eyes a couple times and the three of them reassured her she was not alone. Mary passed away peacefully at 11:30 that evening. William, Katie and Sarah stayed on for a short while and spoke with the night nurse and certifying doctor to discuss what would happen next. The nurse suggested that they went home to bed and return the following day to collect Mary's personal belongings.

The three went back to Katie and Sarah's house and talked into the early hours.

Chapter Twenty Three

The funeral was a very quiet affair. There was William, Katie and Sarah, the chaplain from the hospice who had taken the very brief service, and a couple of nurses had attended. Becky after much discussion with her mum didn't feel able to go. She had never been to a funeral and the thought of it would be too much. With her mums help she sent a card of condolence, which the family greatly appreciated.

The sun shone into the large window of the crematorium, embracing the view across the valley which made for a very peaceful setting. The funeral was over within 15 minutes no hymns but William had brought some of his mothers favourite music including the recording that Becky had made. Katie read a short eulogy and William a poem. There was no wake.

Sarah and Katie drove William back to their home, despite it only being a short journey it took some time to get across Bath. The three of them sat in silence in the car each with their own bubble of memories. Sarah led them into the lounge and opened the patio doors into the garden.

"Come on you two, sit down and I'll fix you both a drink."

"Sarah, you are an angel, leave Katie and come and live with me"

"Sorry Will you're not my type," Sarah laughed.

Once they all had their drinks they started to relax. Katie took a large sip of her wine.

"Oh God I'm glad that's over, but it was so sad she had no friends. I even called into her neighbours but they hadn't had any contact with her."

William sighed .

"I know, but she was never the same after Dad…"

Katie butted in.

"Yes, it really did affect her."

"It really affected all of you," added Sarah.

"I know that was the worst time of my life, God Katie, do you remember that awful counsellor we had? I don't think she was much help! However, we were able to move on, both of us at Uni, meeting new people making new relationships.

Mum just gave up and became a recluse. I feel bad, I was so selfish thinking only of myself, I used to dread going home in the holidays."

"Don't feel bad Will, Sarah and I called in most days, but she seemed content on her own, and didn't want to go out at all."

"Right, enough maudlin talk, let's raise a glass to Mary."

"To Mary," they all said together.

"At least hopefully she is now at peace."

"Come on, I have a nice lunch prepared, it's quiche and lovely home-made bread."

They helped themselves to the food.

"I thought Hannah would've come, or perhaps she didn't know," asked Katie.

"Oh she knew alright, I happened to be at the house collecting some bits when you phoned to let me know I needed to come down."

"Didn't she want to come."

"When I told her, she made no comment. It was probably for the best, Mum really didn't like her."

"You can't say that!"

"Well it's true and I think the feeling was mutual."

"How did you two meet?"

"It was when I did some work with NASA, the local rag did a piece on me. Hannah was a budding journalist very ambitious. I think she thought I was the same, the reality is, I'm really a boring old fart and quite happy with my lot. Hannah thought I should've been running for PM, then of course she got pregnant."

Sarah nearly choked on her drink knowing the pregnancy was a sham.

"So the wedding was quickly arranged."

"Oh poor Will, you're not really that boring."

"To be honest I am, I should've known it wouldn't last when she refused to play the lyric game with me."

"The what?"

Katie laughed.

"When we were kids we invented this game, you try and get one up on each other by quoting some song lyrics, but you have to say oh something like 'as Freddie would say, we are the champions' but you can't say the band name and you can't sing the lyrics, you have to say them and of course they must be in context with your conversation."

"Blimey! I'd be no good I can never remember any lyrics, you two are so brainy."

"Not brainy, just a couple of sad anoraks and to be honest no one with half a brain would play it, you can't judge Hannah on that. I don't expect apart from me you played it with anyone else."

"Don't be so sure there was this girl at school, Sam, blimey I haven't thought about her for years she was bloody gorgeous."

"Gorgeous and played the lyric game! I think time has affected your memory of her!"

"No honestly, she was stunning."

Sarah passed William another drink.

"In the words of some character from Grease 'tell me some more'."

"You're not supposed to sing it Sarah and you've got words a bit wrong"

"Don't listen to her Sarah you're a natural."

"Okay where to start?"

"As Julie would say 'at the beginning'."

"Bloody hell Will, you've started something now."

William laughed.

"Right, well it was the last year of A-levels, remember Katie, I think it was the first time we moved, although you were out of it at Uni. We moved to Keyford and I went to Oldway school for my final year. I went into school with mum before the end of the holidays to meet the head and a couple of teachers. My mock grades were very good."

"Of course, big head."

"Well they were! I met the science teacher Mr Quilter, I remember walking into his office, he was pleasant enough, after a chat about my mock grades he said he had a proposal for me. A few of his physics and chemistry students had not done particularly well and he decided to partner them up with A grade students to help them. I said I was okay with that and he decided to pair me up with a pupil called Sam Thompson. The six form pupils were going back to school on the Monday

and I would start on the Wednesday when the whole school would return. The school had a six form block separate from the rest of the school and we didn't have to wear uniform. I remember feeling so nervous it was awful." William thought back. "We had registration and then we went to assembly, all the six formers sat on the stage luckily I was at the back. The head talked for a bit and then announced the new head boy and girl, the boy was the school rugby hero, a right knob! The girl was Samantha Thompson! I was stunned.
I thought Sam was a boy, anyway I remember looking across to see she was gorgeous, I was horrified how I was going to work with someone like that."

Katie looked at Sarah.

"I don't see a problem."

"You have no idea what it's like to be full of testosterone."

"Oh please, too much info," protested Katie.

"Don't listen to her, carry on."

"Well, lessons started and for the next few weeks we worked together in silence. I completely lost the power of speech, the longer it went on the worse I became and then about 3 to 4 weeks in I was walking home through the park when she ran up to me and said that we needed to talk."

"Oh you poor thing!"

"Well actually it was okay. She explained she really wanted to get good results and I was supposed to be helping. She said she was fed up with people making assumptions because of how she looked. She made me stare at her to prove there was nothing special and then she then did the same to me and oh my God, I've just remembered, she took off my glasses and then she asked me what colour eyes are kids would have!"

"What!" Katie exclaimed.

William laughed.

"She'd been doing autosomal recessive genes her in biology that day, anyway we talked for awhile made a pact that I would talk to her she would do the same to me. When I left her I quoted Leonard Cohen lyric. she didn't have a clue. We became good friends and I told her about the lyrics thing, she was pretty rubbish at it but at least she tried."

"When you say you became good friends what does that mean young man, just how good?"

"Well officer, very good friends but only the once!"

"Please no more!"

"He can't stop there Katie, I need details!"

"No, he's my brother no details!"

"We became friends, I remember gave her a mix tape for Christmas. She gave me this old microscope she got in a charity shop I think, It didn't work, but she said I could put it on my desk when I became a famous scientist, shit… I wonder what happened to it?" William continued. "We saw a lot of each other as we revised for the exams. A couple of weeks before the holidays while her parents were at work we had the house to ourselves. I went over every day we would talk and listen to music. Mum assumed I was at school."

"So no sex then."

"Sarah, no!"

"Well yes I guess it was bound to happen as we spent so much time together, but I couldn't believe she could fancy me."

"Why, you're very good looking bloke, I'd fancy you if I wasn't gay!"

"Because she was gorgeous and I was bloody awful I had a brace on my teeth long hair and thick glasses."

"I don't remember that, I know I didn't see much of you at the time," said Sarah.

"Of course you only met me after the trial. Anyway we made love! It was amazing, we lay on her little narrow bed all day long. Oh bloody hell, the shower, how could I have forgotten that!"

"No! I don't want to know," squirmed Katie.

"I walked home on air, completely and utterly in love."

"Then what?"

"Then I got home to chaos! Mum was frantic she thought I still had exams to do, but school had phoned about where to send my results. She panicked and contacted our support team, they then started looking for me, apparently a couple of plain clothed police had followed me. Mum went mad with me when I got in."

"What you'd lied to Mum? I don't believe it Will."

"Yeah, within an hour of arriving back we were packed and gone. We were told the trial was happening the following week and we met up in Wales. Then It all changed, I completely forgot about her."

"In the words of someone else from Grease 'wonder what she's up to now?'."

"Oh bloody hell Will, what have you done, you've created a monster!"

"I'm loving it, why have we never played it, I'm so good at it."

"Shame you can only remember songs from bloody Grease."

"And Mary Poppins!"

"No that was the Sound of Music! But at least you've tried Sarah, not like Hannah."

"You and Hannah must've had some feelings for each other."

"I don't know, I think it was more lust. She was very persistent turning up to go over a few things asking me where I thought I'd be in five years, of course I was really flattered and probably gave the wrong impression. Before I knew it she had virtually moved in, then she became pregnant and the wedding was arranged, I just got swept along. Thinking back I had no say in the wedding plans. No, in a way it was as if it was really nothing to do with me. I felt so happy giving her the locket to wear, she hated it, it was her friend Cass who persuaded her to wear it."

"Where is it?"

"What?"

"The locket, where is it?"

"Shit! She's still got it, I promised mum I'd get it back."

William continued.

"Well, I think she became so disillusioned with being the wife of a professor, all the garden parties we attended most of my colleagues were a lot older, pretty boring."

"Just as well you didn't have kids."

"Oh that was never on the cards. Hannah didn't want to be tied down with kids. If I met anyone else I think I'll make a checklist of all the important issues, where to live, kids, pets and of course the lyric game!"

Chapter Twenty Four

Two weeks of mourning had passed. William, Katie and Sarah were at Mary's bungalow. She had led a quiet life and despite downsizing there was still an enormous amount of possessions to sort out.

"Right!" Katie took charge. "There are only two bedrooms, let's start there we can go through the clothes and decide what can be recycled or ditched so let's get a couple of black bags and get on with it."

"I don't know that I fancy going through Mum's clothes. Why don't I start in the bathroom."

"Okay Will, sort things like towels and linen into separate bags, is there anything you need as Hannah has wiped you out?"

"Maybe a couple of towels, I don't think I want this very attractive floral duvet cover, very 70s."

"Did we have duvets in the 70s?"

"Of course we did, or were they eiderdowns?"

The packing took most of the morning, Sarah and Katie drove to the nearest charity shop with clothes, shoes and linen. There was still so much more to do. William decided to empty the kitchen cupboards, and by the time Sarah and Katie returned the dining room table and the most of the floor was covered in pots pans crockery and vases.

"Oh my God! Will, there's so much stuff what are we going do with it all."

"I'll start putting it into some sort of order, plates there, bowls here, at least then you can see what you've got," added Sarah.

They got to work and by the evening they had had enough.

"Okay let's leave it and come back fresh tomorrow," said Katie looking around the room.

"Blimey how many vases did your mum have, I don't remember seeing her with lots of flowers."

With that William walked in with two more vases.

"Where were those?"

"On the bedroom windowsill behind the curtains."

"We'd better check the other windows."

They found another four!

"Will would you mind if I kept a couple?"

"Of course not, I may even keep one myself"

"There are three tea sets! Who uses those these days?" announced Sarah.

William had proposed a quick shower and then a pub supper. They arrived at Sarah and Katie's local pub, the Crown, and ordered their food.

"That's the most exercise I've had in ages," said William stretching out the stiffness in his arms. "Thank goodness it's a bungalow imagine if we had to carry everything downstairs, all that lifting I'll be as stiff as anything tomorrow."

"Think of all the calories we must've burned!" replied Katie.

They spent the evening discussing how to manage the clearance. The furniture was old and uninspiring and would either go to a local charity or to the tip. Sarah being very organised had brought a notepad to plan all the things they needed.

"I'll contact a couple of charities to see what they'll take, I don't think there's any value in the crockery, so charity shop?"

"Will do you need anything now you're going to have to restock a new place?"

"No I'm sorted at the Uni, I'll wait till I find somewhere to buy."

The following couple of days were spent sorting, packing, visiting charity shops and the local tip. A Charity collected the furniture and the place was starting to look bare. William had sorted a few things in the little garden shed with Sarah and Katie taking the garden tools. They sat on the floor in the now empty kitchen drinking tea, the estate agents were coming the next day to value the property and put it on the market.

"You know you two were so good visiting mum, will you be sad to see the place go?"

"Not really. None of the houses mum lived in ever felt like home, only our childhood home."

"Well I think we've done a fantastic job I'll get the carpet cleaner from the car and give the place a freshen up."

"Will did you check the loft?"

"The what?"

"Oh Will don't tell me you haven't?"

"Where is the hatch? I didn't notice it."

"Come on let's hope there isn't too much up there."

They looked for the hatch and found it in one of the bedrooms. Sarah had to drive five miles back home to fetch stepladder and a torch. On returning William opened the hatch, it was obvious it hadn't been disturbed for years.

"Well, anything up there?" Katie asked anxiously.

"Not too bad, a couple of cases and a few boxes. I'll pass them down."

"Any vases?" chuckled Sarah.

"Ha ha!"

William passed down the suitcases they felt empty then the boxes, there were eight in total. The three of them sat on the bedroom floor.

"We'd better check if there is anything valuable or recyclable."

They took a box each. Katies was filled with photo albums, their parents youth, their wedding, grandparents and William and Katie as children. A tear rolled down Katie's face.

"Oh Will these are amazing, so many happy memories."

William and Sarah joined her. Holidays as a family the four of them smiling at the camera.

"Look at you Katie! That's when you decided to cut your hair short, mum was so furious!"

"Oh I know I remember having a shouting match with her about it."

"Your mum and dad looks so young and happy. I don't really remember seeing your mum smiling like that since we've been together, she's always looked sad."

Katie's tears were running freely.

"She lost so much, her home, her job, her friends and the man she loved."

William pulled her into a hug.

"Hey come on Sis, she's at peace now and reunited with Dad."

Katie recovered her composure.

"What have you two found?"

"This one seems full of old pictures," said Sarah thumbing through her box.

"Blimey I remember that from our family home, we'll have to keep a couple each Katie."

"There's also some old pictures, Victorian dress!"

"Are there any names on the back Sarah?"

"Yes, William and Mabel."

"I think that's our great grandparents."

"There are dates too."

"Excellent we'll take them home and have a good look through. What have you got Will?"

"Games and puzzles, Trivial Pursuit. I remember these puzzles Katie do you, remember this one 'Don't miss the boat'?"

The box had a picture of a boat with three people on raising their hats, while a man in a top hat and carrying a suitcase ran towards the boat."

"How do you play it?" enquired Sarah.

"I can't remember. Can you Katie?"

"No I just remember we had so much fun playing with Mum and Dad. What else is in there?"

"Some books, Janet and John."

He flipped through them.

"They were awful, I can't believe we learned to read using them, some newspaper cuttings following the trial and its outcome." Katie sighed.

"Poor mum she never got over losing Dad."

William looked up.

"She kept every newspaper report of the event."

"Okay so we'll keep those three boxes, let's have a look at all the others."

There was some random paperwork, their parents degree certificates, old invoices, manuals for electronic equipment that had been obsolete for twenty years and Katie and Williams school exam results and reports.

"Well it says here for your first year at secondary school you were an exceptional student who should be looking towards Cambridge or Oxford! Oh, this is a bit weird, from your English teacher and I quote 'The thing I love about

William is his rye sense of humour and the fact he fixes the television and video! Who was it?"

"Miss Lewis. I think she fancied me."

"Hey I thought you said you were a gross teenager!"

"That was during my O-levels, before the brace, hair and glasses."

"Do you remember this William?"

Katie had pulled an old microscope from the box.

"Yes it's the one that Sam gave me. Pass it here."

"Bloody hell," exclaimed Sarah, "this box has got two vases in it."

She held them up.

"Oh no not more vases, do they look like they might be worth anything?"

"No idea, there is some lovely linen here I'll take that back to sort out at home."

Williams next box contained some of his fathers accounting books and a load of letters all stuffed inside large envelopes. He flicked through them.

"I think these letters are from Mum and Dad to each other, do you wanna have a look?"

"No not here, can we take them home I think they'll be rather poignant"

There were a few boxes remaining and a couple of suitcases.

"Do you think these were Dad's?"

He had picked up a suitcase opened it and held up a shirt.

"Probably. I think they could go straight to the charity shop just check the pockets first."

Katie and Sarah looked through the final boxes. In one Katie found a selection of jewellery and watches, most of it was costume jewellery but a couple of pieces looked quite old. She decided she would take them to the local jeweller to get some advice. Sarah's box appeared to contain items belonging to Katie's grandmother. Old postcards, some handkerchiefs and a couple of diaries which seem to be full of random comments. She picked up an old bible.

"Amazing this must've been your family Bible it's got everyone's births marriages and deaths all written in the front it goes back to 1737. "Katie and William were fascinated.

"We need to add Mum and Dad's dates and our marriages."
William took the Bible from Sarah it was large and heavy, he looked through the dates and then returned it to the box.
"That's for another time"

Chapter Twenty Five

The summer break had started, most of the students had left Oxford, just tourists remained. William was sitting in his office at the University, a beautiful oak panelled room. On his desk was the antique microscope now freshly polished and taking pride of place. It provoked mixed emotions, the best and the worst times of his life. Looking out over the enclosed quadrangle he could see Mr Hedges the porter directing some visitors to one of the other rooms. He smiled to himself, it was probably a scene that had remained unchanged for over a 100 years, he did love the view from the room. In another corner of the quadrangle were his lodgings, he could see the windows from here. He sighed to himself, he had spent the last couple of weeks checking his correspondence, speaking to students, marking work, keeping busy but now he realised he had completed everything and had organised most of the work ready for the following September. Suddenly the view from his window didn't seem so attractive, was this all he had look forward to for the next few months? Looking out onto the quad from two corners? He wished he hadn't given up the house to Hannah so easily, too late now.

He cleared his desk and decided he needed to get out of the University for a while, he needed to do something go somewhere, shit he was 33, divorced and homeless, things had to change. He picked up the microscope it was so tactile his students loved it. He would go and see Hannah, they'd parted amicably so he thought it would be nice to see how she was getting on.

It was a beautiful afternoon so he decided to walk, it was about forty minutes away, this would give him a chance to clear his head.
As William turned into the road and walked towards his old house he was shocked to see a 'For Sale' sign in the garden. 'Bloody hell she hadn't messed around, crikey she's even got a new car', he thought as he noticed the Audi on the drive. He walked to the back door and caught himself checking his pockets for the key, 'silly bugger' he thought. He rang the bell. To his surprise a man answered the door.

"Oh!"

"Yes?" said the stranger.

"Sorry I was expecting Hannah to answer the door."

"She isn't here."

"Oh, who are you?"

"Does it matter?"

"Actually yes I'm her husband, sorry ex-husband."

"Yes, I know."

"Oh!." This wasn't going well thought William. "When did you move in?"

"Why?"

"Just wondered, can I come in?"

"No. If you must know we've been together for over six months."

"Six months! We were still married then."

The man shrugged his shoulders.

William had suddenly remembered where he'd seen the man before.

"You're the estate agent who came to value the property aren't you?"

Before the man had time to answer Hannah pulled onto the drive in a red Fiesta. She got out of the car and glared at William.

"Hi Hannah, how are you? Obviously moving on quickly."

"I wondered how long it will take you to see the house was for sale, I thought you'd turn up. Do you wanna buy it?"

"No I just wanted..."

He was cut short by Hannah

"You better come in, do you want a coffee or tea?"

"Yeah, tea please"

William walked into the kitchen everything looked exactly as it had when he'd left although it looked like it needed a good clean.

"This is Raymond, Raymond this is William."

"We've met. I was surprised to hear how long you two have been together!"

Hannah glared at Raymond.

"You've been here all day, why haven't you cleaned up the breakfast dishes?"

Raymond shrugged and grinned

"Not my house."

"I know you're probably pissed about the price, but there is a real increase in valuation, isn't that right Ray?"

William hadn't been looking at house prices so he had no idea what the house was worth, although he guessed correctly, more than it being valued at the divorce settlement. However he didn't want Hannah to know he was ignorant.

"Well Hannah the fact you've been seeing Ray for six months, while we were still married, he valued the house for you so you could buy me out, and now he values the property only three months later for a lot more. You can't expect me to believe the property market has suddenly gone mad!"

"Well it's too late, it's my house now."

"Is that even legal? I'll be contacting my lawyer."

Raymond started to look a little anxious.

"Hannah I said it was a risk I could lose my job!"

"Oh shut up Ray, it was your idea. He can't prove anything, no way is he going to make a fuss, he's too spineless!"

William was rather enjoying himself he wasn't really interested in the money, it was her attitude that pissed him off.

"Now Hannah you've rather underestimated me, when I saw you obviously trying to fleece me I came prepared. Thank you Ray for giving me the info and this conversation." William pulled a mobile phone from his pocket. "I'll be interested to know what my lawyer has to say when I play this to him."

"What! You recorded it, shit Hannah tell him it was really all your idea."

"Ray shut up, you're only making it worse."

"Maybe I won't bother with a lawyer, he'll probably charge me anyway, but a little copy to the estate agent and another to the paper that's a different matter."

Raymond was now really panicking.

"Bloody hell Hannah he's going to get us right in the shit!"

"For the last time Ray, shut the fuck up!"

There was a pause Hannah turn to William.

"Right William what exactly do you want?"

William hadn't really thought it would come to this in fact he'd only been taking the piss.

"I'd like the locket you have that belonged to my grandmother it's the only thing I have of hers, I doubt you've ever worn it."

"That might be difficult."

"Why?"

"I've sold it."

"When?"

Hannah hesitated.

"About a week ago."

"Who to?"

"I don't remember."

"Hannah if you've got it let him have it," panicked Raymond.

"It's mine!"

"I thought you said you sold it."

"Hannah if that's all he wants and he erases that recording surely it's the right thing to do?"

"It could be valuable that's why he wants it."

"It was my grandmothers I remember when I gave it to you, you were suitably underwhelmed!"

"If Hannah gives it to you, will you piss off and leave us in peace?"

"Yes."

Hannah stomped out of the kitchen went upstairs and in no time she returned and handed over a small jewellery box that contained the locket.

"There you are, happy now?"

"Thank you"

They all stood in awkward silence.

"It's been interesting, I hope the house sale goes well, where are you planning to go?"

"Oh piss off Will it's not your business"

"Good luck to you as well Ray. You can see for yourself what she's like so I wouldn't hold out any hope of a happy future together. I imagine once the house is sold she'll have no need for you."

"Well old man, you're just a bad loser."

William smiled.

"No, you're really welcome to her."

"Excuse me! I'm here you know," protested Hannah.

"Anyway I want to make sure he erases that recording."
William held up his hands in mock surrender.
"Of course."
He took out the phone from his pocket and made a show of carrying out the process of erasing the recording. When he finished he held out the Phone to Raymond and Hannah.
"There you go no recording, all gone."
Hannah stood there with her arms folded.
"I think it's time you left."
William took one last look around, he realised the house didn't hold any special memories for him. He walked out with a smile on his face, his grandmothers locket in his pocket. Instead of going straight back to the University he made a detour into the city centre and looked for the estate agents the house was on with. He remembered how Hannah had insisted on organising the house valuation, William himself had suggested getting two or three estate agents in but she had overruled him as she would sort it. As usual he'd given in for a quiet life and in hindsight, he should have never have let it happen she was right, he was spineless.

He found himself outside the estate agents and scanned the windows looking at all the properties. There it was, 'bloody hell' thought William no wonder Hannah and Ray had been so twitchy it was on 30,000 more than it had been valued for, months before. Acting on impulse or anger he went inside. There were a couple of desks, each were occupied. From the one on his right a woman looked up.

"Good afternoon how can I help you?"

"Good afternoon, I'm looking for something on the outskirts of Oxford possibly a 2 to 3 bed nothing fancy. I rather like the one in the window I think it's in the Rock Road area but it seems very expensive."

"Let me have a look for you, Rock Road, actually we've got a couple of properties there, the one you've seen and another a bit further down on the same side." She turned to her file. "Here we go. Well it seems strange as they almost look identical, same size rooms, in fact the other one has a conservatory but is actually 25,000 cheaper. There must be an error. Hold on a moment."

She got up and went across to her colleague on the other desk. She spoke quietly but William could hear.

"Graham, these two properties on Rock Road, any reason why there is such a big difference in price especially as the cheaper one is actually the better of the two?"

Graham took the file from his colleague and looked at the two properties."

"Well I valued number 7, Ray valued number 19 his valuation is way too much no one will pay that! When is he next in? I'll need to have a word with him."

"I think he's back to tomorrow, unless he's still sick."

Still sick thought William, he looked absolutely fine when he'd seen him.

"Sick? Or with that awful woman," mumbled Graham.

Graham's colleague coughed.

"Graham customer!"

William pretended not to hear. The woman returned to her desk.

"I've discussed the prices with my colleague, there seems to be an error with the printing so I shall take that one out of the window whilst we sort it out. I'd advise a viewing as soon as possible with the property at number 7 as I think it will be snapped up very quickly."

"If I could have a copy of the details and anything else in the area?"

William explained he lived temporarily at the University and now he wanted something more permanent. He thanked the lady for her time and he would read through the details, drive around the area and see if any of them would suit him. They shook hands and William left with a handful of documents. He hadn't planned on buying anything just yet, but thought maybe he should start looking, at least that would fill his days. He began to feel quite excited at the prospect and walked back to the University with a spring in his step.

Back at the estate agents Graham reviewed the property at number 19.

"I don't know what Ray was thinking, this place is definitely not worth £105,000. I'll re-evaluate and speak to the vendor's, this is so embarrassing. Since he's been seeing that woman his mind is definitely not on the job."

At the University William had a shower and got dressed for dinner. There were a couple of his colleagues still residing over the summer, both were older than himself and both were divorced, bitter and resentful. William listened to their complaints and vowed not to be like them. He would find himself a nice house away from the University, perhaps with a small garden and he certainly wouldn't rush into any new relationships. He wished his fellow tutors a good evening, stopped and chatted to a couple of keen students who were spending the summer doing research and then returned to his rooms. On arrival he drew the curtains and and looked out across the quad. Yes he was very lucky to have the opportunity to work and live in such a historic place. He looked around his room, oak panelled, a sitting room leading off to a small bedroom with an ensuite on one side and a little kitchen area on the other. The furniture was old and comfortable, he had a couple of armchairs to entertain his friends, but no one ever called.

William poured himself a glass of whisky, went to his desk and picked up the house details he had collected earlier. Sitting in the large old armchair he looked through them, most were suitable and within his budget, even if his mother's bungalow sold for less than the asking price he also had the money from his share of number 19. He imagined buying number 7 the property just down the road from his old house. The thought actually made him grin he could visualise Hannah's face especially if her house didn't sell. He realised despite being married for four years she meant nothing to him and they hadn't really known each other. Why had he married her? He'd been an idiot, the more he got to know her the more coarse and crude she had become. All her friends were loud and opinionated, especially when they had too much to drink and boy could they drink. He remembered the number of times he had come home to find a few of them settled in for the evening with a couple of bottles of cheap plonk, no food in sight and nowhere for him to work, he would escape to the bedroom. In the morning he would be often find someone crashed on the sofa, usually Hannah too drunk to make it to bed. The following day would be miserable as Hannah dealt with her hangover. William shut his eyes thank God that was over, he raised his glass."Good luck Ray."

The following morning William sat at his desk with a map and planned a route to visit all the roads where the houses were on his list. The weather was good so he thought he would cycle rather than take the car. He knew Rock Road well so he didn't need to go there. Of the other seven alternatives four were fairly close together, the other three were spread further afield.

After breakfast William started out on his reconnaissance. He decided to time the journey as it would be interesting to see if he could to cycle to work. The first house was about 3 miles from the University, it was a two bed terrace right on the road no driveway but well within his budget. The second was just around the corner but it looked as if it needed some work, William was quite practical but wouldn't really have much time once University resumed. House number three was near a busy road and number four near the local sewage works! He cycled back to the University starving and a little despondent. He spent the afternoon driving to the other three properties on his list. All three were definitely better, nice locations with front gardens and drives but he would need to use his car to get to work.

He decided to make an appointment with his bank to discuss mortgages. He was pleasantly surprised to find he could afford a much nicer property than those he'd been looking at and so by the end of the week he was back at the estate agent. As he went in he was surprised to see Raymond sitting at Graham's desk. Susan who he had dealt with before looked up and smiled.

"Oh hello again. How did you get on, interested in any one of those I gave you?"

"When I came in last time it was on a bit of an impulse and I hadn't really checked how much I could afford."

William could see Ray smirking out of the corner of his eye.

"Not to worry let me know what's your price range and I'm sure we can find you something, maybe a bedsit we've a few on our books."

Susan had become quite patronising and Raymond was openly grinning now. William relished the moment a little longer.

"Oh no, what I mean is I can afford something bigger. After talking to the bank and with the money I have my budget is now £150,000."

"Oh well I'm sure I could help you with that, please take a seat." While Susan went to the file to look for appropriate properties William looked around at Raymond.

"Hello there, we've met before, I think you came to value my property awhile ago."

William was pleased to see Raymond blush then he turned back to Susan.

"Well I think I found about a dozen potential properties I'll get them copied off for you and you can let me know if you would like to view any."

William collected his new stash of paper shook hands and left. Once outside he looked at the properties in the window. There was his old house with a new price, £30,000 less! He looked up Raymond was watching him, William gave him a wave.

William decided to repeat his house hunting process by planning a route and cycling around Oxford. It took him all day with a break for lunch at a small café near the river. All the properties appeared to be in pleasant areas and surroundings with drives and gardens, a real improvement on the previous visits although he still liked the idea of living in the same road as Hannah. That evening he phoned Katie and told her about his successful day and invited himself down for the weekend.

Chapter Twenty Six

Friday evening Katie, Sarah and William sat in the local pub garden, they had planned to stay home but it was such a lovely evening. William entertained them with the tale of Hannah and Ray. Katie was horrified.

"So that little bitch had been having an affair! Will you did the right thing, I've got a good mind to go round and give her a piece of my mind."

"I'll come with you, that will freak her out!" added Sarah.

"Thanks ladies you're both amazing but there's no need."

"Did you really record it all? I'd love to hear it."

"Of course not but they nearly shit themselves, also I got Nan's necklace back. I think maybe you should have it Katie."

"No Will, it's yours just choose more carefully next time."

It was a perfect evening eating supper outside and then walking back arm in arm.

The next morning Katie put one of the boxes on the dining table.

"This is the last one, I've sorted all the photos and put them into albums."

Katie showed William her efforts.

"Wow you've worked hard Katie I feel quite guilty, you should've told me, I could've helped."

Katie shrugged.

"Sarah and I have enjoyed ourselves it's actually quite therapeutic."

"Have you sorted all the stuff?"

"Most of it, I've put mum and dads letters in another box, I've read through them. Oh Will, they were so in love, it made me cry.

Tears started to appear in Katie's eyes, William took her hand.

"Hey come on Sis."

"Yeah I know, it's just how it ended, all so sad."

Katie rubbed her sleeve across her eyes.

"Right last box, it seems to contain Nan's stuff."

William looked inside the box.

"Oh my God what's that?"

Katie laughed.

"I think it's some sort of underwear, knickers!"

"How disgusting chuck it away."

Inside the box there were a couple of atomisers, Katie examined them.

"Oh these are rather lovely. I may keep them unless you want them Will?"

"No thanks."

There were cotton hankies edged with lace and embroidered with their grandmothers initials, some random postcards, a mixture of old and new, and the family bible. William opened it.

"You're right Katie we must update this."

William started to thumb through the Bible, a small envelope fell onto his lap.

"Hello what is this? It's addressed to me, well Robert Brown!"

"Who is it from?"

"I don't know, but the writing seems familiar."

"Open it for goodness sake," exclaimed Sarah.

William open the letter glanced over the writing and looked at the end to see who it was from.

"Oh god it's from......Sam!"

William stood up and made his way to a chair, sat down and read the letter through.

"Shit I feel really bad, poor kid."

"So, what does it say?" Katie asked.

"It must've looked like I just wanted sex and then buggered off." said William as he passed her the letter.

Sarah was reading over Katie's shoulder.

"She does sound really upset. What's with the Madonna thing at the end?"

"No idea I was never into Madonna."

Sarah started humming 'Papa don't preach'.

"What comes next?"

"Does it matter?"

"This is all in the past, as you said she's probably happily married now, with a family."

"How come the letter was in Nan's bible?"

"We went over there one day."

"You did what! We were supposed to keep a very low profile, you shouldn't have done that."

"I was so in love, I wanted her to be part of our family and for the family to meet her.

"Oh no I'm in trouble." blurted out Sarah.

William and Katie both look round together

"What's wrong?"

"That's the next line Madonna telling her dad to back off 'she's going to keep her baby'."

The colour drained from William's face.

"Hang on a minute Sarah, are you saying Sam was pregnant!"

The three of them looked at each other. William grabbed the letter back.

"Papa don't preach. You sure you've got the words right?"

"I think so."

"Bloody hell Will, you could be a dad!" exclaimed Katie.

"Yeah right! She's probably just written that to emotionally blackmail him into making contact."

"Yes you could be right."

Sarah and Katie looked at William.

"Well, what are you going to do?"

"Whatever has happened, I feel so bad. I've got to find her and apologise for leaving without letting her know why."

William had lost interest in the other items he was deep in thought. Poor Sam she must've despised him for abandoning her, what if she had been pregnant, would she have coped, would her parents have supported her? He had never met them, how would they have taken such news, why hadn't he gone back to find her. Katie broke into William's thoughts.

"Will, are you okay?"

"I feel so bad what if she was pregnant."

"If she was, she probably ended it when she didn't hear from you."

"I think Sarah is right, don't beat yourself up about it."

"I have to find her,I have to know either way."

"Where are you going to start? Sarah any helpful ideas?"

"I'd go back to Keyford. Do you remember where she lived?"

"I don't know the address but I'm sure when I get there it will look familiar."

Sarah had cooked supper accompanied by a couple of bottles of wine. The meal was delicious but William had no energy to chat as he was completely preoccupied by Sam's letter. That night he lay in bed reliving the moment they had met, all the afternoons they'd sat on that park bench in the sun, rain and even snow. Huddled up talking non-stop, actually Sam had done most of the talking, he loved just listening to her. Why hadn't he gone back after University? He realised he always compared his dates to Sam, no one had ever been as beautiful. He vowed he would find her. He had the whole of the summer to find her. Exhausted from his thoughts he finally went to sleep.

The next morning at breakfast William announced his plans to go to Keyford as soon as possible.

"Hold on sunshine," said Katie. "There is still sorting out to do here it's been over 15 years since she wrote that note another few days isn't going to make much difference."

"Okay you're right. What time is the estate agent coming?"

"About 11.30. We've plenty of time, but we better get over there and double check there are no further surprises."

Back at Mary's bungalow they did one final check over. The estate agent arrived, measured all the rooms and took plenty of photos. After the formalities were completed William and Katie went into Bath for lunch and to arrange an appointment with a solicitor to discuss probate.

Chapter Twenty Seven

William drove to Keyford, his plan was to stay a few days so he booked into a small family hotel not far from his old school.The room was pleasant and after unpacking his things and having a chat with the owner he decided to walk to the school. As he approached, lunch break was just finishing the pupils were swarming towards the building's, a few had been out for their lunch and we're rushing towards the school gates. William stood and stared, just seeing the school uniform brought back memories of walking around the school with Sam.

"Can I help you?" a voice called out.

William jumped.

"Sorry, I was miles away."

He looked at the man who had spoken to him.

"Mr Whitock! Are you still here? You haven't changed a bit."

The old school caretaker smiled.

"When were you here then, I didn't recognise you."

"1985 but I was only here for A-levels."

"That will be it then, why are you here now?"

"I'm in Keyford for work, just got here, staying at the Grange hotel. I realised how close it was to the school so I came up to have a look, doesn't seem to have changed at all."

Mr Whitock stroked his chin.

"Well let's see, there is a new sports block, and the old pool has been covered and it's now heated."

"Lucky kids, I remember swimming in the winter gala, I couldn't believe how cold it was."

Mr Whitock chuckled.

"How about the teaching staff? Many changes there? Mr Jarvis was headmaster when I was here."

"No he retired some years ago we've had a couple since then this one is Mr Thomas came from a school in London got some funny ideas!"

"How about Mr Quilter, he taught science."

"Oh yes he's still here."

"Really? I'd like to catch up with him sometime, I teach science now."

"Oh jolly good. Well I best be getting on now."

"Thanks for your time."

William took another look at the six form block. He remembered standing at the window watching Sam and her best friend, Megan walking into school together.

It was a pleasant afternoon. William decided to walk down to the town centre to find somewhere where he could have a sandwich. He remembered the little teashop that used to be at the end of the High Street. He walked down the road opposite the school this leading onto the main road where there was a zebra crossing now. He remembered the lollipop lady that lived in the house next door to the lane where he walked each day to and from school, she would get stroppy if they ever tried to cross without her. Down the hill, it was like stepping back in time, the path led him to a bridge at the bottom. He stopped on the bridge and watched the river flow underneath him, it was so peaceful. So many memories, Martin , Richard and of course Sam. He wondered what they were all doing now, had Martin escaped the the farm? It would be good to catch up with them, but knew that it would be difficult, too many awkward questions about his abrupt disappearance. His mind drifted to earlier times, his friends in Derby, and knew he would never be able to meet them again. He pulled his thoughts away from the past and looked around at the few cottages, nothing had changed, one still had a plaque above its window that showed the flood level one night in 1968. He walked up the hill to the town, his way home from school had been along the river path to the park, he'd walk that later but now he needed food!

The little tea shop was still there, although he was sure it had a different name. He sat near the window with a sandwich and a cake and wondered what to do next. Should he go to her parents house? Did they still live there? Would he remember the way? He finished eating paid the bill and decided to start there.

As he reached his destination the feeling of stepping back in time increased. He hesitated at the gate, it all looked so familiar, memories and emotions filled his head, was he making a big mistake? No, he'd come this far he had to finally close this chapter of his life. Taking a deep breath he walked up the drive wondering what he would say. So many times he had done this to meet Sam for revision and then after exams, just to be with her. Back then he had always used the side door, but felt he should use the front door now, he rang the bell, a dog barked. He stood for awhile, no one answered. Stupid idiot he thought to himself, they were never there in the day, they had both worked. Looking around he realised there were no cars in the drive. Should he leave a note? Or maybe call back later? Her dad worked in the bank he couldn't really go there, her mum worked in town, he racked his brains she had a studio but where on earth was it? He would walk back into town and look, if he couldn't find it he'd ask at the hotel they would be bound to know.

William walked into the town centre, past the fish and chip shop, he paused, they were closed, he remembered the best fish and chips he'd ever tasted. He moved along the High Street all the while taking in the various names, a few had changed, but surprisingly most of them were still the same. A supermarket now replaced Richards the clothes shop, a few shops further on was the chemist where Sam had worked, had been called Mills &Mills but now it was Boots. He stepped inside and remembered the few occasions he had been able to go out on a Saturday for his mother, walking through the shop so he could see Sam. She always worked on the cosmetic counter on his left, he looked across in anticipation. Idiot of course she wasn't there in fact the cosmetic counter no longer existed it was just glass shelves. He thought he'd better buy some paracetamol so he didn't look like a shoplifter. He picked up a packet and walked up to the counter, in front of him there were a couple of customers being served. Whist waiting he looked towards the pharmacy which was on a slightly raised area behind the counter. There was a large sign giving the pharmacy times and below that a framed Certificate announcing the pharmacist on duty. It read 'Miss Samantha Thompson'.

William stared in disbelief. He looked into the pharmacy area, she definitely wasn't there, he checked the notice again 'Miss Samantha Thompson'.

"Can I help you sir?"

William re-focused on the assistant in front of him.

"Sorry I was miles away, second time today!"

He handed over the paracetamol, his heart was pumping.

"I wondered if the pharmacist was free to talk to?"

"Oh she's busy with a rep at the moment, she shouldn't be too long."

William looked at his watch.

"I've got an appointment, what time do you close?"

"6 o'clock tonight."

"Maybe I'll call back tomorrow."

"Sam doesn't work Fridays, it I'll be Mr Furrows

"Okay well I'll catch up with him tomorrow."

Anxious to leave William paid for his paracetamol and left. He crossed the road walked down an alley between the bank and the Baptist church which led to the park. On autopilot he walked across the park to the bench where he and Samantha had spent so much time. He was trying to gather his thoughts. What if she'd been there, what could he have said in the middle of the shop. It said 'Miss Samantha Thompson' so did that mean she was single?

He looked at his watch it had just gone 3:15 so he had nearly 3 hours before the shop shut. He went through a variety of options in his head. Going back to the shop, going home or the best idea wait until 6 pm and meet her after work. Yes that's what he'd do, that way they could chat once he introduced himself maybe go to one of the pubs for supper, something they never managed to do when they were teenagers.

Now he had a plan William relaxed and looked around him. The view of the park from the bench hadn't really changed. Some of the trees had grown, but the flower beds were still in the same place. The old pavilion was still standing, although now sadly covered with graffiti. A few children came into his peripheral vision, wearing the Oldway school uniform, William had that strong sense of stepping back in time again, sitting there waiting for Sam to appear from his right hand side with her bag over her shoulder, she had such a distinctive walk. His heart used to race at the sight of her, he smiled to himself, such lovely memories.   His reminiscing was rudely interrupted by a football that bounced uncomfortably close to his face. A boy yelled out.

"Frankie you idiot, you nearly hit that bloke!"
The boy ran towards him and grabbed the ball.

"Sorry."

"It's okay no harm done."

William got up and decided to walk back through the park, up Bath Hill to his guesthouse. He walked against the flow of school kids leaving on their way to their various homes. Once back he checked into his room had a quick shower and freshened up. He made himself a cup of tea and sat in his room looking out of the window.

He decided to drive to the shop remembering the main car park was located behind the high street, which he now noticed had become one way so he gave himself plenty of time. There was no need, he was soon at the car park behind the chemist shop. William decided to kill some time as there was a good 40 minutes before Samantha was due to leave so he drove around the town recognising the street names until finally finding Milward road where he and his mother had lived that year. He found house number 12 easily, it hadn't changed the front garden was neat and tidy but the house had a look of emptiness. He looked at the clock on the dashboard of his car it was 1745 time to head back. He parked near the back of the shop again, not too close but near enough to give him a good view of the back door. What if she went out the front? He hadn't thought of that. There was no need to worry the door opened and out walked two women and a man. Was one of them Samantha? His heart started to race, desperately trying to match his memory of her with one of the two women. One was a brunette, the other blonde. Any doubts were soon erased as overhearing their conversation he instantly recognised Samantha's voice, she sounded just the same with her slight Somerset accent he remembered so well.

"I'll give you a lift Cheryl." Samantha offered.
No thought William go with a bloke.

"That would be great." The brunette replied.

The man got into a car and drove away.

William could hear Samantha and Cheryl chatting away and as they walked past, they didn't even register him. William watched them as they got into a silver mini and drove out of the car park still chatting away. William smiled, boy she could always talk.

Shit what was he doing? He needed to follow them, he started his car, swung out of the car park only to get stuck in a queue of cars at a pedestrian crossing, he could just see the mini about five cars in front. The mini got to the end of the road and turned left, all good so far if she turned left at the next mini roundabout she could only go up Bath Hill thought William. A couple of cars turned right so William gained on Samantha. At the roundabout she turned left again excellent thought William, this stalking lark was a piece of cake. Just off the roundabout was another pedestrian crossing, Samantha sailed through the lights as they changed to red causing William to nearly hit the car in front. The lights seemed to take forever, As he sat there he was getting frustrated as more cars joined the traffic behind Samantha.

"Come on come on," William shouted impatiently.

An elderly woman was taking her time to cross, the lights were green by the time she managed it, at last the car in front moved. William drove down the hill over the bridge up the other side just in time to see Samantha turning right along the Oldway. Phew, thought William panic over, from his memory there weren't many turnings and they were on the left as the right side of the road was lined with fields dropping down to the river. Driving up the hill seem to take forever, he reached the roundabout and couldn't believe how many cars were coming from his right. Patience, he thought. Finally he managed to turn, past the Chinese takeaway, houses on the left fields on the right just as he'd remembered, but no sign of Samantha. To his left were a couple of roads and a couple of cul-de-sacs, he decided to try the cul-de-sacs first, frustratingly no silver mini in either. He turned into the side road, the first one was actually a horseshoe shape and went back to the Oldway. William had driven slowly along the road no bloody mini. He soon realised stalking was more difficult than he thought maybe he wasn't such a clever detective after all!

He was becoming increasingly frustrated he couldn't have got this close and then missed his chance he should've said something, bloody Cheryl could've had gone home with the bloke. Right he thought, calm down there's only one more road she could've come down. It turned into a marathon as numerous roads led off Manor Road.

"Shit, shit shit!" he shouted.

William drove down a couple struggling to do U-turns when there was no sign of her, he continued up and down the side roads for nearly half an hour. He pulled the car over cursing his bad luck. Of course it wouldn't have been that easy, he was an idiot to think it could be. God he needed a drink he decided to call it a day and drove back to the Grange all the time checking every driveway for a silver mini.

The Grange provided an acceptable evening meal, William chose the steak and kidney pie and a pint of beer, he slowly began relax. He went into the small bar area where he decided to give Katie a ring and let her know about his abortive attempt to find Sam.

Katie was sympathetic, Sarah was in the background listening in and laughing at Williams tracking attempt.

"Did you get the car numberplate?" she asked

"No I didn't think of that, would it have helped?"

"I may have been able to check on the police computer and found an address for you."

William groaned.

"I'm really not cut out for this detective lark."

Sarah and Katie laughed down the phone at him.

"Chin up William we were impressed you had such success."

"What's your plan now?"

"I'll stay here overnight especially as I'm on my second beer and it's going down rather nicely, then if it's okay with you two I'll come over to you for the weekend as I have no idea if she'll be working or not, then try again on Monday."

"That will be lovely to see you although Sarah is working and I must do some admin."

They chatted a little longer and William sat back in a very comfy chair and enjoyed his drink. He'd been feeling so smug finding Samantha and seeing her.

The following morning William drove to Bath it really was a beautiful city. On arrival at Katies and Sarah he announced he would cook a supper as a thank you for their hospitality. Katie raised her eyebrows.

"Will, I never knew you could cook!"

"Well there's always a first time!"

William cheated slightly and used a jar of 'Homepride' sauce with some chicken, potatoes and frozen peas and carrots. Katie and Sarah were impressed with his effort.

"Do you cook much at the University?"

"No, I have a little kitchenette in my room enough to make myself tea and coffee and a microwave if I want to heat something up, I started experimenting when I got the house, quite enjoyed it, but now I usually eat in the University."

"How about Hannah, you never asked us to come over once you were married."

"How can I put it? Hannah was never comfortable with your relationship."

"Ha ha that was blatantly obvious, she used to watch us all the time, it was really creepy."

"Hey Sarah, you're not drinking? It's not like you especially as I have bought this bottle of wine"

"Sorry Will, I'll give it a miss, we have a serious case on at the moment and I may get called in and I've got an early start tomorrow."

"Okay, more for Katie and me."

The evening past uneventfully. If Saturday had been slow Sunday was a nightmare. William couldn't settle to anything. He was restless, Katie was sitting at the dining table reading through some of her case notes. He was a real distraction pacing up and down the room, randomly picking up a newspaper or magazine and flicking through them. Katie had had enough.

"Oh for goodness sake Will, go for a walk, or better still drive over to Keyford and go for a walk there you may even see her."

"No point I'm going to go over tomorrow afternoon and try again."

William thought about Katie's suggestion, it wasn't a bad idea. As it was only late morning he decided to go to Keyford.

He drove out of Bath it was a pleasant drive and as it was a Sunday and the roads were quiet. Katie was right, now he was being proactive he felt better. He had no problem parking on a Sunday, no pay-and-display, bonus! He walked along the High Street down the alleyway to the park, bugger someone had beaten him to the bench, two women, one had a pushchair and two youngsters, they appeared to be comparing the inadequacies of their respective spouses. Why did people marry and stay with their partners when they got on so badly. William walked on a little way to the next bench, but could still hear them bitching. Then one said.

"Here he comes."

William was curious to see the recipient of the negative comments. An overweight balding man was walking towards them. William watched him approach, bloody hell it was the old head boy Dean! The past 16 years hadn't been kind to him. The blonde girl turned around.

"Where the fuck have you been, I've been waiting ages, the bloody kids have been whingeing, how come you can have a quick drink and I'm stuck here?"

Wow, thought William, she's giving him a really hard time. The woman look familiar, yes she definitely been at school with them, she looked overweight too. Dean and his partner ended up having a blazing row, she appeared to wear the trousers in the relationship.

William listened with interest, he remembered how controlling Samantha said Dean's Dad had been and how Dean would follow him, except it appeared that Dean had met his match with his partner. William remembered Dean bragging about his future but he was sure it was not to turn out like this.

The group walked off ending Williams entertainment. He walked across to 'their bench' it felt soiled by their fat arses and aggressive behaviour. He looked around, come on Sam he fantasised, 'just walk into the park, he imagined her coming over to their bench seeing him and staring in surprise as she she recognised him, the grin spreading across her face and then rushing to hug him.

"Oh Sam where are you?" he mumbled to himself.

He sat for a little while longer watching a variety of people walking, running and cycling past. No Samantha. He got to his feet, it didn't matter, tomorrow afternoon he'd be at the back door of the shop and await her departure from work. He'd make sure he would make a note of the registration number so even if he'd lost her in the traffic Sarah may be able to find her address.

William arrived back in Bath to find Katie and Sarah cooking supper in a state of elation.

"Something I should know?"

Katie and Sarah looked at each other and said in unison "No!"

He frowned, something was going on, well they'd tell him in their own time. In fact his disinterest would really wind them up.

They sat down to eat. Katie had prepared roast ham, new potatoes carrots, peas, broad beans and some lovely parsley sauce. William loved being with the two of them.

"Wine Sarah?"

"Oh no thank you Katie."

William looked up, definitely something going on. He decided to ignore them and told them of his plans for Monday.

"We will both be at work so you will have to amuse yourself all day."

"No problem, I'll probably going into Bath and do a bit of sightseeing."

Monday morning arrived Katie and Sarah had left early. William decided on a leisurely breakfast. He just poured his 2nd cup of tea when the phone rang. It was the Dean from his University, he had known where to contact William.

"William glad I caught you. A bit of a bother here, an ex student of yours, um, Clive Shergold, anyway he's got into trouble with the police. His parents are asking for a, um, character reference from the University, thought he was your, um, student you are the best man for the, um, job."

"Clive Shergold, name doesn't ring any bells. He obviously wasn't a very memorable student. What's the crime?"

"Oh, um, don't know, I'll give you the parents telephone number, you speak to them. Good man, well done. He rang off.

William stared at the phone. That buggered his plans completely, he would now have to go back to Oxford, review Clive's University record, before phoning his parents and finding out what happened.
William contacted Katie's office but he wasn't able to speak to her. He left a message with one of the secretaries to let her know he had to return to Oxford.

It turned out that Clive had been a fairly average student, nothing of note in his attendance or work. He had been involved in a few student pranks but nothing serious. William phoned his parents to find out Clive's crime. It turned out he had been messing about with a friends unloaded air pistol pretending to take pot shots as they were driving through the local village. A passing motorist had reported the event to the authorities. The police have taken the incident seriously and Clive would have to appear in court. His parents had contacted a solicitor who suggested a character reference written by somebody with credibility could help, so they had contacted the University.

After an intense conversation with Clive's parents. William spent the afternoon composing the character reference, by the time he'd finished, printed it off and walked down to the porter to get it posted the day had slipped away. He felt it was too late to drive to Keyford, so would have to go the following morning, staying at the Grange again so as not to bother Katie and Sarah.

Tuesday morning. Before William left he thought he'd better check if there had been any correspondence for him as he hadn't been there for the last few days. He walked across the quad to his study, he couldn't believe it, there was large amount of paperwork that needed his attention. What he thought would take a couple of hours to sort out had him tied up for the rest of the day. Another day gone. Tomorrow he was definitely going back to Keyford come hell or high water.

Wednesday. It turned out to be a puncture that delayed him this time. By lunchtime it was all sorted. He went back to his digs to freshen up, the way things were going, he wasn't going to take any chances. If he left that afternoon he could get to the shop before 6 and would check in at the Grange after he had found Samantha.

With his mind made up William packed his bag and in no time was on the A34 heading south.

The roads were busy he started to worry he wouldn't make it, however he turned into the car park behind the shop at 17.55.

"Phew made it," he said with relief.

Parking the car he realised he was the only one there, it had been fairly full last time. He worried she would spot him as soon as she walked out just after six. 18.05 no sign of anyone, 18.15 William got out of the car and walked to the shop door it was locked. On the glass window next to the door was a sign displaying the shop opening hours. Wednesday closed at 17.00! William took a deep breath and swore to himself. So much for being a detective, he'd made a rookie error and hadn't checked the bloody opening times he could've kicked himself, he kicked the door instead. He double checked the sign,Thursday, yes closed at 1800. Turning back to his car he realised there was no silver mini in sight, no chance of him getting the reg number for Sarah to check. He sat in his car and decided what to do next. It was a good couple of hours back to Oxford, 40 minutes to his sisters or 10 minutes to the Grange, but what would he do the following day with his time if stayed there.

He phoned Katie and explained his predicament she was very sympathetic but had mentioned Sarah's parents were coming to stay on Thursday and she changed all the bedding in the spare room, however he would be welcome to sleep on the sofa. William declined the offer and headed off to the Grange. William settled in had a good supper and a couple of beers and thought of what might happen tomorrow.

Thursday was wet and windy. After breakfast William looked out of his bedroom window and wondered how on earth he would fill his day. He felt as if everything was against him and thought maybe he should forget the whole idea. Even if she was known as Samantha Thompson at work, she must have a man in her life, unless like Dean she had aged and let herself go dramatically in the past 16 years, although the glimpse he caught of her on his first attempt to see her, it appeared not be the case. He then realised how embarrassing it would be if she didn't even remember him! William took Sarah's letter out of his suitcase and read it again, he owed it to her to explain. If she wasn't bothered, he could just tell her the minimum, perhaps he would do that anyway. He had never told anyone about what had happened, he had lost touch with his friends from school, he had never told anyone at University and thankfully he'd never told Hannah. Maybe it was a blessing that Hannah had disliked his family and therefore never had the opportunity to ask them about his past. Imagine her reaction if she'd found out, she would've wanted to write about it for the paper or even a bloody book. He had definitely done the right thing in divorcing her.

The rain had stopped so William decided to go for a walk. He went up to the school, crossed the Oldway, down the lane to the bridge and then took a right and walked along the river to the park. It started to rain again William looked up and could see someone on their bench was it Sam? It couldn't be. He rushed across but in his haste he slipped and fell onto the muddy path. He got up the only thing that was hurt was his pride but he was quite wet. He looked towards the bench the woman had stood not aware of William's predicament and started to walk away. William brushed himself down, he looked up just to see her turn the corner and into the alley that led out of the park to the high street. He followed but when he got to the end of the lane the woman had vanished into the crowd of shoppers going about their business.

Was that Samantha thought William, he was damp from his fall and frustrated he couldn't satisfy his curiosity. All was not lost he would still go to the back door of the shop at 6 o'clock to see if he could catch her there. He still had a few hours to kill, first he would to go back to the Grange get cleaned up and into some fresh clothes then try sightseeing again, Bristol this time, something he was unable to enjoy when he lived in Keyford.

It was 6 o'clock William was sitting in his car with the window slightly open. He noticed Samantha's mini parked next to a blue Mondeo, the occupant was on his mobile phone, a typical rep he thought to himself. Samantha and two other colleagues stepped out through the door of the shop as another car turned into the car park. One of the women spoke.

"Oh it's Dave I'll be off. Cheryl do you want a lift?

After some discussion she accepted.

At last thought William they are going, taking a deep breath, he started to get out of his car to approach Samantha when he heard another voice.

"Hi Sam, you managed to finish on time."

'Shit' thought William she's got a boyfriend, it was Mondeo man.

"Oh hello, what are you doing here?" replied Samantha.

"Well you said you finished at six, I'm staying at the Grange this evening and wondered if you fancied showing me the sights of Keyford and grabbing something to eat."

William couldn't believe it after 16 years someone else was asking her out!

"Well this evening is no good I'd organise to have supper with my parents."

Yes, thought William, on your bike Mondeo man.

"If you let me know when you're coming back in this direction that would be really nice."

No! Thought William.

"How about next Thursday? I could probably get Friday off as I think I'm right in saying you're normally off on Fridays, you've got my card ring the mobile number, let me know if that's good for you maybe I won't need to book the old Grange for the night!"

What! Thought William, it was all he could do to keep himself from walking over and punching the guy. Sam laughed.

"Don't get any ideas I'm not that sort of girl."

Well done Sam, thought William.

"At least not on the first date!"

What! thought William.

"Doesn't today count as our first?"

"No, today was work!"

"Okay, I'll see you next week, doll."

"Bye Wayne."

Doll? Wayne? What sort of idiot was he, and with a name like that, thought William. He watched as Samantha and Mondeo man get into their prospective cars. He was not going to be left behind this time, he started his car and joined the convoy of mini and Mondeo as they left the car park. Thoughts started to go through Williams head, Samantha must be single as Wayne was asking her out. Wayne wasn't local or he wouldn't be staying at the Grange. What were the chances of Wayne staying at the same place as himself and also Sam had a day off tomorrow! The three cars were now driving down Bath Hill over the bridge to the other side, up the hill to the mini roundabout. Right would take them along the Oldway which Samantha did followed by Wayne. This isn't the way to the Grange, what was Mondeo man doing other than trailing Sam? thought William. Now overtaken by a red mist he decided to follow them but in his haste almost caused an accident at the roundabout as he nearly hit a van coming from his right. There was a lot of horn blowing and shaking of fists. William felt foolish, before he could start off again a couple more cars had moved in front of him. Shit he thought he was going to lose her again. He continued up the Oldway but there was no sign of the mini or Mondeo, it suddenly dawned on him he would have to turn off and check the side roads again, a case of déjà vu. This time William decided to take Manor Road and methodically go up and down the side roads but to no avail. He ventured back onto the Oldway and drove up to the last two remaining cul-de-sacs on the left hand side. He knew from his previous experience these would easier to check but no luck. It was never like this in films, thought William, the hero never lost sight of his target and always went the right way and didn't have the bad luck he had had on this and the previous occasion. He drove back down the Oldway having exhausted his options and his patience. If she had Friday off it was pointless him staying in town as he had no chance of finding her, he would stay the night and go back in the morning and return next week before Prince Charming

could seduce her on the Thursday. As William continued down the Oldway he noticed a road sign to a village called Chewton Keyford coming up on his left. He remembered he and Samantha had spent an afternoon walking along the river towards Chewton Keyford, Sam had told him she would have a house there one day. How had he forgotten? Breaking sharply he turned left down the hill towards the village over the river, past fields, before coming to the small hamlet. There was a farm on his left and a very attractive house on the right, followed by a couple of semi detached cottages. He continued on, checking the cottages that appeared on his left and as he approached the final residence a silver mini pulled out from the drive, it was Sam! Thankfully she didn't recognise him or his car and headed out of the village and back out towards the Oldway. William made a note of the house number, and as he
drove on to find somewhere to turn round a blue Mondeo passed him on the other side, it was Wayne!

    William pulled over to assess the situation. It wasn't worth following Samantha and Mondeo man as they were too far ahead.
He recalled the overheard conversation of Samantha explaining to Wayne she was going to have dinner with her parents.
I will go there thought William. If he remembered correctly, he could continue on there would be a turning on his right which would take him over the hill back round to Keyford, approaching from the north side of the town. It was a longer route, but luckily the gods were smiling on him as the traffic was light and despite the distance it took him no time at all. As he entered Queens road he spotted the blue Mondeo with Wayne sitting in it smoking a cigarette talking on his phone. Another black mark against Wayne thought William, Samantha hates smokers, at least she did 16 years ago. William glanced at the house, yes there was a silver mini parked on the drive behind a black Rover. At least he knew that Sam's parents were still a living at the same house and Samantha herself had fulfilled her dream to live in Chewton Keyford. He felt felt very pleased with himself quite the

detective this time but as there was nothing he could do with Wayne outside he made his way back to the Grange.

After supper William went into the bar with a nice pint and sat down ready to call Katie with an update. No answer. He thought back to earlier, why was Wayne waiting at Samantha's parents house he thought she had put him off. His train of thought was broken as Wayne himself walked into the bar. William kept his head down and pretended to text on his phone. Wayne got himself a drink and walked towards William. The last thing William wanted was a cosy evening with his new rival. Saved by the Bell! Wayne's phone started to ring, he answered.

"Alright Fran,.....yes I know.....I'll be back tomorrow late afternoon, yes,........I know it's difficult, okay, Love you."

Why did people have to shout when using their mobiles thought William.

"Mind if I join you?"

William looked up. Wayne stood before him.

"Okay."

"Thanks mate, it's nice to see a fellow rep, the rest of the inmates make it look like a geriatric ward."

Wayne's phone rang again.

"Fran, I'll phone you later,... Oh alright, put her on... Hi sweetheart, be a good girl for Mummy and I'll see you tomorrow because Daddy has to work away sometimes, okay, night night Daddy loves you."

Wayne ended the call.

"Kids aye, you've gotta love em, you got kids?"

William opened his mouth to reply but Wayne carried on.

"See, marriage, all that is fine, don't get me wrong but, well, I've always been a ladies man, so now and again I just have to have a break. Women they don't understand that. Another drink? I'll get these you can get the next."

Wayne got up and moved to the bar. Phew, thought William, his rival barely paused for breath. Wayne returned with the drinks.

"Have you travelled far?" William enquired.

"Bristol, you?"

William thought Keyford was only six miles from Bristol why would he stay overnight, then it clicked.

"Oxford."

"I did some work there once, nice place."

"So you just have a quiet night when you have your break?"

Wayne leaned in and lowered his voice.

"Between you and me, I've got me a nice little Filly all lined up."

He grinned. Over my dead body thought William.

"So where..."

"Yeah well you see I got the dates mixed up she wasn't able to join me tonight but next week it's all fixed."

He took a large slurp from his drink

"So is she married?"

"Blimey no, I don't want some angry husband after me."

Wayne laughed

"I've been caught like that before."

Saved! Thought William as his phone rang.

"Sorry I have to take this, it's my boss."

Wayne nodded.

"Hello,.... just a minute I've got the file in my room."

He gave Wayne a wave and escaped the bar. Katie was on the other end of the phone.

"Will it's me, Katie your sister, have you lost the plot?"

Once in the room William could answer.

"Hi Katie sorry about that I was being bored to death by an obnoxious man called Wayne who appears to be my arch rival, you called just at the right time."

William filled Katie in on his exploits of the day and how successful he was with his detective work.

"So what's the plan?"

"I've not really had a chance to think about it but basically I will call on Sam tomorrow. What time do you think I should go?"

"I don't know, although if you go mid morning she'll have had time for a lay in, if she needs it and if she's not there you can go back later in the day."

"Thanks Sis, I feel quite nervous, but what if she doesn't remember me?"

"You always remember your first love William, don't worry.

Chapter Twenty Eight

William had a restless night, and didn't feel particularly rested when he went down to breakfast. To his relief he saw Wayne checking out, they acknowledged each other.
After breakfast William went back to his room threw his things into his overnight bag. He looked at his watch 9.10 he didn't know what to do with himself. He made himself a coffee and paced the room, at 9:30 he was starting to feel jittery, various scenarios were rushing around in his head. He knew now, she looked and sounded the same, but she could've changed, his memory of her was from years ago. Maybe he should abandon this idea and just go back to Oxford, after a disastrous marriage, he would be an idiot to try and rekindle an old love affair. What had he'd been thinking! William sat on the edge of the bed, he couldn't call Katie she would be at work. Then he thought about Wayne, the bastard! No he couldn't let that happen, whatever happened he needed to warn her that Wayne was married. Maybe she prefers married men, like his ex wife.   William shut his eyes and took a deep breath. Get a grip he told himself. He would just go and see her, explain what had happened all those years ago and leave. Why did he think it was such a big deal, why did he imagine anything would come of it? Because if he was truly honest with himself the more he thought about her the memories of that year came rushing back. The sound of her voice provoked such a wave of emotions.

"As John would say 'my memories of love will be of you'."

It was true throughout all of these dark times Samantha had been like a shining light. He looked at his watch again 10 o'clock. He decided to brush his teeth again. He sauntered down to reception and checked out, it was nearly 10.30 by the time he got into his car. This is it, he thought and proceeded to drive the couple of miles to Chewton Keyford.

Her car was in the drive, he drove passed the cottage and parked. His heart was pounding, why did he feel so ridiculously nervous? William got out of the car and walked into the drive, he had to squeeze past the mini as he made his way to the side door. He could hear music playing, a black

Labrador lay on the grass alongside the path, it thumped it's tail couple of times as William bent down and ruffled its ears, how he'd love a dog.

The door was open, he listened, Leonard Cohen was playing and a female voice was singing along with gusto although an octave higher. William peered in, Samantha, if it was her, had her back to him and was painting the wall. The room was covered in dust sheets, he guessed it was a kitchen by the shapes underneath the covers. This is it he thought before knocking on the door.

"Hello."

Samantha look round, she was wearing marigolds and had a paint roller in her hand. All she could see was the shape of a tall figure in the doorway.

"Hold on I'll just put this down."

She placed the roller in a paint tray then pulled off her gloves and walked towards him. He gazed at her, she had paint splatters on her face and in her hair, but she looked more beautiful than he remembered.

"Sam, I don't know if you…"

He didn't have time to finish.

"Robert Brown what the hell are you doing here?"

She wasn't smiling anymore. Shit, he thought this wasn't one of the scenarios he'd imagined.

"Well?"

"It's a long story Sam, but I found your letter and I wanted to explain what happened that summer."

"Letter?"

"Yes the one you left with my Nan."

She thought for a second.

"Oh, that letter."

So many emotions were flying through Samantha's head. Robert Brown standing in the doorway as if he'd only been gone a week not 16 bloody years, she thought.

"16 years! 16 bloody years you just disappeared I thought I was going mad."

"Sam I'm so sorry."

"Why didn't you phone or write me a note?"

"Sam honestly I couldn't, if I'd been able to I would."

"Why, where were you?"

"We went to North Wales".

"North Wales! " Her voice was raised. "North Wales, don't they have phones or postboxes there!"

"Sam, I really couldn't write or phone."

"Oh God, you've been in prison, haven't you!"

"What? No!"

This wasn't going well thought William.

Tears were coming now.

"16 years Rob and no contact. I think you should leave. You broke my heart back then."

"Sam, I am so sorry I really want to explain why I had to leave in such a hurry."

"I walked the streets of Keyford, I didn't even know where you lived, I went to see your Nan a few times just in case she knew where you were."

William remembered something.

"It was you, she wanted you to have the locket didn't she? The staff told us she given it to a young girl, who handed it in. They didn't say anyone had actually visited her."

Samantha had perched on a stool the only bit of furniture visible.

"16 years Rob, well I'm not going through that pain again."

"Sam, something else I need to tell you before I go. Wayne that rep, he is married with a kid. Please don't get involved."

"What! How do you know about Wayne?"

"Well, I was outside the shop when he was trying to chat you up."

"Hang on, how do you know where I live?"

"I followed…"

"You followed me? Out, now!"

"No, technically I followed Wayne, who followed you."

Samantha took a deep breath and shut her eyes. She opened them again and walked towards him with her head held high.

"As Gloria would say 'go, get out that door'."

William looked at her and grinned, she could never get the lyrics right.

"Samantha Thompson what a complete and utter fool I've been. I've wasted the last 16 years of my life when I should've been with you."

Samantha just looked confused.

"What are you talking about, I've just told you to leave and you're grinning like a Cheshire cat."

William smiled.

"I haven't gone mad Sam, honestly. I can see this has been a shock, but I never meant to hurt you. I would really, really like to explain about the past. You obviously need some time, I could come back tomorrow."

"I'm working."

"In the evening?"

"No."

"Sunday?"

"No."

"Ok, on Monday I will be in the park, sitting on our bench, if you remember it. I'll be there from 10.30 in the morning and I will sit there all day."

Samantha folded her arms.

"I seem to remember your last words to me were, see you Monday!"

William rooted in his pockets and produced a car park ticket and a pen. He wrote on the ticket and handed it to her.

"You can reach me on either of those numbers. If I'm not at the bench you can call me and give me hell," he sighed, "but please give me one more chance."

Samantha didn't trust herself to speak, so she just nodded.

"Bye Sam, until Monday."

Samantha watched him walk down the path and squeeze past her car. The 16 years had been good to him. He no longer walked as if he carried the weight of the world on his shoulders, he had a good haircut, no brace on his teeth and surprisingly no glasses, perhaps he wore contacts. He'd been dressed nicely too, nice jeans and a crisp white shirt, very sexy, wow what was she thinking? She popped into the downstairs cloakroom to get some paper to blow her nose. Oh my God, she thought, as she caught sight of herself in the mirror, she couldn't have a looked worse if she tried. Her hair which had been tied up had partly escaped the scrunchy, she was horrified to see her hair and face were covered in splashes of paint with a particularly bad smudge where she'd rubbed her cheek.

"Shit" she exclaimed.

It didn't matter she told herself, he meant nothing to her and as for that rat Wayne, wait till she saw him, if it was true of course. Rob had no reason to lie so she guessed it probably was. She went back into the kitchen looked at the half finished wall, she really couldn't be bothered now, so she decided to put on the kettle and turn the music up loud, she could do this.

William had spent Sunday evening with Katie and Sarah. He gave them a run down of his meeting with Sam.

"So she still thinks you're called Rob? Didn't you tell her Will?"

"I didn't really get a chance."

"What about the baby?"

"Again I didn't get an opportunity to ask!"

"Was there any sign of a child living there?"

"I only went into the kitchen. The child would be 15 by now."

"Were there any pictures or anything?"

"No I don't think so."

"Don't think so! Will don't give up the day job, you're the worst detective out!"

"That's not fair, I found her, and where she lives. She was painting the kitchen so the walls were bare and everything was covered with dust sheets."

"Ok you're let off."

Katie and Sarah looked at each other. Sarah nodded, William looked at them both.

"Okay, what's going on with you two?"

Katie grinned.

"You're going to be an uncle!"

William jumped up.

"Fantastic, group hug!"

"Will, I hope you're okay with this, you know with Hannah having a miscarriage and everything."

William smiled.

"Katie and Sarah I'm honestly thrilled, and between you and me I don't think Hannah was ever pregnant, I think she just wanted to get married."

"But that was a complete disaster from the beginning," said Katie.

"I know, in hindsight I think she had it all planned, she just wanted the house. I've discovered since she's been having affairs left right and centre. You were right Sarah when you said don't trust her."

"Will you poor thing."

"Yeah, what a bitch" added Sarah.
I think I'd got into a bit of a rut, with work and life in general. Now, I feel I've finally woken up."

"Well I know you think Sam is the one, but please be careful."

William smiled at her.

"Katie don't worry, all I want to do is clear the air between us. If she doesn't want to see me again I might go travelling and have an adventure. All I've done is studying then work, I intend to have some fun."
Katie hugged him.

"You deserve it little brother, uncle to be!"

Monday dawned sunny and bright. William parked his car behind the shop and paid for an all day ticket. He walked through the shop to the High Street keeping his head held high and resisted the temptation to look back and see if she was there. He bought a takeaway coffee at the café next door and with a newspaper tucked under his arm he walked down the alleyway and into the park. Thankfully the bench was unoccupied so William made himself comfortable. The disadvantage with their bench was it was slightly off the beaten track which is why they had liked to sit there, but unless he kept turning around he wouldn't be able to see her approach if she came from the High Street. He checked his watch, half an hour had passed and he'd finished his coffee he should've bought a sandwich he was getting peckish. He looked through the paper but couldn't really concentrate.

"Hello"

She had sneaked up on him.

"Sam! You came, thank you."

Samantha sat down not too close.

"You knew I'd come."

They sat in silence. Finally William looked up.

"This is really hard for me Sam, I never had to tell anyone about this."

"Not even your wife?"

"No, especially not her."

"So you are married."

"Divorced."

"So, why didn't you tell her?"

"Because..," William paused, "Because I didn't trust her, especially with something that had to be kept secret."

She could hear the emotion in his voice.

"But you trust me, someone you haven't seen for 16 years?"

William took a calming breath.

"The Sam I remember was the most trustworthy loyal friend I've ever had," he looked in the eye, "I believe you're still the same person, also you need to understand what was going on at the time, I know I hurt you and I feel terrible about it."

"I used to come and sit on this bench every day whenever I was home in the hope you would turn up."

"You obviously went to Uni then?"

"Yes, Bristol. You?"

"Yes, Oxford."

"I phoned every Uni trying to find you, none of them have heard of you".

"I deferred for a year."

"Oh, that would explain it. So what happened?"

William looked out across the park.

"I'll try and keep it as simple as possible. When we lived in Derby there were the four of us, my mum, dad and my sister Katie we…"

"Hang on, what about Ruth? You told me you had an older sister called Ruth."

"Katie is Ruth."

"I'm confused."

"Ruth is Katie's middle name."

"Okay. So I know people sometimes call themselves by their middle names but she was Ruth then, why are you calling her Katie now?"

"Sam, Ruth, Katie, it doesn't really matter okay? So the four of us lived in a nice house on the outskirts of Derby."

Samantha was staring at him.

"What? Why are you looking at me like that?"

"I was wondering what your middle name is."

"Sam as I said it doesn't really matter can I continue?"

Samantha was still staring at him as he ran his hand through his hair, a gesture that Samantha remembered well.

"Okay if you really want to know, my middle name is Robert."

"Robert!"

"Yes, happy now?"

"No, far from it. If Robert is your middle name then, hang on a minute the teachers all called you Robert. Presumably you wrote Robert on your exam papers. I don't get it, what is your real name?"

William sighed, why did nothing ever go the way he planned.

"My real name as you put it, is William. Now, can I continue?"

"Is Brown your real surname?"

"No, okay no. For fuck's sake Sam I'm trying to explain, please shut up and listen."

He realised he'd raised his voice.

"Shit, Sam I'm sorry, I didn't mean to shout at you, it's just this thing I have to tell you it's…"

Samantha had moved closer and put her hand on his arm.

"No, I'm sorry Rob ..um..Will . I didn't mean to be insensitive, it's all a bit confusing."

Sitting closer she could smell his aftershave, a smile spread across her face.

"What!"

"You still wear Aramis, if I close my eyes and Inhale it's like stepping back in time."

"Shall I carry on?"

He hoped she wouldn't move away from him.

Chapter Twenty Nine

William's parents were slightly older when they started a family. His father was an accountant and had worked for the same firm for many years when he decided to start his own business. William's mother, was a music teacher at the local school, so their home was always filled with music. She had taught William and Katie the piano, guitar and violin. Both of them became accomplished musicians and enjoyed singing, as well as excelling in their academic studies. It was a very happy home.

The first time William was aware something was wrong was the summer of 1985. There was a tension in the house, his parents spent a lot of time in whispered conversations. The family had taken a weeks holiday in Cornwall, William had just completed his first year of A levels and Katie was to start University at Cambridge in the September. The family had always holidayed as one with both parents joining together to swim, surf, play games or go for walks.
On the Wednesday morning Katie and William came down to breakfast to find their mother alone.

"Where is Dad?" Katie asked.

"He's had to sort out some work, so he'll be away all day."

"Why? We're on holiday," protested William.

Mary dropped the box of Rice Krispies she was holding.

"Shut up William, now look what you've made me do."

William was surprised at her reaction, his mum was the most laid-back person he knew, he was even more surprised when he realised she was crying. Katie and William looked at each other and jumped up from the table and knelt down with her.

"It's okay Mum, we'll help you clear it up"

"Is Dad okay?" asked William.

Then a thought struck him.

"Is he ill? Has he got cancer or something?"

Mary blew her nose.

"I'm sorry it's just Dad has been under a lot of pressure lately and…"   "Oh my God you're getting divorced."

Mary smiled.

"That you can rest assured that will never happen, ever. But I think we may be facing a very difficult time and I want you to be brave and mature about it."

"Mum you're scaring me."

"And me" added Katie.

Mary smiled again.

"Come on let's get this mess cleared up and sort out some breakfast."

Williams father, Andrew had left Cornwall earlier that morning, he needed to find a police station. He felt it should be one of the larger cities so he decided Bristol would be his destination.

He found the main police station fairly easily and parked his car. Looking at the imposing building, Andrew almost turned on his heel. However he knew he had to do the right thing, he just hoped they would believe him. On entering the station he saw a waiting area with a couple of people seated. He noticed a large policeman standing at the reception desk.

"Morning sir what can I do for you?"

Andrew felt sick, his mouth was dry, he wasn't sure if you could speak, he swallowed hard.

"I need to talk to someone."

"About what sir?"

The desk sergeant gave an internal sigh, bloody time waster he thought. Andrew swallowed again, come on he thought, it's now or never. Taking a deep breath he glanced over his shoulder to make sure no one was watching him.

"I've witnessed a murder."

"Oh yes."

Here we go again bloody Looney thought the desk sergeant.

"Yes, I need to tell someone about it."

The sergeant looked at Andrew hard. He saw a man in his 50's nicely dressed in chinos, a shirt and jacket, a wedding ring on his finger and a decent haircut. Yet he looked as if he hadn't slept for a while, there were dark shadows under his eyes, maybe he's not a looney, he thought.

"Let me take some details and I'll see who's available."

"Thank you."

Andrew gave his name and address but wouldn't elaborate on what he witnessed in such a public area.

"Take a seat then sir."

Andrew sat, he felt slightly better now that he'd made the decision to report it. A man of similar age to him came through one of the doors. The desk sergeant nodded towards Andrew. D.I. Hadley introduced himself and shook Andrew's hand.

"If you'd like to follow me sir."

He led him into an interview room. There was a table with two chairs either side"

"Please, have a seat. Would you like a drink?"

"A glass of water please."

Hadley moved across to a side table, where he poured out a glass of water from the jug sitting there. He returned and placed it in front of Andrew then sat down opposite.

"The desk sergeant says you want to report a murder, is that right?"

"Yes."

At that point there was a knock on the door and a man in a grey suit entered the room.

"This is detective constable James he will be taking some notes."

D.C.James pulled up a third chair to the table. He took out his notebook and pen.

"For the benefit of D.C.James let's start with your name and address."

Andrew dictated his details to D.C.James.

"Derby! Don't they have a police stations there."

"The truth is, I don't know who I can trust, this man is has a lot of influence back home, if you know what I mean."

"No Mr Layton I don't. Perhaps you'd better tell us what happened."

Andrew took a sip of water.

"I'm an accountant. After working for a large firm of accountants for a number of years, I had had enough and decided to go it alone and start my own business.Things were slow at first, money was tight but slowly I developed a stable client base and a good reputation. About six months ago this man came to my office, he said he was concerned money was going missing from his business. As I said he is well known in the community and I was flattered when he told me he had heard I was reliable and honest. He asked me to review all his accounts going back over a year and report to him as soon as possible. He would pay me a very generous fee with a bonus, depending on how quickly I produced the results.

"Does this Man have a name?"

Andrew took another drink of water to clear his throat.

"Lewis Mathews."

He paused to note if there was a reaction from the detectives, there was none. He continued.

"I had finished all the end of year work from my clients so was glad to take on such a large contract. I visited Mathews at his office and spent the majority of time there, carefully analysing his figures. He has an enormous business empire and it took nearly 4 months to complete my work. I phoned him with my findings and as he had suspected, money had indeed been taken, in fact it was almost £125,000. Matthews ask me how this was possible. I explained who ever did his accounts had moved money around keeping it very well hidden."

Andrew paused again and took in a couple of slow deep breaths.

"Go on."

"This is a dreadful part, he asked me to come to his office the evening of the 15th and bring my findings. When I got there a man on reception took me downstairs to the basement, which I thought was odd. I was shown into what appeared to be a freshly decorated room as there were sheets on the floor. It was brightly lit, there was a small table a few chairs and there were about half a dozen men standing around, and Lewis Mathews himself. Mathews welcomed me. He asked me to sit and show him the data I had collated and explain how the money had gone missing. After I had done this Mathews spoke to a man sitting opposite him on the other side of the room. He turned out to be a Mr Silvers, Matthews accountant.

"Could I have some more water please? Thank you."

D.C.James passed the water jug to Andrew. He pour himself a glass and the continued.

"Mr Silvers looked horrified, and started to say it was all a mistake and I was a liar. I felt really embarrassed and said to Matthews that I was sure my results were accurate but was quite happy for someone else to double check. Matthews said there was no need as he had suspected Silvers had been up to something, he just hadn't realised how much he'd stolen. Silvers then started to apologise and asked for leniency, Matthews made some sort of gesture, the door opened and in walked a young woman. I don't know who she was. Silvers stood up, he called her Lisa, Matthews then said to Lisa what did she have to say for herself, she swore and screamed at him, apparently she had been an accomplice."

Andrew closed his eyes, he could still see it.

"Matthews stood up, Silvers and Lisa were facing him. Silvers was now pleading for his life, Lisa was crying and begging."

"Can you speak up Mr Layton."

Andrew hadn't realised he was now whispering.

"Sorry. One of the men in the room pulled a gun from his jacket gave it to Matthews. He shot them,...Mathews shot them, in the head, first Lisa and then Silvers. I thought I was going to be sick I couldn't move, and then Matthews said something like, 'I'm sorry you had to see that Layton, but I expect complete loyalty from my team'. I couldn't take my eyes off the two bodies."

"Are you sure they were dead?"

"Oh God there was so much blood, and the smell like, I dunno, sort of metallic. Then Matthews told the men to clean up the mess. I realised then why the floor was covered in plastic sheeting, it was used to wrap up the bodies before they were taken out. Matthews was so calm, as if nothing had happened. He said he wanted me to carry on as his accountant and then, just left. I couldn't move, I just sat there for some time. As I collected up my documents put them in my briefcase I noticed this on the floor so I picked it up."

He put his hand into his jacket pocket and took out a small bag, inside was a man's handkerchief covered in blood spatters.

"I think it belonged to one of the men. I don't know if this helps to collaborate my story."

Hadley sat back in his chair.

"Say we believe you what do you want us to do?"

Andrew was surprised at the remark.

"Arrest Mr Matthews for murder of course!"

"And you would give evidence?"

"Yes, the knowledge of what happened is killing me."

"Do you have any idea who Lisa is?"

"I'd seen her in the offices a couple of times when I've been working there, but I don't know her surname."

Andrew proceeded to give a description of Mr Silvers, Lisa and a couple of the men that had been in the room. Finally Hadley concluded the interview and told Andrew they would get his statement typed up for him to sign.

"Leave it with us Mr Layton we will be in contact."

William and his family returned home from their break in Cornwall. Things were almost back to normal, although there seemed to be a constant tension between his parents. When he asked them if there was anything wrong they assured him all was well and work pressure was to blame. One day Andrew confided that he had a particularly difficult client and this was the reason he was working long hours and part of the weekend.

Behind the scenes D.I.Hadley and his team were making discreet enquiries into the disappearance of Mr Silvers, at the same time a woman in Derby had reported to the local police her flatmate Lisa was missing. The investigations began to gather pace.

The school summer term finished, William spent the holidays working in the DIY shop and hanging out with his friends. They played football in the park and flirted with the girls they met. They cycled out to a local lake and swam in its cold waters, it was idyllic but something still niggled at the back of William's mind.

The week before they were to return to school William and his mates were sitting in the park under the shade of a tree. Some girls had joined them and William was making headway with a pretty girl called Claire.

"It's been a bloody brilliant summer, I don't want it to end," said Williams friend Joseph.

"Nor me," agreed William.

"When is your birthday Will?" said Jack, another friend, "Is it before we go back?"

"Yeah next Friday."

"We've got to have a party."

William smiled.

"Brilliant idea we could have a barbecue at mine."

He hugged his new friend Claire.

"Do you fancy coming?"

"Yes," she said looking at her friends, "how about it?"

"Yeah come on girls the more the merrier" said William eagerly.

They made their plans, it would be the perfect end to the holidays. The group split up and William walked Claire home, as they reached her house they stopped and kissed briefly.

"Claire can I see you again?"

"Yes I'd like that, let's meet tomorrow probably best in the park about 10 o'clock"

William sauntered home, he felt very pleased with himself. Claire seemed really nice, school didn't seem so bad, he had excellent results in his mock A-levels, this would be his last year and his mates were taking many of the same subjects as him, and to top it all he was going to have a birthday party!

William was surprised to see a large van on his parents drive, his dad's car was parked in the road. The van had a carpet company logo on the side which was odd. William wondered which carpet was being replaced.

He let himself into the back door and headed straight for the fridge, as usual he was starving. Surprisingly the fridge was almost empty. He looked for the fruit bowl, empty as well. He looked around the kitchen. The worktops were normally filled with every day clutter, cake tins, box of tissues, paperwork, mugs on the draining board, they were all clear. He checked the cupboards, they were empty too. William was puzzled and as he walked into the hallway he could hear mumbled voices coming from the lounge, He noticed there were suitcases and boxes lined up by the front door, what an earth was going on!

He walked into the room, his parents his sister and two men were sitting and talking quietly. Katie looked as if she'd been crying. Andrew looked up.

"Will, thank goodness you're not too late."

"Too late for what?"

William suddenly felt sick something was seriously wrong. Andrew saw the terror on William's face.

"It's okay, these two gentlemen are police officers. I recently witnessed a terrible crime and they have been investigating the perpetrator, things are coming to a head and now they feel we could all be at risk."

"At risk of what?"

One of the police officers stood up.

"There is no need to be alarmed son."

"Dad, what crime? I don't get it."

Andrew spoke quietly and calmly.

"I witnessed a murder, up until now no one knows I had reported it but the police fear they will have to show their hand soon, therefore exposing my identity as a witness. Because of this we are going into the witness protection program."

William stared at his dad in horror. His mother spoke.

"I've packed most of your clothes, but go up to your room and see if there's anything I've missed that you particularly want to take."

William couldn't move, this was too surreal.

"Come on Will," said Katie, "I'll check with you."

She dragged him out of the room and up the stairs to his bedroom. William sat on his bed he felt shellshocked.

"It gets worse, we have to change our names, Mum suggested we use our middle names, she's going to be called Mary, at least it won't be alien to us but the old Bill says we have to take Brown as our surname."

"Brown!" exclaimed William.

"Yes," Katie sat next to him, "Will there's something else, Dad isn't going to be with us."

"What, why?"

"I think it's because you and me are in education and Dad will be the target, so if he is with us we can't continue with school and university."

William put his head in his hands, this couldn't be happening.

"I don't care about school, I want to stay with Dad.".

He was struggling not to cry. His father heard the last part of the conversation as he walked into the bedroom. He motioned for Katie to leave them. He took her place on the bed next to William and put his arm around his son's shoulder.

"Will, I'm sorry this has happened. This has been a very difficult time. I need to be away from you all as it will be easier for the police to keep us all safe. It won't be forever, as soon as they can get this man to court the sooner I can give my evidence and get him behind bars. I really want you and Katie to continue with your education as you have your whole future to look forward to."

William could only nod in agreement

"Now the police are keen for us to be on our way. We are all going to Burton upon Trent to stay in a new hotel it's called a travel lodge or something."

"What am I going to tell my friends?"

"I'm sorry Will you must not contact your friends it could put both us and them in danger. As I said it shouldn't be for too long then when we return you'll be able to tell them all about your adventures."

He didn't have the heart to tell William they probably would never be able to return home.

William reluctantly looked around his bedroom and wondered how long it would be before he slept in his bed again. He collected his guitar, some of his favourite sheet music and a couple of albums.

As discreetly as possible their belongings were loaded into the van. There were seats inside, the family settled in and travelled in silence until stopping at a lay-by where they, along with there overnight bags were transferred to car, which took them on to the hotel. Once in their rooms Andrew called them all together.

"I just want to thank you all for supporting me, I know Katie and William you've only just learnt about it but you've behaved with extreme maturity. I said earlier, I'll be going somewhere different to you, I don't know where you will be and you won't know where I'll be. The police feel that's the safest option and when this is all over we're going to have one hell of a celebration!"

The following morning, they said an emotional farewell to each other. Andrew got into a car with two plain clothes policemen and with heavy hearts William, his mother and sister climbed into another. The cars pulled away in opposite directions. Mary and her children drove in silence for over an hour no one knowing what to say. It was all a bit of a squash as they were also accompanied by two police officers. Finally William broke the silence.

"Where are we going?"

"To a pleasant town called Keyford," replied one of the police officers. "You'll have your own house, you can make it quite homely. We've already moved into the house opposite so we will be nearby should you need us."

"Is it much further?" moaned Katie.

"Yes I'm afraid it is, We wanted plenty of distance from Derby. We'll stop soon and you can stretch your legs."

It was another hour before they reach Keyford. They drove through the town then turned into quiet road. The car stopped at number 12, William struggled out of the car glad to stand upright.

The house was a 1960s semi, one of the officers opened the door for them whilst the other unloaded their suitcases. William helped him take them up to the house.

The front door lead into a hallway with staircase, on the left a door opened into a lounge diner which ran the length of the house, behind the hall was a small kitchen. William noted their other belongings had already arrived.

A police woman took Mary into the kitchen and explained they had done a food shop so they shouldn't need anything for a few days. William and Katie chose their bedrooms, Katie offered to take the smallest as she hoped to go to University and therefore wouldn't be there too long. William took the back bedroom looking over the garden. They both wandered back downstairs.

"I think I'll go out for a walk," announced William, "I really need some fresh air."

"I'm afraid you can't do that." announced the policewoman.

William wanted to argue with her, they couldn't stop him could they?

"I'm sorry it's for your own safety."

"We might as well be in prison!"

William went out the back door slamming it hard. He explored the garden, it wasn't very big, but was seriously neglected. At the bottom was a shed, the door was unlocked, he peered inside. He cursed as he realised he'd forgotten to bring his bike. With any luck they'd be home in a couple of months.

It was another ten months before the case went to trial. In that time William had met Samantha and they had fallen in love. Spending that time with Samantha had given William renewed hope and that day in July when they had finally made love had left him ecstatic.

However that very same day Mary had phoned the school to find out exactly when William's exams would finish as the police were keen to move them again as a precaution before the trial started.

She was horrified to discover his last exam had been the previous week, where on earth was he? She called the police across the road, they immediately went into action radioing others to walk through the town to look for him.

Mary was instructed to pack everything up, a couple of vans arrived to move their possessions. A message came through he had been spotted and appeared to be walking home. The officers followed him at a distance, William oblivious to what consequences his actions had caused.

He arrived at his home and walked through the back door grinning like a Cheshire cat only to be greeted by his extremely angry mother. How could he have lied to her, didn't he know he could've put himself in danger. He wasn't able to explain as 15 minutes later they was sitting in the back of one of the vans as they started a long drive to North Wales where they would stay while the trial took place.

Chapter Thirty

It started to rain, Sam ever prepared grabbed her umbrella from her bag.

"You must've been a very good girl guide."

Sam shrugged.

"I was a Brownie, hated every minute of skipping around and making silly promises, I left as soon as my mum allowed me to!"

William continued with his tale.

The trial was coming to an end. Andrew had given his witness statements for the murders and Lewis Mathews money laundering. The police kept Andrew isolated until the completion of the trial which resulted in Mathews and his associates receiving long prison sentences.

The police collected Mary, Katie and William from the cottage in North Wales and took them to London to be reunited with Andrew. They were put up in a hotel and Andrew would join them within the next couple of days.

Mary was so excited, which lifted William and Katie's spirits. William couldn't believe there was light at the end of the tunnel, they had been advised not to return to their home in Derby but to make a new life in a new area. The police reminded them they must not contact any of their old friends but William decided once they settled he would contact Samantha .

They had a police liaison officer with them at the hotel who announced to the family that Andrew would be returning that day. They waited in the hotel room, William paced up-and-down unfortunately Katie had a migraine and had returned to her bedroom.

The liaison officer's walkie-talkie went off 'he's on his way, apparently he wants to walk here, so they're happy with that, he'll be accompanied by a couple of plainclothes officers'.

Overhearing the message Mary jumped up.

"Which way are they coming?

"From the police station, should take about 45 minutes," replied the liaison officer, "but I'm not sure which direction."

"I want to meet him!

"I'm coming to," added William.

"I'm not sure that's very sensible what if you miss each other."

"Check when he is almost here and find out which way he's coming and we'll go and meet him," pleaded Mary.

The liaison officer reluctantly agreed. William told Katie about their plan but she didn't feel up to joining them.

"It's okay, I'll wait here."

Mary and William sat with their jackets on ready to go. The call came through, they were 5 minutes away and would be arriving from the right of the hotel. Mary and William couldn't wait they were out of the door, down the stairs into the lobby and out onto the pavement, Mary was like a teenager.

"Right let's see who spots him first."

They hurried along.

"There he is, across the road."

Sure enough he was walking towards them chatting away to a couple of men.

"William look, he's grown a beard, that'll have to go!"

"Hey Dad, over here!"

Andrew looked up and saw Mary and William frantically waving, a grin spread across his face as he waved back.

At that moment their view was blocked as a bus followed by a blue van that passed between them. Eagerly William focused again on his father. Something wasn't right Andrew was on his knees, William crossed the road not taking his eyes off his father. As William got closer he could see his Andrews shirt was covered in blood, he tried to shout but no sound came out he fell beside his father and took his hand. Andrew gripped him briefly then his hand became limp. Mary arrived by their side screaming her husband's name, she bent down and cradled Andrews motionless body not wanting to let him go. Around them chaos reigned, police and ambulances arrived but William was oblivious he just clung on to his parents, shocked to the core.

William stopped talking, every minute of that time so vivid, he could picture the logo on the van as it passed in front of them, he could still remember the sounds and smells and the feel of his dad's hand in his.

At some point during his narrative Sam had taken his hand in hers. They sat in silence for a while, then William realised she was quietly crying, instinctively he put his arm around her and pulled her close.

"Sam I'm sorry, I didn't mean to upset you."

Samantha could barely speak.

"No, no I'm sorry, I've wasted so much time, blaming you for all my failed relationships, I always thought they would leave me so I'd dumped them, and all that time you were going through hell. Rob I'm so sorry and I was so angry when I saw you've, you've..."

"Shush, its okay I just want you to know, to understand, I would never have left you. I know I should have contacted you sooner, but I assumed you'd have moved on with your life and forgotten about me."

Samantha could only shake her head and continued to cry. Telling his story William felt a weight had been lifted from his heart sharing his story with Samantha was more cathartic than all the counselling sessions he had attended.

The rain continued Samantha and William sat cuddled together under the umbrella.

"This bloody weather, doesn't it realise it's summer time?"

Samantha didn't respond.

"Sam sadly we're going to have to move, I'm desperate for a pee, where is the nearest loo?"

He was hoping she'd suggest her place. Sam sat up pulling away from him.

"Sorry Rob, um Will, I'm going to find that difficult to get my head around. Where did you park?"

"Just behind the shop."

"There is public toilets in the main car park close by."

They walked to the car park sharing the umbrella, William took her to his car and opened the passengers door.

"Sit here in the dry, please wait for me."

She nodded and climbed into the car, she let her head rest back and closed her eyes. All the years of bitterness and anger gone, she should feel happy but instead felt the most terrible sadness, she still couldn't believe what William had had to cope with. The tears started again, why couldn't she stop crying?

She was glad it was raining at least none of her colleagues were outside on their breaks, she didn't want anybody to see her.

William was relieved to see Sam was still there when he returned to the car. It was obvious she was struggling to digest his news. She remained quiet with her eyes closed and tears running down her cheeks. He longed to reach across and wipe her tears away but the intimacy of earlier was replaced with an awkward tension.

"Sam please talk to me, what are you thinking right now?"

Samantha rummaged in her pockets for a tissue and blew her nose. She turned to look at him and stared for a minute.

"Do you wear contact lenses?"

"Contact lenses?"

"Yes, do you?"

William look confused.

"Is that what you're really thinking about?"

Samantha sighed.

"Ro..Will. I feel like my head will explode with all the thoughts and emotions right now, at least it's a yes or no answer."

Then realisation dawned.

"Ah," he said, "the glasses I used to wear?"

"Yes."

"They were just glass, I remember they were really thick framed they hid half my face, and then that was their purpose, apparently I looked very like my dad."

"Same with the hair?

"Yep, although I think long hair had been very trendy at my old school that summer."

"I suppose the braces were for the same reason?"

"Actually no, I really needed them."

He smiled at her, the questions had reduce the tension between them.

"Sam you always knew how to ask the right questions. Thinking back to how I looked then, I'm amazed you recognised me when I turned up at your doorstep."

"Don't forget I used to see you without your glasses quite a lot, plus I'm reminded of them every day."

"Really?"

Shit she had meant to say that, she smiled to cover her faux pas.

"Yes in Charlie, my dog."

That had been close she thought.

"Can I take you to lunch?"

Sorry Will, I don't think I could eat a thing right now."

"Okay. Can I see you again?"

Samantha hesitated.

"Okay."

William exhaled loudly, he hadn't realised he'd been holding his breath.

"Thank you Sam."

They sat in silence again.

"What are you doing the rest of the week?" William asked tentatively.

"Well I'm working, day off Friday and Saturday."

"I'm on holiday, so I'm free and happy to drive here again."

"No, I'll come to Oxford, I've never been before I just need to sort out, um, dog care."

They arranged a time and place to meet, a pub by the river, William gave her detailed directions which Samantha carefully wrote in her diary.

"What do you want to do now?

"I'll walk home," said Sam.

"Can I give you a lift, it's still raining."

"No, I prefer to walk. As Paul would say 'I need a little more time to think things over'."

"Sam Thompson you are amazing."

She smiled at him.

"It's been really..," she shrugged, "I don't know what to say, I think emotional is the only phrase that comes to mind."

"If you change your mind about Friday or just want to talk or ask me anything, you've got my number just give me a call, I don't want to put you under any pressure but I would really like to see you again."

She nodded, how do you say goodbye to an ex lover? The last time they couldn't let each other go, they kissed and kissed, the memory brought tears to her eyes.

"Sorry I don't know what's wrong with me."

William took her hands in his.

"Sam please don't apologise, I know this must've been like a bolt out of the blue."

She nodded again unable to speak. She squeezed his hands then pulled away to find another tissue.

"Sorry."

"Sam it's okay.

She retrieved her bag and umbrella from the foot well.

"Are you sure I can't give you a lift."

Sam shook head.

"No, I'll be fine.

"Leonard would say 'Hey that's no way to say goodbye'."

"Good old Leonard," she tried to smile.

"See you Friday?"

"Yeah."

She got out of the car and walked away. He sat and watched her for as long as he could, he so wanted to chase after her. He felt terrible for upsetting her so much yet he knew she was the one. Talking to her brought back so many memories and emotions. Recounting what had happened had been hard but he smiled as he realised he loved her, he always had and he always would. Whatever happened between them wouldn't change how he felt. He also accepted that he had never felt anything like this with Hannah, she had made such a fool of him.

Chapter Thirty One

Samantha spent the next few days working, there were numerous times in the evenings when she picked up her phone, sometimes even dialling his number, then bottling out at the last minute. She spoke to her parents and asked if they could cover her family responsibilities as she would like to visit an old school friend away and she may stay overnight. Her parents were thrilled that she was actually having some social time to herself.

On the Thursday evening she felt like a teenager as she packed a small overnight bag, stressing about what to wear. She woke early the following morning and drove to Oxford arriving safely at the pub where they arranged to meet. Arriving early she parked up and decided to walk along the river, it was beautiful. She sat on a bench and wondered whether to phone him and after dithering for a few minutes decided she would.

"Hello."

"Oh, hi it's Sam."

William's heart sank, he was about to leave and was convinced she was phoning to cancel.

"Hi Sam, are you okay?"

"Yes it's just.."

Here we go he thought.

"It's just I've got here a bit early and.."

"Don't move, I'm on my way!"

He hung up and dashed out the door.

Sam looked at the phone.

"Oh, goodbye then!"

She walked back to the pub car park and waited in the car. It wasn't long before William arrived on his bike. Sam smiled.

"You cycled!"

"Best way to get around Oxford."

Both felt a little shy, William chained up his bike and lead Sam into the pub.

"Do you want to eat inside or out?"

"It such a lovely day, outside please."

They chose a table overlooking the river. William got them both a drink and returned with the menu. It was so easy their shyness soon disappeared as they discussed what to eat. William left to order their food leaving Samantha to look out over the river.

"So what are you doing with Mr boring?"

Samantha jumped, she hadn't heard the woman arrive.

"I'm sorry you, are?"

"His ex wife," she paused, "I don't expect he mentioned he was married?"

"Actually yes he has, although I don't know your name."

"Hannah, I'm a journalist."

She was annoyed to see Samantha was so attractive.

"So when did you two separate?"

"We finally got divorced about eight months ago, should've done it earlier."

She sat on the bench next to·Samantha and lit a cigarette. Samantha backed away.

"I must warn you he's so fucking boring. All he does is fucking work, as for the sex," she mimed a yawn, "he's usually to fucking knackered to bother, I don't think we had sex for, well eons ago."

Samantha was incensed.

"You surprise me. To be honest we've only made love a couple of times, but it certainly wasn't boring, especially the last time in the shower, I can't stop thinking about it."

"You're fucking lying."

"No she's not!"

Both women jumped and turned around. William was standing behind them.

"Hello Hannah, to what do we owe this pleasure?" he said sarcastically.

"I've been trying to get hold of you for ages, every time I've called at the college the porter says you're out, you never answer your phone."

"Why?"

Hannah suddenly turned on the charm.

" Oh Will I've really missed you, it's not the same at home without you my love."

William cringed, this was so embarrassing, he glanced at Sam but she appeared to be ignoring them both and was rummaging in her large handbag.

"Hannah drop the pretence, what are you after?"

"Money."

"Money for what?"

"I can't pay the fucking mortgage. You didn't tell me it cost so much to have a house and all the bloody bills. I only need about £1000."

"You're joking. What about your estate agent boyfriend? I thought he was sorting that out?"

"We split up. Come on I know you earn more than me you wouldn't miss a £1000."

William wanted to slap her, but reigned in his temper.

"Hannah you had the house for a song. I even paid off a lump sum on the mortgage to help you. It can't cost you more than £150 a month, why do you need so much?"

Hannah stubbed out her cigarette and lit another before replying.

"You going to buy me a drink?"

"No Hannah."

"I've got into a bit of an arrears that's all. Christ we were married doesn't that mean anything to you?"

"You know as well as I do the marriage was a joke, you manipulated me to get a nice house."

"Bastard. If you don't give me the money I'll drag your name down in the papers, I'll write a story about how you abused me, you'll loose your job!"

Samantha looked up and stared at Hannah. She continued her outburst.

"Oh as for you I'll do some investigating dish the dirt."

"What If there no dirt to find?" Samantha replied.

"Then I'll make some up."

Samantha was horrified.

"You can't do that, surely you need some proof if you're 'dishing the dirt' as you say."

Hannah laughed

"Oh Miss prim and proper. I can do as I like, a good journalist doesn't reveal their source. Once the story is printed the damage is done to your reputation, and even if I retract the story later it will be too late."

Hannah sat back and smiled.

"So I think it will be in your best interests to give me some money I'm not asking for much."

"What you're saying is, you're going to blackmail us for some imaginary crime we've never committed?"

Hannah clapped her hands slowly.

"Give the monkey a banana."

William glared at Hannah.

"You've just admitted trying to blackmail us, we can go to the police and tell them, be a witness for each other."

"Why would they believe you? I'd say I had some dirt on you and you were trying to prevent me from printing it."

Samantha reached into a bag and pulled out a small tape recorder.

"Luckily I recorded everything you've said."

"That's bullshit!" Hannah was startled.

Samantha looked at William.

"I remember I had my dictaphone in my bag."

"You're lying!"

Samantha rewound the tape and prayed it would work.

"It's probably not the best quality but.."

She pressed play, thankfully Hannah's voice came across loud and clear. Hannah jumped up.

"I hate you," she screamed storming off.

William looked at Samantha.

"Sam.."

"You don't need to say anything."

They were interrupted by the arrival of their food, neither of them felt particularly hungry after Hannahs intrusion. They ate in silence then William looked up.

"Do you really still think about making love in the shower?"

"Yes I do," said Sam blushing.

William laughed.

"Her face was a picture when you said that, I could've kissed you."

Samantha smiled.

"I was only too happy to help, I must admit when you told me you were divorced I never imagined you would marry someone like that!"

"It was the worst mistake of my life."

With that William gave Samantha a very short resume of how he had met Hannah, explaining she had told him she was pregnant and he had done the right thing by getting married, although they barely knew each other.

"So you've got a child?"

"No thank god! I couldn't imagine any thing worse."
They sat in silence for a while,
Samantha was grateful she had never got into a similar situation.

"It must have been hard losing your home."

"To be honest, once Hannah had shown her true colours it didn't feel like my home and I felt it was a small sacrifice to pay to get her off my back. Also once we left Derby all those years ago I've never really had a home."

"I'm so sorry, are you renting now?

"I rent rooms at my college, but hopefully I'll be able to buy somewhere soon."

After lunch William took Samantha on a grand tour of Oxford, she thought it was beautiful, enjoying the architecture and the narrow cobbled streets. He then took her back to his rooms at the University. She walked around the lovely dark wooded panelled room noticing the worn leather chairs, examining the old books on the shelves and then squealed with delight when she saw the old microscope on his desk.

"You kept it!"

William smiled unsure whether to tell her the truth, but he felt he should.

"To be honest Sam, I retrieved it after my mum passed away, it had been at her house for the past 16 years."

Samantha stood at the window and looked out across the quadrangle, this was the view William saw every morning. Her thoughts were interrupted by him.

"What time do you have, I wondered if you fancied going out for dinner?"
Samantha smiled.

"Actually I brought an overnight bag in case I wanted to stay."

"Fantastic, have you booked anywhere?"

"No."

"No problem, you can stay here."

Samantha frowned at him.

"Here?"

William laughed.

"Not here in my room, but during the holidays the college is pretty empty so they rent rooms out to tourists, let's see if we can find you one."

Samantha grabbed her bag and followed him out. Within an hour she was checking out her room.

"Sam I'll leave you to you get freshened up and I'll walk back over in an hour so we can go out for dinner."

"I haven't brought anything smart to wear, I would rather go to a pub is that okay?"

"Perfect, see you later."

Samantha sat on the bed, was she silly saying she'd stay? It was all going so well, probably too well but part of her wanted to run away. She decided to phone her Mum and let her know she wouldn't be home until the following afternoon. Her Mum was delighted.

Samantha showered and changed, she hadn't brought much so at least she was spared the angst of 'what to wear'.

Across the quadrangle William also showered and changed in record time, then paced his room checking his watch wondering how much time she would need. On the few occasions he and Hannah had gone out she would spend ages applying layers of makeup and bright red lipstick. He'd hated it, he really hoped Sam wasn't the same. Eventually he felt he'd given her enough time and walked across to her room. He was pleased to see she was ready to go looking lovely and natural.

They walked into the city and enjoyed dinner in a secluded pub then walked back through the quiet streets, William explaining it was very different during term time. Returning to the college they ended up in William's room where they shared a bottle of wine and talked into the small hours.

William was woken by his phone, it was Katie.

"Well, did she come?"

William grunted.

"Will were you asleep? It's gone nine!"

William groaned.

"Yeah but don't worry I had to wake up to answer the phone!"

"Ha Ha very funny, just tell me did she turn up?"

William brightened.

"Yep, we had a great day and she stayed over."

"Oh my god!"

"Katie why are you whispering?"

"I don't want her to hear me."

"Firstly numpty, I can't hear you, so there's no chance of anyone else and secondly she didn't stay here in my room!"

Katie laughed.

"I had visions of her lying in your bed asleep."

William then filled her in telling her all they did, including the almost disastrous lunch with the arrival of Hannah and how Samantha had risen to the challenge.

"Bloody Hannah, she's such a bitch," said Katie.

William finished the call and promised to keep his sister updated. He then phoned Samantha, she sounded bright and wide-awake so he suggested as it was such a lovely day, a walk along the river perhaps with a picnic would be agreeable.

Having procured some provisions, they walked along chatting to each other. They found a quiet spot away from the town, William produced a rug so they sat and enjoyed their lunch. They lay side-by-side, not quite touching watching the light clouds and listening to the gentle of ripple of the river and the hum of bees.

William turned on his side to face Samantha.

"Sam, thank you for coming it's been better than I could possibly imagined," he paused, "I've told you stuff that I've never told anyone else, you've had the rather horrific experience of meeting Hannah and now you know of my failings there…," he paused again. " what I'm trying to say is I haven't much to offer you at the moment no home…"

Before he could carry on Samantha interrupted.

"The answer is yes."

"Hang on you don't know what the question is."

"William Brown, I feel so replenished and mellow I'd agree to anything."

"Anything?"

"Yep."

"I could be proposing to rob a bank or skinny-dipping in the river or even marriage!"

Samantha rolled onto her side to face him.

"Ha, That shut you up," said William triumphantly.

Samantha smiled.

"Careful what you wish for."

"Samantha Thompson, are you flirting with me?"

He gently pushed her hair back from her face then very slowly leaned forward and kissed her, to his delight she responded.

Sometime later Samantha looked at her watch and groaned, she really didn't fancy the drive home and wished she could stay longer. They walked back to the college hand-in-hand and made plans to meet up again.

Chapter Thirty Two

Over the next few weeks they met up on Samantha's days off, either in Oxford, Bath or halfway between the two. Samantha didn't want William to come to Keyford, she said she was too well known in the town and didn't want the gossip. He was happy to go along with it but felt she was keeping part of herself from him, he hoped with time she would trust him enough to drop the barriers.
Samantha knew their relationship was doomed to fail unless she let William into her life properly but she was terrified of the consequences. Just as when they'd been teenagers he respected her boundaries and didn't put any pressure on her. She would lie awake in bed and run scenarios through her head.

The weeks were flying by. Samantha was unable to see William one week, as she had promised to visit Megan in Italy. He so wanted to go with her, but realised she wasn't ready for that.

Samantha had a wonderful time and over a bottle of wine told Megan about meeting up with William a.k.a. Rob again. Megan was amazed as Samantha gave her a brief account of what happened to him.

"Do you believe him?"

"Yes, I went to the library, they've got an archive of all the national newspapers going back years and of course I was able to narrow it down within a couple of weeks. I found the story, there was even a picture taken after his dad was stabbed and in the background you can just make out William supported by two ambulance men."

"Bloody hell Sam, does he know about…"

"No!"

"So what are you going to do?"

"I need to talk to Mum and Dad, get some advice."

On returning home Samantha did just that, as usual her parents supported her and helped Samantha put her thoughts in order and talked through everything that worried her.

The following weekend Samantha visited William in Oxford this time she stayed in his room. They spent much of the day in bed, it was like being teenagers again this time without the hurried fumbling. The next morning before leaving, Samantha took hold of Williams hands.

"I wonder whether you'd like to come to mine next week?"

William grinned.

"I'd love that Sam."

He held her tight he really didn't want her to leave. Their relationship had certainly moved on, but he worried what would happen once term restarted, it was going to be difficult.

William was due to arrive at 11 o'clock. Samantha had spring cleaned the house, hiding things away in drawers and putting shoes and coats away. Satisfied everything was tidy she checked the home-made soup she was making. The weather had changed and it was raining heavily, she hoped it wasn't a bad omen.

Samantha had spent many evenings compiling a scrapbook which she clutched to her chest, where could she put it? She didn't want to leave it for William to find, in the end she took it upstairs and hid it under the bed.

William phoned to say he was running late, Samantha was becoming more and more agitated until eventually he arrived just before lunchtime. Samantha produced the home-made soup and some chunky bread. They sat down and started to eat.

"Sam are you okay? You remind me of when we first made love you were like a cat on a hot tin roof!"

Samantha struggled to eat any soup.

"There's something I need to show you."

William was feeling a little alarmed as she took him through to the lounge.

"Wait there."

Samantha left the room and returned holding the scrap book. She sat down next to William on the sofa, she took a deep breath, this was it she thought.

"This is my life since you left me all those years ago."

Reluctantly she handed him the book.

The first few pages were local newspaper cuttings from the Upper Sixths first day, the swimming gala and A-level results. There were William's Christmas and valentines cards, pictures from the photo booth at the ice rink and the sketch her mum had done. William looked at her and grinned.

"Well obviously these were before you left," said Sam.

He turned the page and gasped. A very young Samantha , pregnant, another one of Samantha looking very tired holding a tiny baby. He kept turning, each page was another year, the baby became a toddler, first day at school, loosing her first tooth, swimming badges and finally a teenager looking uncannily like her mum apart from the dark eyes.

William hadn't said a word he looked at Samantha. She couldn't read his expression at all, she looked back at the latest photo of her daughter.

"I called her Rebecca, after your mum." she said quietly.

William ran his hands through his hair.

"I need some air."

With that he stood up and walked out. Sam heard him drive away, shit what had she done, she sat down heart pounding, it had taken all her courage to tell him about Rebecca, she knew it was going to be a shock for him, but hadn't expected him to run away.   William needed some space, he pulled into a lay-by, his head was swimming. He took some steading breaths and phoned his sister praying she'd answer. Katie listened and could hear the distress in her brothers voice.

"Stay there Will, I'll come to you."

Samantha hadn't moved from the sofa, she couldn't believe it, she thought she'd done the right thing, but was she wrong? Had it been too soon, or too late? No, she couldn't of told him earlier she needed time to get to know him and trust him. She slowly went through the scrapbook. It had taken her ages to compile, she thought it was the best way to show him his daughter growing up, but obviously not, perhaps she should've told him first, but she hadn't been able to say it. Samantha looked at the clock on the mantelpiece she'd been there for nearly an hour, shutting her eyes she thought, face it Samantha he isn't coming back.

"Bastard!" she shouted at the room.

Picking up the scrapbook, she took it back upstairs to her bedroom and put it under the bed. Siting on the edge of the bed she put her head in her hands and sobbed until she was completely exhausted. When she finally stopped she decided that was it, she was never ever going to let another man into her life. William had left her for a second time, no way was he is going to let him hurt her again.

Picking up her phone she checked to see if there was a message from him, nothing. Her fingers hovered over his name, then instead of dialling the number she deleted it.

"Sod you William Brown I never want to speak to you again."

She dragged herself off the bed and went back downstairs, replacing the photos of the daughter she'd hidden. She wandered into the kitchen and saw Williams overnight bag where he had left it on his arrival. She gave it a kick for good measure.

Rebecca had gone to her grandparents, Samantha had told her about her father and his sad life. The plan was Adeline would bring Rebecca home to meet him when Samantha phoned. Now she couldn't really face talking to her so she sent a text saying William had to return to Oxford, she didn't know how to explain to her that he had run out on them both. Catching sight of herself in the mirror she was horrified to see she looked so dreadful. Rebecca mustn't see her like that so she went to the bath bathroom to freshen up.

Katie found the lay-by William had stopped in, she got in his car. He looked like he was about to throw up.

"Will, talk to me, what happened?"

William put his head in his hands.

"I must have sucker written across my face, it's just like Hannah all over again. She's lied to me!"

"Oh Will I'm so sorry, you've been so happy, what did she say?"

"First time we met I told her everything, all about Dad, the trial, everything, but she didn't say a word."

"To be fair Will it would've been odd if she suddenly told you then 'oh by the way you've a daughter'."

"I know, but the next time when we had lunch and Hannah gatecrashed, I told her all about Hannah and how she lied telling me she was pregnant, I'm 100% sure now that she wasn't."

"Will, no way could she have told you then in the pub garden."

"Katie, she had loads of opportunity since, I knew she was holding back."

"I'm a bit confused, what did she say exactly when you asked her?"

"Asked her what?"

"Whether she'd had your child of course."

"When did I say I'd asked her?"

"So you've never asked her out right?"

"No."

"Okay so technically she's never lied as she's never denied it."

"That's not the point."

They sat in silence for a while then Will groaned.

"Oh no! I've just remembered, after that disastrous meeting with Hannah, Sam asked me whether I had a child. I said something like, I couldn't imagine anything worse….what I have I done?"

"The thing is little brother, you should remember, since finding that letter you've had time to think about her, planned to find her and you'd thought about what you were going to say. As you said, Sam was really shocked and not particularly happy to see you. She's probably had to work hard, being a single mum, getting her degree and keeping a job. Not only did she get pregnant in her teens, but in her eyes you had abandoned her."

Katie paused to let her words sink in. William put his head back and closed his eyes, he knew she was right.

"So what exactly did you say before you walked out?"

"Just that I needed some air."

"What!"

William turned to look at his sister.

"I was so shocked, I just had to get out. Shit I'm such an idiot."

"I've never met Sam, but right now I want to give her a big hug and apologise for my brother."

William closed eyes again.

"I've ruined it haven't I, she'll never want to speak to me ever again."

They lapsed into silence again.

"How do you feel about her Will, I mean hand on heart."

"It's quite simple really, I love her."

It was Katie's turn to look at her brother.

"Will do you really mean that? You've only been together for a short while."

"I loved her with all my heart when we were younger. Meeting her again it's like..,"

He struggled to find the words to describe how he felt.

"All I can say is, it's just so right, I've never felt like this with anyone else, I just want to be with her."

"Then tell me you moron what the fuck are you doing sitting here? Get back to her, talk to her."

"Will you come with me?"

Katie rolled her eyes.

"Do you think that will help?"

"Katie I just need a bit of moral support right now and I need someone to stop me making a fool of myself."

William started the car and headed back to Samantha's cottage. They parked up and walked into the kitchen. Katie was delighted to meet Charlie the Labrador who gave them both a warm welcome.

William called Samantha, and went to look for her, Katie decided to stay in the kitchen. Samantha was in the bathroom trying to freshen up before her daughter came home, she heard her name, her heart gave a little somersault. Why was he back, her mum was on her way she needed to get rid of him. She came out of the bathroom and ran straight into William, he threw his arms around her.

"Sam I'm so sorry it was just a shock, 'I needed a little time' as Paul would say. I also needed a bit of advice, which I've had from the head of my family."

Samantha looked puzzled.

"Will, you need to go Rebecca could be back any minute!"
"Good, I'd love to meet my daughter."

He took Samantha's hand and lead her downstairs to the kitchen.

"Samantha meet my sister Katherine ."

Katie was on the floor cuddling Charlie, she lept up and gave Samantha a hug.

"Call me Katie it's lovely to meet you Sam, I hope you kneed him in the balls!"

Samantha's yes opened in surprise and she smiled.

"Nice to meet you Katie I've heard so much about you."

Katie looked at Samantha, it was obvious she been crying despite her best efforts, Sam's eyes were red and puffy.

Suddenly the kitchen door flew open and Rebecca burst in followed by Adeline.

"Its raining cats and dogs out there... KATIE!" squealed Rebecca, "what are you doing here?"

She threw her arms around Katie.

"Becky?"

Will and Sam looked on in confusion.

"You know each other?" said Sam puzzled.

"Katie is Mary's daughter, you know the lovely lady at the hospice and you must be Will, I saw your photo on her locker."

Samantha looked open mouthed at Katie, William and Rebeca.

"Oh my god!" exclaimed Katie, "She recognised you, on her last day, she finally knew who you were."

Rebecca looked puzzled.

"That's what she kept saying to me I know who you are."

" I don't understand," said Sam, "I thought your mum's name was Rebecca, I saw it in the family Bible."

"It was Rebecca," replied William, "she changed it to Mary and never changed it back."

It was Rebecca's turn to look confused.

"I don't know what you're talking about."

Sam ignored her daughter for a moment and made introductions between Adeline, Katie and William. Adeline stared at William making him feel uncomfortable.

"Mum stop staring you're creeping him out!"

Rebecca giggled.

"Don't worry Will, when Nana's like that it means she wants to paint you."

"Really?" said a concerned William.

"She painted me lots of times, it's soooh boring having to stay still for ages."

"Sorry Will, I did ask Sam years ago to ask if I could paint you. I even did some preliminary sketches."

It was Samantha's turn to look shocked.

"Really? You never told me Mum."

Adeline smiled.

"I've lots of sketches of interesting faces."

She turned to Katie and gave her a long look.

"I'd love to do you as well."

Katie look really pleased.

"I'd love that."

Rebecca was asking William about his musical performances.

"Mary told me you were a brilliant musician."

Before William could reply Samantha butted in.

"Becky love, you know we talked about your dad and I explained what had happened."

Rebecca nodded.

"Well.."

Rebecca looked at her curiously.

"Yes,"

"Well love, Will is your dad and I've only just told him about you!"

Rebecca looked confused again.

"Will? But Nanna said my dad wasn't going to be here."

Samantha smiled at her daughter.

"Don't worry we had a crossed wire."

Rebecca digested the information and suddenly felt very shy. The five of them stood in awkward silence, Katie came to the rescue.

"Will said you'd made a beautiful album of photos can I see it?"

"Of course go sit in the lounge I'll get it," said Sam.

Samantha retrieved the scrapbook from her bedroom and found Katie, Rebecca and William sitting on the sofa. Katie was doing a brilliant job dispelling the awkwardness of the situation.

"Can I show them Mum?"

Samantha handed the book over. Katie teased William about his long hair and glasses in the newspaper cuttings, it didn't take long for Rebecca to find her confidence and soon all three of them were chatting like old friends. Samantha went into the kitchen, Adeline had made a tray of tea and a home-made cake she'd brought with her.She looked at her daughter and noted her red eyes.

"I thought he'd gone." she said quietly.

"Long story Mum, he just needed a bit of time out to take it all in, I wasn't sure he was coming back."

Adeline held her daughter tight.

"Is he okay now?"

"I hope so, but we need to talk."

Adeline smiled.

"I'll take Becky back with me and give you some space."

"Thanks Mum".

"Mum, Mum!" called Rebecca.

Samantha carried the tray into the lounge.

"What love?"

"Katie is my auntie and I'm going to have a cousin and.." tears filled her eyes, "Mary was my other Grandma!"

"That's wonderful." Samantha replied.

They sat and chatted for some time then Katie looked at her watch.

"Oh my goodness, I need to get going."

"I'll give you a lift back to the car." said William.

"No need," said Adeline, "come on Becky it's time we left we can give Katie a lift."

Rebecca was torn she really wanted to stay but was happy to go with Katie.

William helped Samantha clear the tea crockery. They sat at the little kitchen table, their hands reaching across to each other.

"Sam I'm so sorry about earlier, it was just so unexpected I didn't know how to react."

"Will it's okay, honestly,I've been wanting to tell you for ages the longer it went on the harder it became."

William reached into his pocket and brought out a small parcel.

"I brought you a gift."

He handed it over, Sam carefully unwrapped it, the box look familiar, she opened it and gasped. She looked up and grinned at him as she lifted the locket out of the box.

"Grandma wanted you to have it Sam"

Tears welled in Samantha's eyes.

"It's really Rebecca's."

"I didn't know about Rebecca, I brought it for you." "Thank you Will, you have no idea how much this means to me."

William looked deep into Samantha's eyes.

"Sam I can't believe we've arrived at where we are now. We've both had our own lives apart but somehow we've still been connected. Something out there has brought us back together and even though I don't know how this will end, It, what ever it is, is so strong It has control of the overwhelming feelings I have for you and I know you have for me, what is it Sam, what is it?"

Sam brushed her fingers gently over William's cheek.

"As John would say, 'Perhaps love'."

The end

Printed in Great Britain
by Amazon